Flights of Angels

My thanks to Pauline Tattersall, Professor Rodney Coates and his wife Gillian and, of course, my family, who support me in all things. Thanks too, to David Crystal for his encouragement and to the Ucheldre Repertory Company who helped me bring Shakespeare to life in Anglesey. Most of all, thanks and apologies to William Shakespeare, whoever he was.

A fond farewell to Ziggy Stardust and Thomas the Tank Engine.

Flights of Angels

The Third Nicholas Talbot Adventure

M Stanford-Smith

HONNO MODERN FICTION

First published by Honno
'Ailsa Craig', Heol y Cawl, Dinas Powys,
Wales, CF64 4AH

1 2 3 4 5 6 7 8 9 10

ISBN 978-1-906784-38-6

Published with the financial support of the Welsh Books Council

Cover design: Simon Hicks
Cover image: © Andrew Davidson

Printed in Wales by Gomer

Hamlet: The rest is silence.
Horatio: Now cracks a noble heart. Goodnight, sweet
      Prince, And flights of angels sing thee to thy rest.

Hamlet. Act iv Sc.ii

Author's note. The happenings in the battle of Strathyre are modelled on the contemporary reports of the clashes between the MacGregors of Rannoch Moor and the clans around them. The chieftain was indeed taken prisoner and was treated, and reacted, in the manner described. A truce was made and immediately broken. After the intervention of King James an edict went out to disband the clan, ruling that anyone bearing the name MacGregor could lawfully be killed on sight. A clansman changing his name would be spared. This edict was not repealed until the middle of the eighteenth century.

Prologue

Christopher Marlowe, poet, playwright and wretched ex-patriate sat huddled in the chimney corner, still cold in spite of the glowing peats on the hearth. Outside the pele tower, the Scottish haar clung damply to the stones, and a vicious little draught crept under the door, lifting the rushes and rippling the arras that clothed the walls. His mittened fingers were too numb to hold a pen and he was thinking aloud instead of writing, building the images in his fertile mind. He was thinking of the place he had so rashly left behind, the warmth and sparkling light, the colours, comfort and culture of Italy. He had only come back to see his *Hamlet* performed, goddammit, and here he was in the wilds of Scotland.

The journey here had been hateful, bucking and pitching through the North Sea from Gravesend to the Firth of Forth, marooned in a tiny cabin while his companions struggled outside with the winds and tides. Nicholas Talbot was angry with him, he knew, for making this journey necessary. No, it was not entirely his fault, there had been another threat Marlowe did not yet understand. He had been given another name, Christophe Malheur, his host's idea of a joke. There had followed a gruelling journey riding beside the carts in gathering snow, with frequent stops to dig out the wheels and the impacted hooves of the horses. As for what followed…

"Devil take him," he said aloud. "Was it really worth it – are my plays worth all this? Am I allowed to see them, hear the applause, hear them shout my name? No. The great William Shakespeare takes it all. Damn you, Niccolo, I curse the day you began all this."

PART ONE

Chapter One

The day was fine after the storm, the roofs and towers of the Castle standing up granite-grey against the blue. The early morning sun glistened on the tidewrack flung far up the shore, the firth, still running high, was a choppy mass of creaming wavelets. It was crammed full with shipping come in to shelter, fishing boats and wherries, here a French galliasse and there a troop ship flying the lilies of France, riding high in the water. A Dutch barge bobbed and creaked next to a fleet of cockleboats, the smell already beginning to taint the air. A sleek caravel flying a black and gold pennant below the cross of St George nestled up to the quay.

A man stood on the cobbles, hands on hips, tall and bulky in leather jack over quilted doublet, long legs planted apart in thigh-high boots, cropped chestnut hair parted all ways by the wind. Sir Nicholas Talbot, Lord Rokesby, just twenty-four years old, star sign Scorpio, come to seek safe haven and claim the lands ceded to him by the King. He was counting heads.

His party disembarked in good order, the Rokesby trading vessel *Snipe* had brought them with all convenient speed and in foul weather from Gravesend, and his contingency plans were going forward smoothly. His cousin and squire, Young Colin

Melville, came ashore first and doubled off to find Sir Robert Carey. Carey had promised them armed men to escort them on the rest of this precipitate journey. The reason for all this haste? Twofold.

News had come to the new Globe theatre on the south bank where Nicholas was playing in the first performance of *Hamlet*. Lord Mowbray, Nick's most ardent enemy, had escaped from the Tower and Christopher Marlowe, supposed dead in Deptford, had turned up, risking his own life and others' to see his play – double jeopardy. Nicholas had brought his family and Marlowe pell-mell to the safety of his estates in Scotland. He needed his hands free to deal with Mowbray once for all, in his own time and on his own terms.

Nick counted. His wife Rosalyne, composed and darkly beautiful, had their son William by the hand; his other boy Jack, the elder by six months, was trying to help Mistress Melville, their nurse, down the gangplank. Mistress Melville, thin and erect, who needed no help, was allowing it. Kit Marlowe, looking murderous and cold, Tim Trelawney, who was skippering the ship back to Deptford, Betsy, Rosalyne's woman, still grizzling. Perhaps send her back.

Nicholas wished Tobias Fletcher had come after all. Toby had been his close companion in every escapade for seven years, and he missed him. It had been thought best for him to stay and safeguard their interests in Richmond. Jock the MacNab, was already back with his kinfolk in Strathyre, an archer like Tobias, and a man to be reckoned with. The luggage now, what little there had been time for, and the horses. Oberon, the grey, Nero the black Friesian, Caesar, the gift of King James. Hotspur, the new-schooled colt. Shadow of the Wind, the Arabian for Rosalyne, stepping daintily down the wooden planks, led by Hugh d'Arblay,

Nick's other friend at court. D'Arblay had pleaded to come; he had squired Nicholas at the tournament and knew Mowbray of old. All safe ashore.

D'Arblay took charge of the horses and Nick rounded up his flock ready to settle them in a nearby inn to await the escort. Rosalyne, his bride of a few crowded months, came to stand straight-backed beside him, her cloak wrapped close about her, the brisk wind blowing strands of black silk across her face. He looked at her, suddenly doubtful. She was bred to court life, fashionable society, fine clothes. How would she fare here, snatched rudely from their elegant house in Richmond? Of course, she would not be languishing in the wilds of Scotland; part of his plan was to present her at the Scottish Court and bring himself once more to the notice of the King. Nicholas did not like what he had heard of the correspondence between Cecil and the Earl of Essex. The question of the succession still seemed balanced on a knife-edge and he had made an independent decision to keep an eye on things. His money was on James: he did not trust Cecil to keep his promises.

He shaded his eyes to gaze up at the Castle. No Royal flag flying. That probably meant the King was on a Progress – James' word for a hunting-party. He sighed. At least it wasn't raining. A touch on his arm and he glanced round to see Rosalyne smiling up at him. She had abandoned the stiff forms of court dress for soft woollens and practical boots, and looked nothing like the court lady of Richmond.

"What next, my lord?" It was such a neat parody of Tobias Fletcher that Nick burst out laughing.

"I'm writing the script as I go along, my lady," he said. "Another uncomfortable journey, I fear, then home of a sort."

"I am minded of Petruchio in the play, who so shamefully mistreated his bride. Do you seek to tame me, Nicco?"

Relieved, he answered in similar vein. "A little test, Rose. You were in danger of becoming spoilt." He had half an eye on Young Colin who had been stopped by a figure galloping in along the shore, plaid flying. The man came on, Nick's cousin running after. Nick went to meet him. The horse slid to a halt in a shower of pebbles and his rider leaned down, panting for breath.

"It's no' fit," he gasped. "The MacGregors are out. Jock MacNab says nae bairns or wummin—"

"The MacGregor—"

"It's the season. Jock says—"

"A moment. Get your breath, man, it's not a tale for the dockside. D'Arblay, take my lady and Mistress Melville up to the Castle for shelter. I'll follow."

About to protest, Rosalyne caught his eye and inclined her head. By the time the horses were saddled and the small party mounted and riding off up the ginnel that led to the Castle gates, the messenger had collected his wits. Leaning now against his sweating horse he said what he had come to say. Watching his two seven-year-old sons craning round elbows to see, Nicholas listened. The tale was enough to make him wish they had not come, flying from one danger to run headfirst into another. About to bring the exhausted messenger into the nearby tavern, he paused.

"What of the Highland lad I sent to make ready?"

"Harry Munro is deid."

"Dead!"

"Killed. Aye, and his sweetheart with him. Killed and burned."

A black rage and grief was building in Nick's head. Harry Munro, the boy who had risked his life to bring him out of that

6

tunnel at Calais, who had written to thank him for his happiness and his bride in the "most beautiful place I ever did see", dead. Murdered on Nicholas' land and in his service.

Presently he said, in a voice grown thick, "I will come. Get yourself rest and food. I must bestow my womenfolk and find men. I will come."

Young Colin was at his elbow, his face white and furious. "The Palace at Linlithgow is the place, Nick. My father will see them safe and there will be kinfolk wishing to back you."

"Give me a moment to think. Have this man seen to." Nicholas walked a few paces away, thinking of Munro's eager freckled face as he set off for his homeland after five years in captivity. He saw him in the dawn light, coming with a capful of mushrooms and a scarf full of eggs, resourceful, brave and merry. Murdered. After a while Nick mastered himself and began to plan.

Young Colin's idea was a good one. The Palace of Linlithgow was a Melville stronghold, not more than two days' ride south. His cousin Charles Melville was there with his uncle – Rosalyne and the children would be safe. He needed men, he did not know what might lie ahead, the escort promised by Carey would not be enough.

Kit Marlowe was standing nearby with Caesar and mounts for himself and Young Colin, listening. He had been told the tale of Calais – an expression of Nick's had stuck in his mind – "to lie in cold obstruction and to rot…" He knew his Nicholas and was in no doubt what he would do. He was equally certain that he himself was not going to be bundled off with the women and children. After his solitary sojourn on the *Snipe*, he felt like a good fight. Young Colin came out of the tavern and the three men mounted to ride up to the Castle. They rode in silence, Nicholas still struggling with his anger and grief and wondering how to break the news to his wife.

In the event, he did not have to. News had come already to Walter Abercrombie, Keeper of the Castle in the King's absence, and Rosalyne came to meet him with a cup of wine.

"You will wish to speak with Sir Walter, my lord. You have lost a friend, I am sorry. I pray you, be easy about us, we will go or stay as you think best. We will talk later – and Nicholas, none of this could have been foreseen. Monsieur Malheur, you will wish to see where we are to lay our heads tonight." With her usual smooth efficiency, she had taken charge of domestic matters and Marlowe, with an amused grimace, allowed himself to be led away. He would be speaking to Lord Rokesby later.

Abercrombie, a burly man with wiry salt-and-pepper hair cropped close to his skull, an ally from Nick's last visit to Scotland, sat across from him on the other side of the fire and gave him what other news he had.

"You were not to know, Rokesby, what neighbours have come to Rannoch Moor. The King will be displeased – the MacGregor have long been a trial and a nuisance wherever they go. Driven out of the north, they chose to settle west of Loch Rannoch, and rather than tangle again with the Campbells, they foraged east, where there was least resistance. Wild men, the whole clan of them, and there's little sustenance to be found on the Moor, a hostile country at the best of times." He leaned over to fill their cups. "His Majesty would like them contained. A bill to outlaw them is before the Assembly but there is no sitting before the new year. He would wish men to be provided – if you are willing."

"How many?"

"Aye, well, there may be a wee difficulty there. I expect news from Carey regarding the – um…"

"Border problem?"

"Quite."

Nicholas sat nursing his cup, letting the silence prolong itself. He was not drinking. His stomach, still in turmoil, was growling with hunger. It seemed he had entered on cue to deal with this marauding clan. It certainly had not been part of his plan. If it were not for Harry Munro he would not entertain the idea for a second. But Munro's death made it his fight, and he waited for Abercrombie to speak.

The door opened and a steward entered with servants bearing steaming platters of food, followed by Rosalyne, his two sons and their nurse.

"Your pardon, Sir Walter. The boys wish to bid their father goodnight and these matters are best not talked of on an empty stomach." She smiled cheerfully at Abercrombie and gave the children a little push. "Make your goodnights and then go with Mistress Melville." The small domesticity broke the developing tension as Nicholas did not doubt she had intended, and he set aside his untasted wine to open his arms.

There was a tramp of booted feet outside and under the doorway stooped a svelte figure in cramoisie velvet, wondrously tailored. Sir Robert Carey, deputy Warden of the Marches, doffed his feathered cap in a sweeping bow.

"My lady, welcome to Scotland. Your servant, Sir Walter." He turned to Nicholas. "So, my friend, you took my advice, my heartiest congratulations. Sorry to have missed your wedding. And these are your boys – fine lads both. You come in good time, Nicholas, things have quietened for the moment, men can be spared."

"Delighted to hear it."

Carey cast a shrewd glance at Abercrombie.

"I see I have interrupted you. My lady, had you not come in such haste, I could perhaps have warned your impetuous husband that his property may not be what he hopes. Now we are graced with your presence, we shall offer you what humble entertainment we may..." The urbane flow lasted while Jack and William were quietly spoken to and reassured and allowed titbits from the table. Having achieved their object, Mistress Melville and Rosalyne made their curtseys and shepherded them out.

The three men eyed each other and Abercrombie suddenly burst into laughter.

"Rokesby, the Lady Rosalyne puts me to shame. You must have a poor idea of our hospitality. Eat, man! You come with your lady and your bairns looking for peaceful welcome to your own lands and we offer you war. I ask pardon. And I am sorry for your friend."

Carey had sat to the table and was helping himself to the savoury-smelling stew. He looked up.

"What friend is this?"

The tale was soon told and, beguiled by the smell of hot food, Nicholas presently drew up a stool to eat. Over the stew and dumplings, the men thrashed out a plan. It was agreed that Linlithgow was the safest place for the women and children, and taken as read that Nicholas would ride north and west with as many armed men as he could muster, to deal with the MacGregor. Before they had finished, Abercrombie was called away and Carey got up to fill his pipe and light it with a coal from the fire.

"These pressing matters aside, Nicholas, I come to bring you news of that other little matter. Your real reason for coming here.

Mowbray. You were wise to choose your own ground, Nick. I am reliably informed that Essex was indeed behind Mowbray's escape. And the man Poley – you mind him – is with him. Last I heard they were seen heading north."

Nick sighed. This was not good news. Poley was the one man who would recognise Kit Marlowe. On the other hand, the man owed Nicholas a life.

"At least Mowbray will not find many friends here to aid him," he said. "He can have little enough money to buy them – Essex will not help him there."

"Cannot, rather than will not. My sweet clutch-fisted cousin Elizabeth has threatened to take back the winery that keeps him afloat. He is in dire trouble, Nick. You and I are both better off here."

"You think so? He and James correspond."

Carey stared at him. "You know that for a fact? My God, give me honest reivers any day. You know where you are with them."

Nick laughed at him. "And you a courtier, Robin? Have you lost your hopes of advancement – surely now is the time."

"My Queen-cousin is sick and the vultures are gathering. I shall wait and see. Now, my friend, I would suggest you leave your womenfolk with me and go on ahead to see what is left of what our generous James has gifted you."

"My lady may have different ideas. She is a constant blessed surprise to me."

"I told you so," said Carey smugly.

Sir Robert Carey, son of Henry Carey, the Lord Hunsdon who had attended Nick's wedding, had once again been posted north to police the Scottish Borders. Always at loggerheads with his brother John, the Lord Warden of the Marches, he had nonetheless made a name for himself among the warring clans as a fearless fighter and a canny adversary. If things had "quietened for the moment" it was entirely due to him. As good as his word, he had brought armed men, horses, and wagons, and arranged for an assortment of Melvilles and MacNabs to meet them on the way.

"I've yet to hear what the Douglasses think of the lands being ceded to you," he said. "Didn't you upset someone in France?"

Out of the frying-pan? thought Nick. *I should have remembered what it's like up here.* On the whole, he preferred a straightforward band of marauding Scots to the devious plans of Mowbray. He meant to bring the man out of hiding and meet him face to face – he'd had a bellyful of the man using others to do his work.

"I wasn't looking for this kind of trouble," he said.

"It seems to find you, my friend. I wish you luck."

When he went to find their bedchamber at last, sore at heart and suddenly dog-tired, Rosalyne received him with gentle looks and comforting words.

"Come to bed, my lord. No idle questions and vain entreaties, I know what you must do. We shall be safe with our kinfolk." She was helping his fumbling fingers with points and buttons, and he caught her to him.

"This is hard for you, sweeting, not what I intended—"

"Never mind now. Let us make the most of what time we have."

They had not shared a bed or been private since the night before the play, in Richmond. On board ship, the women and children had shared a cabin, and Nicholas had been kept busy on deck. Her calm serenity had amazed him and now she took him in her arms with trembling urgency. They made love with a fierce tenderness, and he held her close.

"What is it, sweetheart? What do you fear?"

12

"I do not want you out of my sight – so many enemies – you are going into God knows what danger."

"I am forewarned. There will be men enough… Rosalyne, I brought you here to keep you safe from Mowbray and now I must leave you in the care of others. It breaks my heart. I would keep you by my side, but this fight – none of my choosing – is no place for you and the children. Stay strong, Rose, I will send."

"I am no different from any soldier's wife, Nicholas. You have good cause to go, and you must go in good heart. Rest easy, my love, your care should be only for what you have taken in hand."

Chapter Two

Strathyre, south of Loch Tummel

In a corner of the smoke-stained pele tower, a makeshift bivouac had been set up, and in it a man was working. Bow-legged and squat, with a round bald head and large ears, he had long gone by the name of Hob. A leatherworker by trade, and never in one place for very long, he had learned on his travels to turn his hand to anything. He mended pots and kettles, saddles and fences and gates, and until his dog died he had been a welcome rat-catcher. He had come to Strathyre in the aftermath of the MacGregors' massacre, and made himself a snug billet in the deserted steading. One or two families had begun to venture back to their crofts and Hob's various skills were called for. He had dug himself well in, but lately there had been strange comings and goings that unsettled him, men riding fast and alone along the valley and through the hills. Much as he had come to like the place, he was beginning to think of moving on.

He stopped hammering and set aside the mended kettle. In the sudden quiet he caught the jingle of a bridle and the sound of hoof on stone. There had not been a horse in the valley since the MacGregor came. He hastily tipped the bucket of water over his fire and sidled round to the blanket he had hung across the broken door. He listened through the ringing in his ears. No sound, he had imagined it, the place must be full of ghosts. He shook his head, pulled aside the blanket and stepped out into a silent semi-circle of bowmen, their arrows implacably centred on his chest.

In their midst a tall individual with a proud high-bridged nose and blowing russet hair sat astride the largest horse Hob had ever seen. The man spoke. The voice was resonant and controlled, with music in it, the tone amused.

"Alone here?"

Hob nodded, showing the whites of his eyes. Two of the bowmen circled the tower, others went into what was left of the longhouse. They came out shaking their heads and the rider dismounted. Hob noticed that his leather jack and breeches were well-worn and cared for. A recent three-cornered tear needed attention, the steel plate showed through. *Steel, not iron*, thought Hob, in spite of his terror. *A fighting man, with money.* He pulled off his cap and louted.

"Welcome to Strathyre, sir," he said.

"And who are you to welcome me to my own house?" said the rider. Hob was relieved to hear the laughter in his voice.

"Hob, sir, at your service." He noticed that the bowmen had put away their arrows but kept their bows strung in their hands.

"No call to keep 'em strung, sir," he said. "No-one here but me. Nearest folk is down by the bridge that was."

"You survived the raid?"

"No, sir. I came after."

The man lifted his voice and called. Like the ghosts Hob had imagined, men rose from the heather and gorse, and more rode out from between the trees.

"As you see, Hob, you have guests. More will come to put the place to rights. And the fear of God up the MacGregor."

Hob beamed. "Count me in, sir. I seen what they done."

"You work metal?"

"I make harness, sir. Turn my hand to most things. Your gear could do with a mend."

The strong-boned face split in a grin. A sandy-haired youth in half-armour rode up, a sloe-eyed man with black ringlets brushing stirrup-leathers beside him.

"All clear, Nick. Do we make camp? Who's this?"

"Our Jack-of-all-trades, it seems. Hob by name. Leave him be. Set up our quarters in the longhouse, the men camp to the west. Kit, take MacNab and set a guard, if you please."

Hob quietly lost himself in the bustle of a sizeable body of men settling in. Latrines were dug, a cook-house set up, tents, shelters and horse lines mushroomed in the fields to the west of the tower, and stabling was found in the outbuildings for the officers' horses. When Nicholas came in the last of the light to inspect the damage to the tower, he found it swept and garnished, all trace of Hob's habitation gone. Lanterns were lit; a fire burned in the huge chimney breast, his pallet and campaign chest lay along one wall with his gear neatly arranged. Hob was bringing in his folding table and chairs. Mistress Melville and Rosalyne had overseen the provisioning of the wagons, they had sent hangings and a carpet, decent platters and jugs and flagons, blankets and furs. The men had been equally well provided for; Nick had seen them warm, dry and fed.

"If you will sit, my lord, I'll bring in your supper presently," said Hob. "The other gentlemen have eaten." He set up a chair by the fire, dusted off the seat with a flourish, and turned to pour

16

from a jug warming on the blackened hearth. He set a stool beside the chair and stood back. At any moment, Nick thought, he would perform a jig.

It had been a long hard day after a gruelling ride, and Nicholas had been saddened by what he had seen, but for the first time in a long while, he wanted to laugh. It was a moment he would have liked to share with Rose. He sat down and took the mug of hot spiced wine and allowed his self-appointed batman to pull off his boots and bear them away. He unbuttoned his doublet and stretched out his legs to the blaze, warming his toes, thankful to sit for a while and do nothing. He thought over all that had been done and presently got up to rummage in his chest for paper to write tomorrow's orders for the day. Finished, he sat with them on his knee and paused, thinking. *How many times has my father done this? How often have I seen him in just this situation, taking thought for men under his command. He never meant this for me – he sent me away to be turned into a gentleman.* Nick snorted aloud. *A little short-sighted for once, father. Money and position bring their own tasks. Noblesse oblige – hah! We shall see how well you taught me.* He put aside his notes and sat nursing the wine and gazing into the flames. *How had Jack Talbot felt about taking men into battle,* he wondered. *All my battles have been my own; I've risked my own skin, no-one else's. Who cared if I got it wrong? This was going to be very different.*

Hob reappeared with a platter of steaming food balanced on a flat loaf of soda bread. He put it on the table and drew it to Nick's side.

"One of the gentlemen would like a word, my lord?" It was a question – Hob was obviously determined to defend his moment of peace. Nicholas nodded, and Hob drew aside the blanket with a comical look of resignation.

Kit Marlowe ducked under his arm, black eyes sparkling with mischief. He lifted his hands to Hob. "A minute only, I promise you." And as Hob withdrew, "You have acquired a good guard dog. Excellent. Go on as you have begun. Like it or not, Niccolo, you are our leader. A captain must behave like one." He pulled up a stool and poured himself wine. "I have been talking with MacNab. He wants to know—"

Nicholas thrust his sheaf of notes at him and went on eating. He was ravenous; all he had had all day was a hunk of bread and cheese pushed into his hand by Young Colin. Marlowe read, looked up and smiled.

"I beg your pardon, my lord Rokesby. I should have known better. After all, her Majesty's erstwhile Ambassador to Venice must know his onions. You need an aide-de-camp. With your permission, that will be me. I see you have appointed your lieutenants and all is in train." He reached across to refill Nick's cup. "If anything daunts you, sweeting, remember this. These men are not pressed men nor are they mercenaries. They are Scots, here of their free will to right a wrong. They set an example to the clansmen hereabouts who might otherwise hang back. You know this, Niccolo, and I know you. I could not let you go to your rest with this charge heavy on you."

Nicholas should not have been surprised at the insight. He should have remembered that Marlowe was a man with long experience in the field, a fighter quick to quarrel, not a soldier but a poet with a poet's understanding of humankind. Of all the men here, he was the only one to have been brought willy-nilly, embroiled in something no concern of his. And his life was the one Nicholas had sworn to protect. He met Marlowe's eye and the man laughed.

"What does my Hamlet say? I need not remind you, it is your motto, after all. Like you, I am ready. This is meat and drink to me, Niccolo. Give me a sword and paper and ink and I am content."

He has a lifetime's experience in taking care of himself in difficult circumstances, thought Nick – Marlowe had not been Walsingham's spy for nothing.

Hob came back with meaningful looks and Kit got up with a laugh, took the sheaf of orders, clapped Nick on the shoulder and was gone.

Next day began early, with Hob bringing in porridge and bread and ale. Nicholas found his fighting jack had been neatly repaired, and smiling, he shrugged it on and went out into the cold pre-dawn light. His orders were being carried out, patrols and guard duties allocated, the horse lines busy and men clearing an area for weapon practice. Nicholas meant to weld this dysfunctional crew of independent Scots into a disciplined – and surviving – fighting unit. He wanted the neighbouring chieftains, when they came, to see his clear intention. Following orders, MacNab had ridden off with others of his clan to invite the Menzies, Murrays and Robertsons to a meeting. Nicholas took Young Colin with him to explore the terrain.

As Harry Munro had said, it was a beautiful place. The sun was up now, rising over the horseshoe of hills to the east, dispelling the eddies of mist over the water. Loch Tummel lay as far as Nick could see, a widening stretch of gunmetal slowly turning pink, dividing a green and purple valley bordered by dark forest. Above and beyond the trees rose the hills, grey and green and lilac, the tops catching the growing light. Streams and white falls fed the river and lake, an island tufted with trees was reflected in the still water. The black scars of the burned homesteads were an abomination.

They rode in silence along the shore, to where the Tummel narrowed into a small torrent to flow into Loch Rannoch. A bridge had been built here, the stone piers now supporting a skeleton of burned and broken planks. Nicholas had his book out, mapping and making notes.

"Get this mended?" offered Young Colin.

"Afterwards," came the grim answer. "I want the devils contained."

They rode on along the wider reaches of Loch Rannoch towards the mountains towering to the west beyond the furzy brown of the Moor with its rocks and green bogs. Here Nicholas called a halt and they dismounted to let the horses drink. Bodiless larks sang and curlews called, a fish plopped in widening rings that rippled the reflection of the hills, the trees in their crimson and gold livery dipped and whispered in a wandering breeze. A deer came out of the forest and looked at them. Nick fell under the spell; he felt he had come home. He could bring up his sons here – teach them to fish and handle a horse, fly a hawk and hunt. He would teach them the names of plants and birds and beasts and show them the poetry of the landscape. They would grow straight and strong…

Young Colin was watching him. "Aye, well, you should see it in winter," he said in matter-of-fact tone. "Pretty, I grant ye, but hard living."

And before that, some hard dying, thought Nick, brought back to earth. He turned back, leading his young horse for a while, coming at his chosen battlefield from the MacGregor territory.

Presently he remounted and trotted on, stopping where the floor of the valley narrowed to get out his notebook and draw. Young Colin stayed quiet. *Him and that crazy Malheur – two of a kind,* he thought.

MacNab was back when they rode into the fast-growing camp. "They'll come," he said.

Chapter Three

The Parley

Nicholas surveyed the men gathered in the big square room at the foot of the pele tower. Above them hung the charred rafters of what had been the upper floors, above that the high stone roof, blackened with fire. The three chieftains sat with hands on spread knees, each with two liegemen standing behind with their hands on the hilts of their great swords, point down on the stone. They were all eyeing this newcomer warily. On their way in, they had seen the orderly camp, men at their arms practice, working parties busy about the buildings and cleaning out the great well in the courtyard. Others were shooting at targets set up in the field and a group of men were at work sharpening long stakes. They waited.

Marlowe, sitting to one side with a notepad on his knee, suddenly saw Nicholas afresh, through their eyes. The image so long held in his heart of a thin fresh-faced youth, cheeks downy with a proud new beard, green eyes eager and sparkling, was overlaid by the changes seven years had brought. He saw, as they saw, a tall long-legged man standing before them, not much older than their sons, with the wide-shouldered build of an athlete, in workmanlike gear showing signs of long service. The clean-shaven strong-boned face was marred by a white scar from eye to mouth, and the high-bridged nose lent a touch of arrogance until you noticed the wide sensuous mouth bracketed with laughter lines. The eyes were as he remembered, long and green, put in with a sooty finger, the crescents beneath ready to crease with amusement.

Nicholas was not amused at the moment. These powerful men had been made welcome, food and drink had been brought and left untouched, and now he stood before them, thane of Strathyre, and realised he had forgotten to ask MacNab the correct form of address for a Scottish chieftain. He fell back on his father's way of speaking to his captains.

"Gentlemen, neighbours. You know why I am here. We are met in a common purpose to avenge our dead and drive out this threat to our peace. I am the incomer, gifted these lands by the King, but I am prepared and ready to take arms against the MacGregor. To that end I have brought armed men and horses, some sent by the King who is eager, as we are, to see this nuisance abated." He paused, looking each man one by one, in the eye.

"I have one thing more to say. This action will be undertaken with you or without you. If it be with you we shall undoubtedly prevail, but there can be only one leader. The plan is mine and the responsibility and vengeance is mine. I claim that right. Those of you who mislike fighting under my command, may leave now with our thanks. No-one will think the less."

There was a long silence. Marlowe silently applauded. *Well-spoken, my sweet boy. My Hotspur without the stammer.*

Murray was thoughtfully combing his beard with his fingers. "What is this plan?"

Marlowe picked up the chart lying on the table and flattened it against the wall. Nicholas drew his poniard to point. His exposition was lucid and concise, delivered in a manner calculated to draw them in. He laid down his poniard and turned back to them.

"As you see, gentlemen, I wish to take the initiative and bring the enemy to where we want them. Time is pressing, winter will be upon us; we want a short sharp fight and an end to it. Give me men and two weeks and we shall be ready."

"How will you stop them coming at you from the other side of the loch?" asked Murray.

"You saw the stakes being sharpened. There will be archers behind them at the broken bridge." Marlowe had brought the chart to the table, and the three men gathered round. They began to ask questions, Nicholas poured wine and it was accepted. He caught Marlowe's eye and Kit winked. Presently, the eldest of the three, Murray, straightened and lifted his cup.

"The odds are great. You need more men than I saw outside. The Murray will come."

"And the Menzies." They turned to look at Big Tom Robertson, the largest landowner present, in both senses of the word, who nodded his ginger head.

"Archers?" said Nick. Big Tom expanded his chest.

"My boy is the best."

Longnose Wattie wins the papingay every year, thought Nick with a fleeting memory. They got down to it then – numbers and time and place – the question of leadership was not discussed.

The chieftains left, feasted and rather flown with wine, and Nicholas took a deep breath. The thing was now possible. Marlowe came to him with the notes he had taken, and set his arm round Nick's shoulders.

"Go and take Nero for a gallop," he said. "It will fadge."

Chapter Four

Time was pressing indeed. It was already autumn; they had met with flurries of snow on the way here that had given way to an Indian summer. It could not last. Nick wanted this battle to be conclusive, no dreary skirmishing lasting the winter long. He had given himself two weeks to turn a mob of excitable Scots into a disciplined force that would obey his orders.

Over the days that followed Marlowe watched emerge that strange charisma that binds men to their leader. No-one questioned Nick's authority: he was thane of Strathyre and knew what he was doing. His orders were crisp and clear and delivered in a voice that would have charmed an asp.

His discipline was not charming however. The first man caught thieving was publicly flogged and afterwards tended by Nicholas himself. A rapist was hanged and cut down just alive. The next would not be spared. Any malcontent was given the choice to get down to it or leave. No-one left, and with competent aides like Young Colin and MacNab, the motley assortment of king's men and bloody-minded Scots was slowly brought into a fighting corps. The difficulty facing Nicholas now was how to bring the enemy out of Rannoch Moor.

He had come in from training one blowy morning and was at his desk with a lump of bread in his hand, grappling with the problem, when a shadow darkened the threshold of the new-made door. He looked up to see a white-faced d'Arblay framed in the doorway, supporting himself on the post. A slender lad ducked under his arm, and came to stand in the centre of the room, a gallant stripling with his hand on his sword. Nicholas, gazing into his eyes, saw only his beloved wife, a Rosalind, a Beatrice, and fell in love with her all over again. He stood and spread his arms and, with a sob of relief, she ran into them. A servant coming in with food dropped the tray and backed hastily out.

Nick was laughing. "Put off these lendings, sweet, as soon as you may. The whole camp will know me a lover of boys!"

"Did I not fool you, Nicholas?"

"Not for a moment, my sweet warrior. My heart could not mistake you. What in God's name…"

"Don't blame Hugh. I made him bring me, the boys are safe with our kinsfolk – I had nothing to do but fret. I can be of more use to you here, Nicholas, I promise you."

"A rose in a field of thistles. We shall see…"

The arrival of the thane's wife brought a number of changes. Marlowe saw some of the strain go out of Nicholas. Standards of behaviour and cleanliness went up; the evening meal taken with his officers began to resemble the dining table in Richmond. She relieved Nicholas of many of the small domestic concerns and the food improved. Careful not to encroach on Hob's jealously guarded preserves, she conferred with him to tempt an appetite grown fickle. She seemed to enjoy what she called "Hobnobbing" and between them he found his position and wellbeing firmly established. It amused him mightily. He kept his fears for her safety to himself; he could not be angry.

Word came from the Campbells to the south of the Moor, who were staying strictly non-combatant – until they saw who was winning – that the MacGregor was massing. It was the time – the spring sowings had been trampled but not destroyed and now the harvest was in, fruit gathered and the fertile valleys ripe once more for plunder. That same night, Nicholas sent out a scouting party to find out for himself. Born and bred in the Border country, the blood of cattle-rustlers flowed in Young Colin's veins, and he brought back report more important in his eyes than the alarming numbers gathering to MacGregor's banner. He knew where the stolen cattle were.

"Not much pasture on the Moor," he said. "They're in the valley at the furthest tip of the Rannoch."

Nicholas leaned back in his chair and grinned at him.

"And I suppose you want to go and steal them back," he said. He thought for a moment. It would be the spur he needed to galvanise the enemy. "It would roust 'em out," he said. "Give 'em a taste of their own physic."

Young Colin was almost dancing with eagerness. "Let me go, sir," he begged. "A few picked men and it's a done thing."

"If t'were done, it were well done quickly," murmured Marlowe, scribbling in his corner.

"Very well," said Nicholas. "Get your rest, pick your men and go as soon as it's dark. I'll follow with the staking party."

Scouts went out during the day; Nicholas wanted no hint to reach the MacGregor. The sharpened stakes were loaded into carts, and a band of archers warned to be ready. MacNab would be in charge of these – Marlowe had managed to convince Nicholas that his place was here at the head of his men if things went wrong. The raiding party left in the dark of the moon, vanishing into the night with hardly a sound.

Time passed slowly. Nicholas paced up and down outside the pele tower, sick with nerves. Rosalyne busied herself inside, she knew better than to plague him, and she had her own preparations to make.

One hour passed, two. A faint silvering showed the coming of moonrise when a small vibration in the ground stopped Nick in his pacing. It grew to a rumour then to a drumming, the sound of hooves and beasts lowing. The herd of cattle swept round the camp, driven by Young Colin and his whooping, shouting men towards the enclosure made ready. Nicholas forgot his position and ran and whooped with the rest, rounding up strays and finally shutting the gates on the milling cattle. He flung his arms round his lieutenant.

"You did it! By God, cousin, you've earned a dram or two for this – come, bring your men. If this doesn't bring them out, I don't know what will…"

MacNab came back with the dawn. He had left his archers to watch and wait by the ruined bridge, and reported all quiet. Nicholas left the raiders to take their reward and go to their beds, and returned to his quarters to make his dispositions. Rosalyne was waiting with his favourite negus and Hob, to pull off his boots. He kept them on.

"Go to your bed, man. When you're rested, get my armour ready." He turned to take his wife in his arms.

"The fuse is lit, Rose. Will you do as I asked and go with the other women up into the hills?"

"We have our own arrangements, Nicholas. We shall be where we are needed. Come and take your rest while you can."

"Presently." He kissed her and drained his cup and went out to see that all was in motion for what was to come. Much later, he came to find her in their bed. The first floor of the tower had been mended and their chamber was warm with the westering sun.

Their coming together was sweeter and more deeply felt than either could have imagined. Wild for each other, they toppled over the cliff together, and after that first real reclamation, the time passed in love and laughter until Nick, roused to a height of passion he had never before experienced, took her with him beyond thought.

The bed had no hangings and the moonlight reached in to where they lay stunned and breathless. He put his hand on her belly to feel the deep shudders still running through her and stroked up to finger away the tears.

"Hush, love, lie quiet. Nothing to fear."

"Nothing." She stretched an arm to draw him close and he slept at last. The sounds of the rousing camp outside woke him to see her smiling down at him, her skin flushed and her hair tumbled about her. His breath caught and the hoarse actor's voice spoke the lines…

"'And now good-morrow to our waking souls…' I can see myself in your eyes, your image is stored in my heart. Do I please you – do you love me, Rose?"

"You have shown me the meaning of the word."

"You clothe me in armour-proof… My love, I must go. The MacGregor will not wait on my lingering here."

"Go then, and please me in one more thing…"

"And what is that, for pity's sake?"

"Eat your breakfast, or you'll upset Hob."

Chapter Five

These scars we had on Crispin's Day

At the end of that day's preparation, she came to him where he sat, his sword at his feet, high on Fairy Mountain, where Harry Munro must have sat many times with his sweetheart. She gathered her skirts to sit beside him.

"I have not come to weaken you, Nicholas. I would keep vigil with you, I am grateful for your life to the boy who was killed." He did not speak, but put his arm about her to draw her close. They sat in silence, watching the sun go down flying banners of purple and gold, mirrored in the still surface of the loch. They could see right down the narrow blazing length of the Tummel with its wooded islet to where it narrowed and widened again into Loch Rannoch. Beyond, lost in purple haze was Rannoch Moor, the domain of the MacGregor. They would be massing now. The meadows south of the Tummel, soon to be the field of battle, lay peaceful and green; the forests on either side wore their autumn livery of scarlet and copper and bronze, burnished by the setting sun. The dew was falling, the colours faded and the long northern twilight began. The air grew chill and he wrapped her in the plaid he had brought with him. They lay close, still and quiet. Presently he slept a little, his head in her lap, rousing in that dead hour of night when men see ghosts and dream of death…

She held him tight in her arms, unspeaking, until the stars began to pale. He raised his head and stood up, smiling down at her.

"When you can see a grey horse at a league, dawn is not far off. It is time." He helped her up and they stood close for a moment. She put a hand up to his face.

"If intellect and a brave heart and a right cause can win battles, the day will be yours. Put on your armour and come back safe."

Oberon was tethered at the foot of the crag, the ubiquitous Hob huddled near his warmth. Nick spoke a word of thanks and took Rosalyne up before him to ride down to the camp. Scouts had been out all night to warn of a night attack; to Nick's surprise the marauders had waited, gathering at the end of Loch Rannoch. He moved among his men, speaking quietly, stowing letters in the front of his shirt, taking the hands of those who offered them, thinking of Marlowe and his tale of Agincourt. His wife stayed at his side, and presently sat to note down the shy words and messages for those who could not write them. The sky began to lighten and she went with him to buckle on his armour. Kit Marlowe stood in the shadows watching, committing it all to memory.

Nicholas had left his elaborate jousting armour in Richmond, preferring more freedom of movement. Over quilted linen went a shirt of mail and over that a suit of plated mail, armour-proof with embedded horizontal strips of steel. Shoulders and upper chest and arms were protected with etched and embossed pauldron and vambrace, the whole affair weighing 45 pounds, less than his fighting jack. Mail-hose and shin guards and codpiece made up the rest, and Rosalyne took up his helm and stood holding it. Hob slotted the last buckle and clicked his fingers. A servant appeared with a steaming jug of wine and Nick's bronze goblet engraved with vine leaves. Rosalyne set the helm on the table, pulled off the thin gauze that bound her hair and tied it to the plume. She poured the aromatic wine.

"Something to stiffen the sinews, my lord?"

Nick smiled at her. "You leave little need for that, sweet. Drink a toast with me – Harry Munro and Strathyre."

They shared the goblet and she stood back from him.

"You have found a cause, Nicholas."

Awkwardly, he found his discarded pouch and took out a letter addressed to her.

"Put it with the others. You are my cause and my strength, Rose. Remember that."

The sun would not shine that day. Lowering cloud threatening the first snow of winter was building in the east, the lakes were a shining sheet of pewter between the dark forests. A darker shadow still was massing where the Tummel met Loch Rannoch, Nick could hear the rumour of a much larger body of men than he had been led to expect. The MacGregor had waited through the night for reinforcements. The growing light revealed at least eight hundred men, bare-arsed and barelegged, like most of his own men, armed with axes and swords and the great two-handed *claidheamh-hor*. Eight hundred against his three. He had thirty cavalry and a company of archers among the three hundred, and a promise of help from the Campbells in the south. "I wouldnae bank on it," MacNab had grumbled. "That's a muckle o' MacGregors. They'll likely bide and see who's on top."

The air was full of a pulsing roar, like thunder, or storm-waves on shingle. His own men for the most part stood quiet, eyeing the strength of the opposition.

Nicholas sat in seeming calm at the spearhead of his men, a black and gold tunic hiding the gleam of his armour, the plume and scarf of his helm floating in the wind off the lake. Nero was armoured at head and breast over a padded saddlecloth that came down past his knees. Behind him waited d'Arblay and Kit Marlowe in mail and breastplate with the rest of the mounted men. His foot soldiers, some in fighting jacks and brigandines, the rest with plaid looped and belted over their shirts, stood shifting, but staying in their ordered lines.

His gauntleted hand went up to keep them still – it was essential to his plan that the marauders made the first move. The MacGregor were milling about, uncertain – this was not their kind of fighting. Some of the youngsters in Nick's command ran out, turned round and flipped up their shirt tails, baring their arses in the face of the enemy. It was enough.

The MacGregors came on in a wave, screaming their war cry. *Ard Choille!* rang and echoed round the valley. Nick's men stood firm, he dropped his hand, and a whickering cloud of arrows hissed into the yelling horde from the archers hidden in the woods and the reeds of the lake. Yells turned to screams and the impetus was lost as men fell and hindered those behind. Another rain of arrows, another and another and Nick drew his sword, raised it and stood in his stirrups.

"Strathyre!" he roared.

Nick urged Nero from a slow trot to a canter to a gallop and led the charge, his men streaming behind him, straight into the centre of the dismayed clansmen. His blood was up, he was screaming with the rest, using sword and axe, guiding Nero with knee and spur. "Munro!" he yelled, laying about him. A figure loomed up before him, the great two-handed sword swinging down on him. Nick's sword scythed across, hand and claymore flew off, cartwheeling in a spurt of blood and the man went down with a shriek under Nero's hooves. Another took his place, and another and he forged on, in the grip of battle frenzy now, sword and axe red and dripping, deaf and blind to all save the task in front of him, to drive the enemy back to where his bowmen were waiting, their arrows gone. Now they came out of the trees in a yelling wave, wielding hammer and claymore, impacting the enemy still more, driving them towards the lake, where stood the men of the Menzies. Seeking room to stand and fight, the MacGregor turned back and for a breathless moment their battle cries were stilled. A dark forest had come up behind them and stood motionless. Many of the MacGregor screamed and ran into the lake to be cut down by the men waiting there, a well-aimed shower of arrows came from the moving wood and Young Colin's men dropped their branches and charged on foot. Seasoned fighters all, the MacGregor were given no room to use their fearsome weapons, surrounded on all sides and pressed together. Nick's strategy was working. The monstrous din echoed back from the sides of the glen, setting up a ringing inside Nick's helm. Hacking and slicing, he and his small band of cavalry forced their way to where Red Rory MacGregor was trying to rally his men and drive a way through. Nick seized him by the hair and Marlowe downed him with the flat of his sword. Their leader gone, the rabble turned into a rout, Young Colin and his men pursuing them over the bodies of the fallen as they ran for home. At the end of the lake, they turned to make a stand – they were Highlanders and fierce fighting men – they were not going to give up.

Out of the west came the Campbells, wild hair flying, bent now on taking revenge for all they had suffered at the hands of these raiders.

At that moment, a crossbow bolt took Nicholas full in the chest, sweeping him off the plunging Nero, under the trampling feet. Hence he knew nothing of the end of the battle, he did not see Marlowe leap down to stand over him and fight off his attackers, the next he knew he was lying stripped of his armour, his pulped shirt stuck to his body with blood and sweat. Someone lifted his head and put a cup to his lips and he saw his armour at his side with the bolt still in it. It was hard to breathe, he tried to move and the pain hit him. He cried out and Rosalyne said, "Lie quiet, it is not as bad as it feels. The bone is not broken, the man said, but you will feel it. The worst is over, sweetheart – the mail made a mess but it is off now." Her voice was steady, and her hands; silent tears were streaming down her face. "The battle is won and you are alive."

"Get me up. What the hell are you about—"

"Lie quiet, you'll start the bleeding again."

He still struggled to sit up. "I must know – let me be, woman…"

Kit Marlowe came into his blurred line of sight and lent an arm. He looked like the devil incarnate, his face a mask of blood from a cut across his forehead, his eyes sparkling and his hair wild and bloody. The attempt to rise brought the sweat out on Nick's face.

"Well, my *parfit gentil* knight, we seem to have prevailed. Ah, you are going to heave up your guts. Good. Now perhaps you will heed your good lady. Rest a little until you are tended to, you young fool. Nothing is so urgent that it will not wait on you. The Campbells came, just in time to chase the buggers back where they belong, with their tails between their hairy legs. By god, it's no wonder men fear these Highlanders, they all fight like demons."

While Kit was speaking, Rosalyne had been busy with water and cloths, easing away the remains of Nick's shirt. He looked down at himself. The bolt had driven armour and mail into his flesh and made a deep groove over his heart. The blow had knocked him out. There was an interesting pattern of red and blue, like criss-crossed paper cuts, where the mesh had bitten into the skin. The groove was not deep but the bruising was extensive and stiffening, it was hard to breathe. He shifted and found another painful area where his shoulders had hit the ground. His sword-hand was swollen and shiny red. He felt that was enough for the present and closed his eyes. Hob was there with basin and fresh water and he and Rosalyne began carefully to tweezer out the fragments of linen driven into the cuts. It was an exquisite torture and he heard Marlowe's voice – *no, he must remember not to call him that. Malheur was too much trouble; it would have to be Kit. Kit was saying,* "Do you remember Hotspur's speech, my dear? You know, so indignant over the perfum'd popinjay and his parmaceti for an inward bruise? You never played it after all, did you? You were going to stammer 'www-wound…'"

"Of course I remember."

"'My lord, I did deny no prisoners—'" prompted Marlowe. Nick took it up in fitful gasps and doggedly went on to the end of the speech. His tormentors were deft and quick, it was soon over and Rosalyne was holding his head, giving him water and something hot and spicy. For some reason it made him very sleepy and the last thing he saw before he slept was his wife and Kit exchanging complicit smiles.

He was not allowed to sleep for long. He was woken abruptly by MacNab blundering into the tent with Young Colin. They were arguing with Kit.

"It's the MacGregor. They've dug the execution pit – Rokesby should be there—"

"They must be stopped," said Marlowe. "It's the last thing we want. Make the man a martyr and it's all to do again."

"Come and talk to them. My lord, you should have a say—"

Nicholas was struggling up; it was surprising how much all the little cuts hurt. Rosalyne stood, her mouth in a tight line, and watched as the men got her husband on his feet and handed him his sword. They left the tent and Marlowe stretched out a hand to prevent her starting after them.

"Let him finish what he started, my dear. He will need you later, when the tally comes in. He can manage till then."

It was not far, the pit had been dug a few paces from the burial ground and the barn where the wounded lay. Red Rory MacGregor was tethered like a beast in the pit dug for his beheading, snarling defiance. Marlowe came swiftly up, and stayed with eyes on Nicholas where he stood isolated now, still in his leg-armour and shredded blood-soaked shirt, leaning on his sword. The other chieftains were ranged on the other side of the pit, Menzies, Black James Murray, MacNab and the big carrot-haired Tom Robertson. Young Colin was there, representing the Melvilles, thoughtfully cleaning his sword.

Nicholas surveyed them and then turned his head to look down the length of the loch. Men were working among the heaps of dead and wounded in the reeds that fringed the water and he caught sight of d'Arblay, one arm bandaged to his side, trying to attend to the horses. As he watched, one of the animals went down in a fountain of blood and d'Arblay turned away, his head bent. Nero still stood, head hanging, exhausted, and d'Arblay leaned against him, his face in the long mane. The sun was setting in crimson bars of cloud, working its magic so that it was hard to tell where the spreading tide of red in the green water ended.

"Well, my Lord Rokesby, what do you say? You led us today. We have waited for you. Your voice is needed." This was Robert Menzies, the most aggressive of the four, whose lands, after Strathyre, had suffered most. Nicholas fought for breath.

"I say, treat with him. Seal a pact that will keep him in his own lands. There has been killing enough." There was an angry murmur and the man in the pit laughed and spat and stuck up two fingers. Black James Murray started forward, his sword swinging up, and Nicholas shouted, "No!" The pain it gave him sent him to one knee and Marlowe stepped forward and spoke.

"I know the mind of this man here, the architect of this day's victory, and I know what he would say if he had the breath to say it." He bowed to Nicholas, who was on his feet again. "If you will allow…" He turned to the others and raised his silver voice. "Execute this man and you will make not an example, you will make of him a martyr. Men will rise in his name, rise and rise again to take revenge on this generation and generations yet unborn.

"Make of yourselves judge and jury and what is to become of the law of the land? MacGregor is outlawed already, and his kin. If you seek revenge only, send him to the Courts of Justice, give him to the laws of Scotland. If you seek recompense, what recompense can there be, worthy of those who have died, but a peaceful settlement? My Lord Rokesby would say let this chieftain carry back a promise, his word that he will make no more inroads on the peace and plenty of this place and the people who live in it. If he will make no vow, give him to the law." He paused and looked round. Many of the clansmen who had fought the battle had come to listen.

"We are men. We are come near the beginning of a new century. Let us be men who will look forward, not men who seek to mend one wrongdoing with another. Are we barbarians? Let us cease wrangling and rebuild our homes and educate our children in the ways of a civilised people. This man was the captain of our enterprise today. Listen to him."

This broadside of rhetoric, worthy of Cicero, was met with the stunned silence it merited. Red Rory MacGregor appeared totally bewildered. *He understood one word in three,* thought Nick. Robert Menzies glanced at his fellows and addressed himself to the young man who had planned the battle.

"Is this what you would say?"

Marlowe had given Nicholas time to gather his strength. His trained and beautiful voice, quiet and perfectly distinct, carried to all the men listening.

"I would say there has been slaughter enough. This man expects rough justice, I think he would welcome it, to give reason and excuse for his kin to go on as before. If he will not yield to parley, take him to the courts. And I ask you, now that your blood has cooled, which of you will wield the axe? Blood will have blood, they say, and this act will cry out bloody murder. Which of you will be a murderer?" He spoke to the man crouched in the pit.

"I say to you, there would be no dishonour in this pact. Know that if, once given, it is broken, these men will show no mercy to you or your kin." A low growl went up and the prisoner shouted something unintelligible.

"Take time to reflect," said Marlowe. Nicholas saw the chieftains draw together and then part to gather their clansmen

39

about them. He had done all he could and turned away to walk slowly and carefully back to where Rosalyne was waiting for him. Men spoke to him, and smiled, and touched lightly, some followed on behind. He reached his tent, stepped inside, the flap came down and he pitched into a bottomless pit of his own.

Two days later he was back at his table, at odds with his wife and the King's Physician, arrived that morning. He was in his shirtsleeves, the weight of a doublet was more than he could contemplate. Under the linen and bandages, the flesh of his chest, scored across and across like a piece of crackling, was extraordinarily painful, and the blow over the heart had shaken him more than he cared to admit. The upper left quadrant of his body was one huge inflamed bruise, his shoulder blades were not much better. The actor's trick of breathing helped, and as long as he sat still he could manage. The previous day he had visited the wounded, moving among them with words of praise and encouragement, a strange whining in his ears. One or two would not last the night and he spoke to the women tending them. One man he knew, one of his own and he lowered himself awkwardly to sit by him. He had been still sitting there holding the dead man's hand when Rosalyne came to find him.

The tally of the dead was far less than he had any right to expect, and he sat now writing the report demanded by the King. In fact he was not writing, but dictating. Like most of his men, his sword-hand was still too stiff and swollen to hold a pen. Rosalyne sat beside him, tight-lipped and angry, taking down the words. He had been told how the fight had ended, and how Marlowe had stood over his body till the last. He knew that MacGregor had signed a pact and been taken to the edge of his lands and left. Either the man had understood what had been said or he decided to save his skin. Red Rory MacGregor might be a raider and a natural killer, but Nicholas did not reckon him any kind of a coward. Now there would be peace. It was time to take stock, see the families of the injured and dead provided for and start to reclaim the lands they had fought for.

Something was nagging at him and he put his seal to the report and sent for Jock MacNab. Rosalyne went with a whisk of her skirts.

"Who among the men carried a crossbow?"

"None," said MacNab, surprised. "All longbowmen. Was that what took ye?"

"The Campbells?"

"They didnae come till after. And I never saw a MacGregor with any but an axe and *claidheamh-hor*. They like infighting, a good dint wi' a blade."

"Then was I targeted, do you think? Deliberate?"

"They dinnae think like that. I doubt they expected what they got – or what they were up against. Are you thinking what I'm thinking?"

"An assassin – Mowbray? Here?"

"Or his hireling. You want we should look for him?"

"In this country? He'll be long gone – halfway over the Border by now. No, double the guard, put the word out."

"It's no' good ground for a Southerner, if it's him. Nights are cold, he'll need shelter. I'll have some men take a wee look."

Nick gave his short nod and stood up carefully.

MacNab grinned. "There's none will blame ye if ye take to your bed awhile. Give yourself a chance, lad, you'll heal quicker."

"I'm going to the horse lines."

Rosalyne pushed open the door with her hip and entered with a tray of bandages and hot water. Nick groaned and MacNab left, chuckling to himself. His money was on the wife.

Chapter Six

Aftermath

It was a week before Nicholas could breathe deep again or hold a pen and he spent each stubborn day at his desk, with Kit Marlowe beside him to write his reports, and the letters and dispatches that went to the King. Word went to Charles Melville in Linlithgow and to Tobias in Richmond.

Nick leaned back and stretched cautiously. "I want to bring the boys here," he said. "When we've finished clearing up. You never really met them, did you?"

Marlowe thought of his isolated cabin-prison on the *Snipe* and grunted. Nicholas was still speaking, confiding some of his thoughts on that first ride along the lochs. Marlowe shook his head.

"You are such a misfit, my dear. You sit there with a chest like a piece of lacework and talk of fishing and flowers – a romantic idealist. Like Ralegh. Perhaps you should have been an explorer."

"I wanted to be an actor."

"Same thing."

As movement became easier, the next task was dealing with the aftermath of the battle and the rebuilding that must be done. The families of the dead and wounded were to be provided for and he spent painful hours in the saddle in worsening weather doing the rounds. Rosalyne fed him, bathed his wounds, bandaged him and let him be.

A messenger arrived, muddy and tired, and gazed round open-mouthed at the scene of the battle and the busy camp. He had brought letters from Cecil and one with writing and a crest Nicholas recognised with a sinking heart. If the Queen herself had written he was in trouble. There was a packet from Tobias Fletcher and he took it indoors to read first.

The Lord Admiral Sir William Talbot, Jack's godfather, had come to Tobias as the only person likely to know Nick's whereabouts, with news and a warning. "Stay away."

> *You left just as the fun started. Essex is back from Ireland and has whistled up a whirlwind. He has upset the Queen in some way, on that very first day, the twenty-eighth of September.*

He must have been crossing the Irish Sea as we passed the Tyne, thought Nick.

> *Sir William was at the meeting in Essex House that same day – all Devereux' friends were there and listening to his boasting, and Ralegh, with Cobham and Shrewsbury, and Grey with that turncoat Thomas Howard, all sat apart.*

Not the Cobham I knew, thought Nick. *Wonder if the son is as tricksy?*

> *Your uncle sat in on the arraignment in the days that followed –*

you knew he was on the Council – and heard Essex accused of contemptuous disobedience to the Queen in returning against her express wish, proceeding in Ireland contrary to his orders, presumptuous letters, entering her bedchamber in rash manner and making and suborning many idle knights. Sir William says E stood throughout at the end of the table in proud and haughty mien and answered gravely for three hours. He thought he could handle the Queen, Nick, and turn her to name him to come after. He failed. The Court has now come here to the palace at Richmond, this day of the second of October for your information, and Essex is confined to York House in the keeping of the Lord Keeper of the Seal. E and his friends fear he will be sent to the Tower.

My lord Cecil has made him an official Visit and said he would do anything to further his good. Cecil now says he will not be reconciled but will bear no malice. Rich, eh Nick? Thank God this man is no longer your paymaster. Essex still has many friends and the love of the people. The Queen must decide soon what to do with him or there will be the rising he hoped for. I pray you, stay where you are. My love and duty to your lady wife.

The rest of the packet dealt with business matters and added a commendation for Tim Trelawney, for what, Nick had no idea.

Among the letters was one from Robert Cecil, and surprisingly several from Robert Poley. The first of these was encrypted and read like a report from the Watch, erratically spelt and lacking punctuation. Poley's short stint at Cambridge did not seem to have done him much good.

My lord, At request of my Lord C I proceeded to enquire into wherabouts of M and let it be know about I was friendly to his cause having no love for your worship begging pardon I take the liberty of mention munny the which I am in hopes of your honor repaying nowing M to be short of funds In due time I came to hear of him and his recent doings May I say here my lord I thank God for your Preservation'

He is damnably well-informed, thought Nick. *Cecil's web spreads far.*

I am crept into M's confidence not in time I beg pardon to prevent the aforesaid infortunate occurrence I trust this finds your good self recovered. We are situate in Northamptonshire whre M had lands bfore his downfall.

There followed precise directions to a village outside Macclesfield.

He is ingorged with rage my lord sometimes I think not in his wits he halfkilled the man that failed with the crossbow If your lordship is in pursuanse of the matter the Pot of Feathers Duncton will find me Yr Obnt Srvnt R Poley Encl. To prove goodwill

Why in the name of all that's wonderful is Poley interesting himself in this affair? thought Nick. He had not thought the man to have a shred of gratitude or loyalty in his makeup. *Expects to be well-paid, no doubt,* was his uncharitable thought. *A trap? Very like…* He did not trust the man supposed to have murdered Marlowe. He may not have been accused of wielding the dagger but he was involved in the plot. He unfolded the page enclosed with the letter and read it, the hair rising on his head. It was a letter to Mowbray from the Earl of Essex and in the wrong hands meant trouble of the worst kind.

Ireland

Mowbray, my very good friend,

With God's good grace you will be free by now and making your way to me. I pray you Ned, be not governed by your vanity and bitter hate to seek out young Rokesby. He will be on his guard now and unassailable by a man alone. No, friend, come to me covertly, I tell you again we may need him. I had great hopes of him and he has proven me right, he has made one fortune and married another. He has the ear of our turnabout Queen and old and ugly as she is she looks on him with favour. Would I had bound him to me sooner, he must needs be seeking power. Let me but come at him again and he will be of use to us – do not kill the goose that may yet lay us golden eggs.

The Queen forbids me to return without her express permission Ned, but in God's name how much longer can I stay in this bog-ridden place? I make no headway against Tyrone and my enemies at home spread lies about me. She keeps me short and complains always of my spending – can I make war without the sinews thereof? If I am to win through I must act. My friends, and I count you among them Ned, urge me to force my way in and confront her with a fait accompli. I shall offer Rokesby a place on my Council: if our miserly Queen does not renew my monies from the winery we need his gold. Spare him for me.

Your friend in all things, RD

Nicholas read with mounting horror. The letter, part arrogance, part whining, and wholly incriminating, was written in Devereux' own hand and in clear. This settled the matter. The situation must be dealt with; it had gone far enough. The other letters from Poley dealt directly with the developments in the attempted coup mounted by Essex and its possible aftermath, much more informative than Cecil. *Little Robin still sitting on the fence,* thought Nick. *Must be getting a mite uncomfortable.*

Cecil's ciphered letter was short.

Stay where you are.

"I wasn't going anywhere," said Nick.

I have told her Majesty you are absent on matters concerning the defence of her realm, which I tell her she should hold at more importance than her whim.
 How to influence Elizabeth… thought Nick.
 Keep away from the taint of my lord Essex. Serve James.

"Tuh!" Nick tossed it aside. Rosalyne came in shaking out her shawl.

"It's trying to snow," she said. "News?" Nicholas handed her Tobias' letter and slid his knife under the Queen's seal. As he expected, it was a very nasty letter, the sort Elizabeth was famous for.

My lord of Rokesby and Richmond, thane of Strathyre
 You have left our presence without word or permission and abandoned us in our hour of need. You were looked for at the play – which I thought a tedious thing – and some jackanapes took your part. I am told you are on our business, defending our realm. How many men, I wonder, take their wives and children on such a dangerous ploy? If you feared the displeasure of my lord Essex, I tell you our displeasure is by far the greater. He broke into our

48

bedchamber as he did before and I told you of, in all the mud of his journey and myself not dressed. I spoke him fair to rid me of him and my thoughts were black. My Robin is flown too high and so I am repaid. I am mistook in all I seek to draw to me. Ralegh and his Bess – does your wife wear the breeches, my lord?

Your absence is untimely and you know right well that had you sought leave in this time of trouble it would not have been given. You left no word and this is the greatest impertinence…

The letter went on in this vein for several pages. Nicholas was not surprised; he had seen her letters before. She was never sparing of ink and paper or repetition. She ranted on,

This is not the first time you have acted without due warranty from us. Have a care, my lord. Without word in your own hand I know not what to believe. I am bedevilled by greybeards who advise me one way then another. My poor silly Robin has put himself and our person in jeopardy and that lord Rokesby who seemed honest is absent from us. You are not impregnable to our anger, Rokesby. Disobedience does not go unpunished. Make yourself known. ER.

Nicholas handed the letter to Rosalyne.

"She is not happy," he said mildly. "Am I wounded unto death? Have we the plague? Have I had a vision and turned Papist? My excuse had better be a good one."

"Make no excuse. Tell her the truth. I notice she does not command an instant return, she must believe some of Cecil's lies. She is old and shaken and lonely, Nicco. She needs comfort. Tell her the truth and make love to her."

He took some trouble over his letter. He told her the truth and forbore to remind her that a great deal of Mowbray's enmity she had brought about herself by, first, giving him Mowbray's confiscated lands and then the woman Mowbray desired above all things. She knew that well enough. The lovemaking took the form of a gentle scold that she should doubt him and a sincere wish that he was at her side at this time of Essex' return. He ended with a promise to come as soon as the fight was done – *with my shield or on it*, he added in the fulsome language she enjoyed. He genuinely felt for Elizabeth. He had heard the cruel things Essex had said of her behind her back, faithfully passed on to her by those of her ladies who had enjoyed the favours of Robert Devereux. Her body was failing her and she hated it.

He sent a message to Robert Carey. There was a man to console her.

As far as King James was concerned, Nick's task at Strathyre was done with the taming of the MacGregor, but for the new master of this little kingdom it was just beginning. The king's men and the clansmen departed, the tenants and crofters returned to their devastated homes to begin the task of rebuilding. They worked fast to get roofs on houses and barns, bring in fodder and fuel and roots from the fields before winter. Nicholas sent for Mistress Melville and the boys.

The bloody morass of the battle field would not recover its green until spring: men and horses dragged the harrows over the churned-up ground to be ready. There would be little grazing and Nicholas put off bringing down the livestock from the hills until byres were repaired and made fit. Instead he ordered areas of brushwood cleared and planted with winter wheat, oats and barley. Repairs began and Jack and William arrived to the sound of the woods ringing with the blows of axes and the whine of saws.

Hob's jaw dropped at first sight of Nick's offspring. They were of a height and he took them for twins. No-one troubled to disabuse him of this idea; they both bore the name Talbot, Nick had formally adopted his son William on his marriage. It was some months before Hob discovered they were born of different mothers (Young Colin could still be indiscreet in his cups.) Childless himself – as far as he knew – he was enchanted with this addition to his new family, as he saw it, and extended his loyalty accordingly. With so much practical work to do, Mistress Melville suspended lessons for the moment, and the boys ran wild. Or so they thought. In fact, their father took the opportunity to take them in hand and begin to make his dream reality. He took them with him into the fields and woods and to fish in the lakes, sharing his own boyhood skills and his feel for the place.

The two boys, so alike in feature, were very different. Jack was the one who needed watching, he would run full-tilt at any adventure and Hob was forever pulling him out of some scrape, laughing and filthy. It did not take long for Hob to realise that the more imaginative William was the most likely instigator of these adventures, but, like his father, had the gumption to know when to stop. The answer seemed to be to put them to work, which they did with a will. It was all new and exciting for them after the palace at Linlithgow.

They gathered bundles of reeds from the lakeside for thatching, helped fill cartloads of stone to be brought up to the tower. They caught fish for the table and learned archery with the MacNab. Nick watched them begin to grow and become strong and independent and rejoiced with Rosalyne to see it. She and Mistress Melville worked alongside the other women to see the men and beasts fed and housed, the care of the wounded their particular province.

That first experience of the aftermath of the battle had been a horrifying one for Rosalyne, it had taken all her fortitude to face it. All very well to use her skills of running a large household to band together women and resources, but when the first casualties came in, some with hideous wounds, she wanted to run away. Commonsense and the experience of the others had come to her aid, and she managed – until her own husband was brought to her unconscious, perhaps dead. She found a strength she had not known she possessed: she was not going to lose this man who had taken her by storm.

Now she stood with his arm about her watching their children – Jack was as much hers now as William – shooting at a target.

"They grow apace, Nicholas. This is what you wanted for them."

He nodded and looked down at her, smiling, picking off the wool stuck to her skirts.

"What now, my lady? Stuffing pillows?"

"I am learning to spin, if you please. A most relaxing exercise – I am happy to tell you your plaid is of the most refined and subtle colours. I shall not be ashamed to wear it."

"After all this, I should hope not. I am proud of you, Rose, and shall be proud to see you in our colours. Black and gold or the Melville plaid, you have made them your own."

The days were shortening but the season prolonged itself, the sun going down every evening in a fume of red. The men and women of Strathyre made the most of it in a fever of husbandry. The Devil's Breath had not yet touched the blackberries, and Nicholas took an hour or two's holiday away from more demanding pursuits to take his family up the hill to pick them. Mistress Melville made a small expedition of it, packing a basket with oatcakes and cheese – what could be better with blackberries? – apples and cider and giving it to Hob to carry. He looked down his nose – what a fuss over a few berries – but in the end succumbed to the gentle pleasure of it. The food disappeared almost at once of course and for Jack the novelty of picking soon wore off. William was intent on finding only the best and in an effort to outdo him, his brother overreached himself and fell with a roar into a welter of bramble.

His efforts to scramble free made matters worse and it took the combined efforts of Hob, William and the two women to get him out. Nicholas had strayed away to find mushrooms and came back at the double to find one son trying hard not to laugh and the other red with temper and purple with juice stamping off down the hill. Anne Melville rolled her eyes, picked up her basket and followed him. At a nod from Nicholas, Hob went too. (Standing order No.1. No woman or child to go unescorted.) Very soon the boy stopped and waited, his back turned. His nurse caught him up, spoke with him quietly and Jack nodded, took her basket from her and carried it back to where his father stood hands on hips, watching.

William had picked up Jack's basket and quite a lot of the scattered berries. Jack shook his head.

Nick grinned at him. "I dropped my mushrooms. Come and help me find them, they don't fight back – unless they're wrong 'uns of course. But then you will know that from Rokesby. Why don't we teach William? There was a time when a little local knowledge saved my life."

This face-saving proposal met with gracious approval and Nicholas set off into the woods, his children running ahead.

Hob wondered. He had not quite worked it out yet.

The barns and byres were ready and the harvest gathered in before he learned the full story and wondered the more. Young Colin boasted also of the English Court and the triumph of the Tournament and Hob worried. Surely his lord and master would not turn his back on all that. He worked on making himself indispensible.

Winter came like the onset of the MacGregor, hurling hail and sleet and snow, in a storm that stripped the leaves from the trees and drove everyone to shelter.

As the hail turned to icy vertical rain, filling the gutters and making a small waterfall off the roof of the tower, a sodden and half-drowned body of men rode in, plumed hats draggled and bent, the fur of their cloaks smelling like a mew of wet cats. Johnnie Erskine, Earl of Mar, had come in person with a message from the King.

Once welcomed in, fed and dry and settled, Nick heard the burden of his song.

"Our Jamie is pleased, Nicholas. He makes of Strathyre an earldom and you thane of Cawdor. The lands run between his at Peebles and the Lyons' of Glamis."

Marlowe pricked up his ears. *Thane of Cawdor. Hmm. Strathyre and Cawdor... no, does not flow.*

"What was the other place?" he interrupted. "Glamis..."

Mar looked round, surprised.

"Monsieur Malheur is a poet," said Nick hastily. "He saved my life in the battle."

"Ah."

Marlowe smiled at him, all dark Gallic charm.

"His majesty would welcome you also, sir. A hero, and a poet."

"*Je regrette, milor.*" Marlowe produced a rattling cough and spat into the fire. "My health will not permit. His majesty will excuse me."

Mar shrugged. "A pity. I am sorry to hear it." He turned back to Nicholas. "Your presence and that of your good lady is required at Court. Your children and their nurse will be welcome."

Rosalyne came in with more wine in time to catch the last exchange. She caught Nick's eye and lifted a shoulder a little, resigned. Mar rose.

"Countess, you will be a ravishing ornament to our Court," he said with a graceful bow.

"Thane of Glamis and Cawdor, perfect rhythm," muttered Marlowe. He sat in his corner, rapt, his lips moving, oblivious to the rather forced celebration going on around him. Johnnie, Earl of Mar was no more pleased than Nicholas at this development. Rokesby was a rising star who would bear watching.

"I have no clothes," said Rosalyne, confronting him in their bedchamber that night.

"No more have I. That is the least of it, I have unfinished business."

"Mowbray? What news of him?"

"Gone to ground, goddammit. Now I think of it, perhaps this is no bad thing. You will be protected at Court, he cannot come at you there."

"But we had such plans—"

"One thing at a time, sweetheart. I suppose I should have expected something like this – James likes to scatter favours. One thing, I shall be in a better position to set matters in train. We'll find him. Think of it sweeting, we shall have the boys safe with us."

Young Colin pleaded to be left behind, he had his eye on Black James Murray's eldest daughter, a dark-haired, blue-eyed beauty.

The chieftain smiled on the match, he reckoned the young Melville to be a bonny fighter and the Melvilles were powerful at Court.

"Intercede for me with my uncle, Nick," said the eager suitor. "To be related to the Murrays is no' bad."

"I can't see him objecting," said Nicholas. "We'll be back for your wedding. I'll leave you in charge. Look after Kit for me."

Chapter Seven

The Court at Edinburgh. The turn of the century

The small cavalcade trotted into the city to find Tim Trelawney waiting for them with the rest of their belongings from the ship. Rose would have at least one dress suitable for presentation, thought Nick. He would content himself with his remaining serviceable doublet and his Order of Merit. Trelawney was obviously full as an egg with news and Nicholas took him aside.

"Why are you not in London with Master Fletcher? He had plans for the *Snipe*."

"I didn't see sense in going back empty-handed, sir. I heard tell of a cargo up north in Peebles, salt and dried cod and coal. It's a gold mine, sir. I took a full cargo to Amsterdam and brought back furs and necessaries to London. Good profit. Master Fletcher sent me back here with a full cargo for the Court, and your clothes from Richmond and orders to stand by." It was not the first time Nicholas had reason to be grateful to Trelawney for acting on his own initiative. He smiled and clapped the young man on the shoulder.

"Well done, Tim. Tell me more of this 'gold mine'."

Rosalyne looked for him in vain to tell him of the quarters set aside for them, and the wardrobes full of clothes. He was deep in conference with Trelawney; the budding entrepreneur had brought a packet of letters and orders for goods. Nicholas was reminded abruptly that he was a man of business: he felt like a juggler continually adding plates to those already spinning. Fortunately he had a partner in Tobias Fletcher worth his weight in dried cod. Trelawney was proving a welcome addition to the ranks.

The more pressing matters dealt with, he rewarded his enterprising messenger and went to find Rosalyne where she was rejoicing in a welter of reclaimed finery. He embraced his excited offspring and sat with his arms round them listening to the tales of their doings. Jack was in a fine temper, and when Mistress Melville came presently to bear them off to their quarters in the Queen's nursery, "They're a lot of babies!" he said scornfully.

"Robbie Scott's all right," said his brother. "And Will Argyle."

"Mphm," said Jack. "They're not in the nursery, though. Do we have to be in the nursery, father?"

"You are just next door, child," said Mistress Melville. "Come away now. Bedtime."

"I wish it was bedtime for us, Rose," said their father as they were dragged protesting away. "Bowing and banqueting is our portion."

"Botheration indeed," she said. "I love the letter B. So – useful."

Queen Anne, no beauty with her thin lips and long pointed nose, and peevish with early pregnancy, eyed the ravishing new addition to the Court a little warily. On Robert Cecil's principle of knowing the whereabouts of any possible hazard, she appointed Rosalyne, Countess of Strathyre, as a lady-in-waiting. There was no gainsaying it and the children were absorbed into the Royal household, together with other noblemen's sons and daughters. Mistress Melville was kept busy, much in demand for her ability to tame the tantrums of the three-year-old Princess Elizabeth. Red-haired and wilful, god-daughter to the English Queen, she reminded many of the elders at the Court of Mary of Guise, in her young days at the French Court. The child's naming was one of James' many overtures to Elizabeth. Nicholas began to look about him for a tutor. Dr Knowles, Nick's own old tutor, was now retired, and had been given a well-found little house on the outskirts of Lower Rookham, with gardens to potter in, and some pasture, with a comfortable married couple to see to his needs. The boys needed taking in hand.

Nick was lucky enough to find a young man fresh from the Universities of Paris, related to the Crawfords in the West and the Percys of Northumberland. Their first meeting was propitious. Tom Percy had come from a visit to his cousins in Carlisle, a well-set up young man near Nick's own age and Nick found him well-grounded in the classics, a handy swordsman and a notable musician. He was moderate in his views, had no interest in politics but a profound enthusiasm for botany. He had no money and no sponsor and when Nicholas spoke of Strathyre and offered generous terms and a period of trial, he accepted and began straightaway on the task of extricating Jack and William from the Queen's nursery.

In this he failed. His songs and passions beguiled not only his two pupils, but the rest of the Royal brood, and he would be seen like a fairy piper leading a crowd of small children into the fields and woods, showing them birds and beasts to the accompaniment of the *Eclogues*, reading tracks in the snow and re-enacting old battles to the tune of the *Iliad*. Nick felt he had chosen well.

"We made him do Agincourt," boasted Jack, coming in with a red weal down his cheek. "We told him about the Battle of

Strathyre. Father, why is Henry Stewart allowed to hit me and me not hit him back?"

"Because he is a Prince," said Nicholas. "And he is not as big as you."

"He had a big stick!"

"Perhaps he feels he needs one."

Jack considered this, his head cocked to one side. Presently he said, "When he's as big as me, can I hit him back then?"

"No, because he will still be a Prince."

"Oh. But anyone can still hit me."

"You'll manage. Princes can't stop you using your head. What about a game of chess?"

Jack stuck out his bottom lip. "Ask Will."

Nick looked thoughtfully at his mutinous son. Jack was well-grown for his age, taller than his half-brother, physically strong. He would soon be entering his godfather's household to begin his training for the Court or the Navy, away from the petticoat government of Mistress Melville, Rosalyne and the Queen's nursery.

Not before time, thought Nick, staring at the back turned to him. The boy was standing very straight, arms folded, glaring out of the window.

That's sons for you, he thought. *Breeched before you know it, leaving, out in the world.* Perhaps Rosalyne would give him a daughter to watch over and keep safe. He looked across at William. So different, a studious boy, his head bent over his drawing. He would keep William by him a while longer.

In all this time, Nicholas was in frequent attendance on the King, with Mowbray like a nest of scorpions in the back of his mind. He wrote something of this to Marlowe, together with the recent news and Kit seized on the phrase with glee. "Scorpions," he muttered, "yes." His current work was sticking in places and he wanted his Mercury back to speak the words aloud for him.

The King, always careless of formality and preferring to hunt and listen to poetry rather than struggle with ciphers, opened up his correspondence with Cecil privately to Nicholas. After listening to another of the flattering letters, codeword 10, James sighed.

"All very well, but I find I cannot entirely put my trust in Master Secretary Cecil. I am told he favours the Spanish claim."

Told by whom? wondered Nick. Familiar with Cecil's habit of hedging his bets, he tried to be reassuring.

"A smokescreen, your Majesty. A diversion to muddy the water – a rumour spread by my lord Essex."

James shifted uneasily at this and Nick thought, *Bang in the gold.* He went on, "My lord Cecil well knows the people will not stand for a Spanish Catholic queen. Nor would our queen allow it said."

"Does she say so?"

"Yes, your Majesty. She has said, 'None but a king shall follow me.'"

"Master Secretary speaks of Essex."

"Robert Devereux is a threat to himself, not to your Majesty, surely?"

"You think so?" He sat with an elbow on the arm of his chair, his chin sunk in his hand. At his side was the red leather box in which he kept his most private papers. Presently he roused and fumbled out the key.

"He writes to me." He unlocked the box. "Here, see what he says."

"Your Majesty, I don't—"

"You have saved my life once, and my throne twice over, Strathyre. Am I to trust only in my nobles? Men of self-interest like most of their kind. Your uncle Melville? A good man and he is in England doing what he can. Read. According to you and my lord Cecil, I have nothing to lose."

No, but I have, thought Nick.

Chapter Eight

Scotland 1600

The dawn of the new century was celebrated with an elaborate banquet. The long T-shaped table was piled with dishes and platters – roast boar, venison, capons, oysters and a roast swan with all its feathers stuck back on added their pungent steam to the smoke, perfume and sweat rising to the groined roof. There was ale, whisky, wine, mulled wine and fortified wine; flaming puddings were brought in accompanied by pipers and in blessed intervals a lutanist played, unheard in the growing din. Barons and chieftains, come in from outlying estates, were seated down the stem of the T and Nicholas, separated from Rosalyne, sat at one end of the top table, she at the other between Argyle and the Earl of Mar. Henry Argyle was paying her marked attention, he noticed, even attempting to feed her titbits with his fingers. She contrived to be drinking from her cup or turning her head to listen to Mar, those fingers did not reach her lips. *She is in beauty tonight,* thought Nick. All in violet, the gauze fan of her collar making a background for her dark hair, spangled with amethysts, she had been careful not to outshine the Queen. Anne of Scotland was in full fig, tissue of gold paned and quilted with pearls and rubies, a tiara of diamonds trembling on her wire-wool hair. Nick smiled to himself. *Wonder what she owes John Challoner for that lot?* He knew his fellow businessman had distanced himself from the Scottish Court since the debacle over the letters last year, but that did not mean he was not still the Queen's jeweller – and her main creditor.

Toast after toast was drunk, voices grew steadily louder and a drunken lord leaned across and shouted something to James. The King was on his feet in an instant, calling for his horse. Trumpets sounded, everyone who could still do so, stood up, a bench went over and, whooping and calling, there was a stampede for the stables. A midnight hunt!

James was never happier than on horseback, his disproportionate body showed to best advantage in the saddle, his spindly legs became part of his horse, his fine torso erect and commanding. This was better than meat and drink to him. Nicholas paused for a word with Rosalyne as he passed in more leisurely manner. He was drunk but not to the detriment of his horsemanship, no need for her to worry.

The night was clear and very cold, the stars bright and hard in a black-velvet sky. Far to the north, a gauzy curtain rose and fell, fading before a rising moon. The snow was deep-packed and firm under their hooves as the glittering array of horsemen issued from the castle, torches flaring, clattering down the steep streets and out into the country. Servants were scurrying to load sleds with food and flagons to follow the hunt as it streamed over the whitened fields towards the black of the forest, and Nick took his time saddling up Nero and following on. He took no weapon save his poniard, content to feel his horse moving sweetly under him, sure-footed and willing, and to enjoy the eye-watering wind, bracing and welcome after the heat of the banqueting hall.

Invigorated, he hallooed as they set up first a hare, leaping and zigzagging over the snow, then a small snort of wild pig. Shouting and yelling, too drunk to be a danger to any but themselves, a lone fox drew them back towards the river, where a crowd of townspeople had come out to watch. The servants had come up with the sleds and one bright spark began to kick a bag-pudding about. A servant was sent scampering for a proper ball and Mar shouted for two teams.

The Scottish game of *footbal* played by torchlight on the sandy shore of the firth looked from the outset more like mortal combat than sport. There were no rules to speak of; the game was played on foot, the object simply to get the blown-up pig's bladder between the rocks at either end of the beach. Mar led one team and Nicholas the other, each side seeming intent on mayhem, cheered on by the townsfolk, laying bets. Rosalyne and Mistress Melville, muffled in furs, watched with some of the other Court ladies, all of them looked down upon by the cold stars. The Queen was not present, and James sat his horse apart from the rest.

"They are all mad," said Rosalyne as Nicholas downed Argyle in a flying tackle and stood up grinning to be flattened in turn by Johnnie Erskine.

"Just children," said Mistress Melville comfortably. "Men-children. It's as well to get out their wild humours."

There are other ways, thought Rosalyne, watching her husband go down on the ball under a heap of yelling Scots. The bladder had to be replaced three times and the thing was only deemed to be at an end when the last available ball went floating out to sea. The casualties were carted off and Nicholas came up laughing, with a fine black eye developing, wiping a bloodied nose on his sleeve.

"No telling who won," he said. "And we're all too drunk to care."

"Johnnie Mar cares," murmured Mistress Melville, watching him limping up the shore. Nicholas shook his head.

"Fine sport," he said. "We'll do it on horseback next time – with a ball that doesn't explode."

Life went on at Court, time spent in hunting, hawking and feasting, and sitting beside the king reading aloud.

Nicholas began to fidget.

"We should return to Strathyre, Rose," he said. "I long to be there for the coming of Spring. Do you pine for Richmond, my lady? Or can you be content here awhile longer – even after the reason for our coming is over and done?"

"I love Strathyre, Nicholas. To me it is the place where we truly found each other. I have made friends there, the boys will grow strong. No, my lord, I shall not stay here at Court, I shall come back with you. Only one thing troubles me. Would you wish the babe that is coming to be born a Scot?" If she hoped to surprise him, she was disappointed, Nicholas knew and cherished every part of her. To please her, he was astonished and delighted, picking her up and carrying her to the couch under the window, calling for wine.

"Give me a daughter, sweetheart, made in your image, and I shall be the most grateful, the happiest lover in Christendom."

Before they left, word came from Poley arranging a meeting. It meant a short detour on the way back to Strathyre and Nicholas decided to take a small, armed escort in case of trouble. His last interview with the King was an uneasy one. A man had come to Court with another appeal from Essex for James to raise his forces

66

and leave for the border to wait for reinforcements. Essex, with his friend Mountjoy, promised help and men from Tyrone in Ireland if James would commit himself to an assault on the throne of England. The messenger was still hanging about the palace waiting for an answer. Nicholas, asked for counsel, advised that James do what he did best, delay in answering and make no commitment or statement to anyone, least of all to my lord Cecil. On no account should he think of an assault of any kind.

"This is old stratagem, your Majesty," he said. "Come too late. My lord Essex is in no case to carry out such a plan and I hear Mountjoy is like to renege on his promise of aid. He is enjoying success in Ireland where Essex failed. I doubt he will risk a promising career now." *Poley has his uses*, he thought, *before Essex sneezes, I know he has caught cold.* "As long as Robert Devereux has nothing from your Majesty in writing, all will be well." James would not meet his eye and Nick's heart sank. The last thing he wanted was to be sent to London to meddle in the affair. Reluctantly James agreed to let him go and deal with his own problems with the proviso that he must hold himself in readiness and come if needed.

"There are those who suspect you, my thane," he said. "My nobles mislike it that you can command such a band of men to follow you. I have no such fear. You and your men would stand at my back, I know it."

"Your Majesty has only to sit quiet," said Nicholas. "A time of masterly inactivity, I think, as your advisers suggest, with Essex handled as you would a hot coal. As so often before, he has ill-timed his effort, it is aborted through his own misjudgement. Be patient, your Majesty, the crowns of England and Scotland will be yours." He suffered a tearful embrace and left to take his leave of a cynical Johnny Mar and bid farewell to the only man he had found to trust at this Court of Scotland.

The meeting with Lord Abercrombie took place in a small anteroom leading off the old statesman's bedchamber. No-one else was present. He did not invite Nicholas to sit and himself paced between window and door, his hands behind his back, his robe jutting out behind him. He came to a halt finally in a familiar stance before the fire. He fixed Nicholas with a steely eye.

"I like you, lad," he said. "I like what you have done and what you are trying to do. But I should warn you, there are those here at Court who are wary of your rise to power." Nicholas made to speak and Abercrombie held up a meaty hand. "Power is what you have, Rokesby of Strathyre and Cawdor, like it or not. Some of the Privy Council have proposed that you join us, others are bitterly opposed. You have your lands, wealth, your trading ships ply our ports. You have valuable connections abroad and the ear of the Queen. You have a trained body of men who would follow you. Not only that, you have a wife who makes you the envy of the younger element around the King. All these things are dangerous. Leave Court now and you make yourself vulnerable."

"I have a more pressing enemy, my lord. I did not come here seeking power or a place at Court. It was a sanctuary for my family. A mistake, evidently. If I maintain a small force, it is for their protection."

"I know that, and men of sense know that, but in any Court there are always warring factions and men jockeying for position, looking to the future. How long do you give the Queen?"

The abrupt question took Nick by surprise.

"A year or two, perhaps more if this business of Essex does not bring her to despair."

"There you have it. There are those who see you feathering your nest, with an eye on position in the new government of England and Scotland. Would your lady settle for less?"

The notion seemed to Nicholas so ludicrous that he would have laughed if the old man had not been so in earnest.

"I can only say I have problems enough, my lord. I seek only time and place to bring up my children and keep my promises."

"Wealth and position do not interest you?"

"Enough money to keep my wife content and my sons provided for, a position that offers me freedom – what more can a man want?"

"In an ideal world, very little, I grant ye. If your wife is so easily pleased. Perhaps your ideas of freedom are perilous ones, Nicholas, keep them to yourself, the time is not yet. Very well, go and slay your dragon and then return to take up the responsibility you have laid, will you or no, upon yourself. We need young men like you."

Nicholas had a great deal to think of as he prepared for the journey. The long-held idea of a united England and Scotland was one that affected him profoundly. So far, he had simply taken each obstacle as it presented itself, it was time perhaps for the larger picture.

I must make time to look ahead, he thought. He would consult with Kit, if that wayward poet was not in the throes of composition.

James' queen professed herself to be heartbroken at the loss of her lady-in-waiting; Nick suspected she was far more upset to lose the services of Mistress Melville in the nursery. She lent her travelling coach, much cushioned and bedizened with hangings and rugs. Rosalyne flew into a passion when Nicholas insisted she travel in it with the boys and Mistress Melville, giving him a side of her tongue he had only suspected.

"To be cosseted so is intolerable," she raged at him. "I can ride and shall ride for weeks yet—"

"I know of no place to rack up for a night and you will not ride nigh on thirty leagues. If you wish to come to Strathyre, let that be an end to it."

She was still fuming when they set off in a determined drizzle of rain only an hour or so later than Nicholas intended, the boys also wearing mutinous faces at not being allowed to ride their ponies. Paying no attention to their complaints, Nicholas set off towards home with a clear conscience and a strong escort.

The meeting place arranged with Poley was a few miles south of the road to Strathyre, and Nicholas sent his party on, taking only one man with him to mind his back. The track led off through a belt of trees crowding a narrow glen. Nero's hooves trod soft on a carpet of pine-needles, ladders of weak sunlight barred their way and the branches dripped and rustled after the rain. They came to a plank bridge over a tumbling stream and ahead lay a ruined croft as promised. At the edge of the trees, Nick stopped to listen. Over the babble of the water came a frenzied barking. Nick signed to his man to stay where he was, dismounted and crept over the bridge into the cover of the tumbledown wall. The barking stopped and he froze, crouching by the rotting gatepost and drawing his poniard. He caught the choked breathing of a man at the end of his tether, ending in a sob, before the dog set up a keening howl that tore at the nerves. Nick found a chink and peered through. Among the nettles and sprouting grasses of the yard lay the body of a man, his clothes a fantastic patchwork of moleskins and ratskins, a crossbow dangling from his belt and a dagger between his shoulder blades.

70

A filthy terrier had his nose clapped to the doorsill, his tail clamped between quivering back legs, teeth bared, and growling. He was obviously a notable ratter, as the man's clothes bore witness, and he seemed to have cornered a human rat. Nick sank back on his heels and considered. A trap? He signed to his man to keep watch and stole round to the back of the croft, where eyeless windows stared across empty meadows, and eased his way up to the opening where the door had been. Someone groaned and Nick risked a quick glance round the door. Poley was sitting hunched on the floor, nursing his hand. He was alone. Nick straightened up and walked in. Poley yelped with fear and fell back against the wall. Blood stained the side of his jerkin and he fumbled for the pistol lying on the floor.

"Trouble?" said Nick.

"Christ's nails, my lord – you'll be the death of me!" He was grey-faced and sweating and Nick, kneeling beside him, offered his flask.

"What happened?"

Poley took it and gulped greedily. One hand bore the marks of the terrier's teeth and blood oozed from a wound in his side. Nicholas waited. In fits and starts the tale came out.

"I've been rumbled," said Poley. He had been followed by the rat-catcher with the crossbow, he said, sent to meet with Nick and finish the job he had botched on the battlefield. After a desperate fight – according to Poley – he had been overpowered and slain.

"That bloody dog—" he complained. Nick smiled grimly. The dagger in the assassin's back told rather a different story. He listened to the rest of it. This was Mowbray's last throw – again according to Poley – the man was sick and still in hiding, waiting for the summons from Essex.

"He'll wait a long time, my lord. Essex has been released, on his oath to return to his own house and stay quiet. I hear he is still encouraged by his friends to make an attempt, indeed he may be foolhardy enough to do so, but without money, Mowbray is out of favour, especially if he kills you. Our Robin would still count you among his friends, my lord. As they say, who is not my friend is my enemy. Mowbray can rot for all he cares."

"Where is Mowbray now?"

"I don't know, my lord, I was betrayed. But never fear, I left a man to watch, we shall have news."

The terrier was becoming frantic, scrabbling and barking, and Nick got to his feet and pulled off his cloak.

"For God's sake cut that creature's throat," said Poley. "He'll have the sinews out of your leg."

Nicholas made his way round to the front of the croft with his cloak bundled in his hands. The terrier abandoned the door and flew at him. Nick dropped the heavy cloak over him and picked him up. He held the struggling little body tight to his chest and spoke to it.

"You're a fighter," he said. "And a loyal one too. Will you change allegiance, I wonder. Come now, steady. I do not want to harm you." He raised his voice and called to his man. Poley came slowly round the corner of the building.

"Your assassin needs burial," said Nick. "Take him inside, there are stones enough. I should take back your dagger – just in case."

The terrier was lying in his arms trembling now, Nick could feel the thin ribs heaving against his chest, and the rapid drumming of his heart. It was not in him to kill the animal and he made room for it to breathe. He freed one hand and felt in his pouch for the purse of money. Poley had paid for it in blood.

"Make yourself scarce," he said. "I did not ask for your service, but I thank you for it. News of Mowbray may find me at Strathyre and will be well rewarded. You will find a bread poultice will draw out the humours in your hand." He walked back over the bridge to where Nero waited patiently, mounted, and set the shivering bundle in front of him on the saddle-bow.

"Your master tried to murder me," he said to it. "I cannot regret his passing and it seems we must still be on our guard. Will you bite the hand that will shortly feed you? We shall see."

Chapter Nine

By the pricking of my thumbs

In the warm, snug workshop, part of the stabling tacked onto the side of the tower, it was fuggy with the odour of leather, metal and the pungent reek of harness oil. Hob was putting the finishing touches to the pony-sized saddle he was making. Its twin was ready and waiting on the saddle horse at his elbow. He had chosen a simple stamped design; he had the notion that the big man disliked fuss. You only had to look at the way he ran the place. And take those children now, always in here under his feet... Well, hardly children, they had grown that fast. They might have different mothers, but they both had the man's sunny expectation that a task attempted was a task done. At the double. And the silly thing was, you tried not to disappoint. Why else was he, Hob, still working at this time of night?

He had mightily resented being left behind while his family went off to Court, but he had come to understand why. This Master Malheur was seemingly very important to my lord Rokesby and Hob had come to see it a privilege to serve him. Hadn't he stood over Hob's master in the battle? And spoken for him?

"He's a moody devil, mind," he said to himself. "But the words in him, now. Does you good to listen to him when he gets going.

The way he puts things – makes you think." He picked up the smaller punch. "And the lady, wouldn't want to disappoint her neither. Got that way of looking at you as if you're really there. No, I'm glad I stayed – even if it is bloddy Scotland."

Someone went past the door at a run.

"That's that carrot-headed loon. The language of him – best flow of curses I ever heard." He looked at his handiwork. "A bit of gilding, now? No." He got up and put the beautifully worked saddle next to the other and shrugged into his sheepskin. There would be hot food in the mess-hall and talk round the fire. Self-appointed body servant and childminder, Hob stroked his hand over his work, took down the lantern and went out into the wind.

Marlowe had celebrated the beginning of the new century alone. Now, he huddled over the smouldering peats with a tumbler of the local whisky at his elbow and cursed Nicholas Talbot root and branch. A southerly wind had come to turn the snow to slush and mist and creep its tendrils under the door. Just recovered from a bout of tertiary fever and kept awake by a troublesome cough, his plays lying neglected in his chamber, he brooded.

Trouble was coming, he could smell it. Elizabeth was dying slowly, too slowly, and with her passing there would be great changes. James, well-known for always choosing the middle way, would be tolerant of the Catholic faith, as he was here in Scotland. The trouble was, the militant Catholics did not want to be tolerated, they wanted to reinstate the old religion and drive out the heretic Protestants. A faction calling themselves Presbytes was making itself felt and Kit doubted the King's strength to withstand both Churches and the State. James' wife was Catholic and his son and heir sickly. James would always rather hunt than sit at the council table – he liked to be liked.

The first years of this new era would be difficult. The matter of Robert Devereux was still to be settled, and Elizabeth was risking unpopularity in her delay in dealing with him. Marlowe worried that his beloved Nicholas would be drawn in over his head. The young man had become necessary to him, his daemon; he had wrought a change in his words, his writing and in Marlowe himself. Kit had begun to see through his eyes, suffer when he suffered, rejoice when he rejoiced. Kit did not want to see him torn apart between his steadfast ideals and the wolves seeking power. He sighed.

"There's little enough I can do, stranded here…" he said aloud. "Or anywhere for that matter, I do not exist." He began to think again of his work, he could feel the fit coming on him again, the words gathering at the door, clamouring to be let out. He had his characters, the plots were secondary always, borrowed, stolen, plundered from questionable histories. The words, the people, the action – that was the thing. In the miserable cold his thoughts had returned often to Italy and the sunlit Inland Sea. His Scottish play was hanging fire; he needed another element that, for the moment, eluded him, something more than the raw ambition of the woman. In his first jealousy he had modelled her a little on Rosalyne, until Rosalyne herself had come to Strathyre dressed as a young gallant. That had fed his imagination and opened his eyes to the thing between her and his Niccolo. *I am a selfish bitch,* he thought. *I cannot grudge him that.* But a woman as strong and sensual as she could take over a man, seduce him, suck out his soul. The nightmare couple of his play had no children – a babe had been lost. Good idea that, it made a vacuum that had to be filled. Nick's wife had children – would she stay content with what she had? She had such power, it would be a strong man who would withstand it. Perhaps both she and Nicholas had met their match. For Kit, what was between them cast a light, coming like sunshine to illuminate what might be.

Jealous fool that I am, I have cast her as villain, he thought. *A sorceress. What if…* His mind strayed to another sorceress, a tale he had been toying with in his dreams of the tideless sea, an Egyptian queen, and a lusty Roman general. "This is what I am come to," he muttered. "I must live my passions through theirs, one foot always in the shadows – that way madness lies." The pain in his side came again and he shivered. *I must have conflict,* he thought. *Nick's enemies come from without – no drama in that for me. No, take away the marriage of true minds and what is left is mine to play with.* The door in his mind opened and the words crowded out, flooding his imagination, jealous men, flawed heroes, powerful, ambitious manipulative women, childless and vain, without that saving grace he saw in Nicholas and Rosalyne. The room had grown chill and he shivered again. "Bloody Scotland!" he said.

One of the bloody Scots ran past the window at that moment with a shout, horses trampled, harness jingled and next moment the man himself walked into the room, banging moisture off his heavy cloak, his exaggerated actor's face ruddy with cold, unshaven cheeks glittering gold. The room suddenly shrank. He pulled off his cap, found his square of linen to blow his nose and threw off his cloak to kneel by the fire and put his arms round his friend.

"A godforsaken place, eh, Kit? I begin to wonder when we shall see the sun. Soon, I promise you. What is this? Sitting in the dark with this mean fire – I'll have Hob's hide—"

"I sent him away. I needed quiet, but I see any hopes of that are blasted." The door banged open again and the two boys ran in followed by their mother, their nurse, their tutor – the room was suddenly full of people. Kit stood up suddenly, flinging his arms wide and shouting with laughter.

"So," he cried. "No more peace – we shall be merry! Wine there! There shall be cakes and ale and feasting. The Master of Strathyre is back!"

There was wine and feasting indeed, Hob excelled himself; he had been waiting and pining for this moment. The fire banked up and the room warm, the saddles presented and admired, the boys clamoured for a story before bed, they had slept most of the way in the coach. Mistress Melville sat nodding in the corner. Rosalyne spread her rosy skirts by the fire. Nicholas took his seat on the floor with his children and began.

"The stiff brocaded skirts of the Sultan," he said, "and his fat turban with its jewel and stiff feather, were seen no more, he had gone to war with the Turk. The waters of the tideless sea were alive with the oars of the war galleys. What was poor Sinbad to do…?"

Marlowe sat in his chair by the glowing peats listening to the spell-binding voice painting the scene and thought, *I should never have allowed them to drag him away from the playhouse.* It was not only the beautiful flexible voice; it was the presence and the understanding that coloured it. In the poet's inward ear rang his own words as Nick would render them, sonorous and slow, despairing, a man in ruins, the woman who had been both prop and spur now failed and gone.

The Queen is dead, said the messenger in his head. Kit imagined a long pause, Macbeth turning away downstage, the next two lines a mutter, a dismissal, a denial. A pause again to gather thought, then the voice slowly gathering strength.

Tomorrow and tomorrow and tomorrow...

You could almost feel sorry for the man. Kit looked at the little group round the fire, listening as the wind howled round outside and the tale of Sinbad unfolded. He watched the rapt faces, Rosalyne had her hands clasped under her chin and he was reminded of Angelica in Venice, beguiled by Nick's tales. Hob stood in the shadows with rounded eyes and his mouth open and the two boys sat still and quiet.

He wanted to cry out, *Not these words – mine! How was I to know he would grow into this? A boy of sixteen, his voice not yet seated, still lanky and unformed, how was I to know? Fool that I was, I thought to seduce him, make him mine, and I could only do it with words. Hah! He was more formed than I knew, shaped by his beginnings, a lover and a fighter already. Now look at him. I may plume myself on my part in this man's creation, he listened to me then – not any more, I fear. Time I went perhaps, be my own man again.*

The story over, Nick stood up and stretched, stooped to kiss his sons goodnight and strolled to the table to pour wine for himself and Marlowe. Kit smiled up at him.

"Well, my Hotspur, what shall we enact tonight?"

Nicholas yawned. "Another bedtime story. I've just ridden fifty miles."

"When has that ever stopped you? But I won't keep you, your lady is warming your sheets."

"A pleasant thought. What is this I hear – you have been ill?"

"Nothing to matter – the better for your coming."

"Spring is on the way, Kit. I saw birds with wool and twigs flying to nest, soon the swallows will come, they have builded under the eaves, still there from last year. The airs here suit them, I'm told."

Something in the voice and the face seemed to burst the iron band that Kit felt round his heart and his eyes sparkled with tears. Nick stooped to put his arms about him.

"Have you been so lonely, Kit? No work to beguile you – I am a thoughtless brute – but you may not be seen—"

"Soon I shall be so changed that M. Malheur will pass in the shade. I do well enough. With your coming the juices flow again – much food for thought, sweeting, we will talk tomorrow. Get to your bed, I have things to do."

"Now I bethink me, I also have something to do. A wayside scrap, an unconsidered trifle, abandoned to live if he could and die if he couldn't. I must see if he still lives and breathes."

"Yet another hanger-on? Are you not sick of us?"

"You frighten me, Kit. What ails you that you can say such a thing? You have been too long out of the sun, you are not well. We must look to it."

You are my sun, thought Marlowe. *Like the lovesick Helianthus I turn towards you, and must hold my peace.*

Chapter Ten

Strathyre, May 1600. Sweet lovers love the Spring

It was a halcyon day, full of the songs of spring, the air was alive with the sound of birds: the cock on the dung heap, the doves round the dovecote strutting and preening and cooing their throaty invitation, the invisible larks sang high in the sky over the birds flying to nest with twig and grass and wool. Green shoots were showing in the fields, the slopes were dotted with lambs, kingcups and early purple orchids starred the banks of the many streams. The trees were beginning to lose their stark winter outline in a dark fuzz of coming leaf.

Marlowe was missing.

Cursing, Nicholas sent out a search party and saddled up Oberon to look for him himself.

The truant was sitting on the hillside doing nothing, his play almost finished; a dark play for a dark winter of the soul. The low northern sun was warm on his face, reflecting bright daggers off the waters of the loch and a fitful breeze carried the sweet-almond scent of the gorse, brash gold on the hillside as he sat looking down the glen where the moorland began.

He had his two characters drawn now, what Rosalyne and Nicholas could become if you added in two fatal flaws, overmastering ambition and the inability to deal with the result. Powerful and dangerous, both of them, the Lady Macbeth and her lord, bred in this wild and violent place. Nicholas, with his wife to help him and his children to rear, was making of it a peaceful demi-paradise, Marlowe's Macbeth was a destroyer. The poet needed something else – a catalyst to wake the terrible ambition lying waiting. His gaze wandered over the hillside across the river and sharpened. Three old women, seemingly come from nowhere, were at the burn with their baskets of linen. As he watched, one of the three stood, waddled a little apart, straddled and let down a stream of yellow liquid. It steamed into the ground and she sighed. Another of the trio suddenly cackled and pointed in his direction. The old besom looked over her shoulder and flicked up her skirts at him in a grotesque parody of a flirt, screaming with high-pitched laughter.

Kit shuddered: he was rooted, fascinated, this was what he had been reaching for. The three of them were up now, singing and capering: he looked away from the old creatures' hairy legs, goat-legs, Pan's legs, the devil's, and when he looked back they were gone. For all his logic and reason, he was jolted for a moment, the hair rose on his scalp, his hands tingled. *By the pricking of my thumbs…* he thought. A moment only, commonsense told him they were simply hidden in the ditch. He looked about him, fixing the place in his memory. The standing stones, the swirls of mist over the water, the black tussocky stretches of moorland rearranged themselves in his mind. The scene was set.

Words and phrases swam up like carp from the depths of his imagination and he pulled out his notebook – like Nicholas, he was never without one – to write it down. It grew chill, and he wrote on…

He could hardly see the page. He looked up to find the sun going down and dusk closing in. He shivered, suddenly alone and exposed in this desolate place where he had conjured up such terrifying thoughts. A flight of rooks startled him with their cawing overhead and he watched as they clawed their way across the sky into the dark of the woods. "Night thickens," he said aloud. "Night thickens...got to remember it." He called to his patient horse; Corsair was well used to his vagaries by now. This time however, the animal jerked away from him and went cantering back the way they had come. Cursing, Marlowe started to run after him and stopped when he saw the reason for the animal's disobedience.

Nicholas, Corsair's rightful owner, was at the foot of the glen, riding through the stand of firs that marked this furthest end of Loch Rannoch, the faithful terrier, now known as Butcher, panting behind him. Corsair pranced up to greet him and he leaned down to catch the trailing rein. He did not look pleased.

His voice was mild enough when he spoke, but Marlowe was not deceived.

"You are aware, are you not, that you are in MacGregor territory?"

His voice is violet, thought Marlowe, *with a touch of bronze. What a waste – he could play my Othello, my Thane, my Antony, when I get round to him.* He saw with dismay that Nick had come fully armed, on Oberon, expecting trouble. The resonant voice sharpened.

"Up with you. You are waited for."

Kit mounted without a word. He knew Nicholas in this mood. He felt like Jack caught in some dangerous misdemeanour. Nicholas turned Oberon's head and led the way at a canter. Marlowe followed, thinking, *Ill-met by moonlight – no, done that…this was the battleground…moorland…when the battle's lost and won…*

He was still juggling words when they came to the mended bridge over the Tummel. Nicholas turned to wait for him.

"Never," he said, "never go without escort and *never* go on to the heath. Understood? Rose was worried."

We can't have that, thought Kit waspishly. Nicholas walked away with the horses and Marlowe hurried to his quarters, on fire to write down the ideas that would change the whole mood of his play: ghosts and witches and godless anarchy. He paused a moment. *The time is out of joint for such a theme,* he thought. *Murdering a monarch. There is trouble enough over the last one.* He shook his head. *It's a crowd-pleaser. Its time will come. Get it down.*

Later, wrapped in a plaid by a glowing fire, a cup of hot broth in his hands, it was hard to believe that only that morning he had been revelling in the burgeoning season, ripe with promise. He was thinking again of Venice and the Princess Angelica and Nicholas.

"She loved him for the dangers he had passed," he mused. "That was it. Not just the man – hypnotised by the tales he told." She had inspired the play still lying unfinished in his chamber. He conjured up a picture of Angelica, lint-fair hair and eyes blue as the Aegean, named the most beautiful woman in Venice, coming from Nick's bed flushed and laughing… He was still amazed at Nick's womenfolk and what they had achieved. You had to admit he was good at women. The beauty in Venice, and now this raven-haired witch who had him under her spell.

"Cyprus," he said aloud. "On the Inland Sea, a man of Africa. A subtle Venetian…" He pulled out his notebook, instantly lost to the world.

The door opened and Nick's wife entered carrying a tray, a manservant behind her with a brazier of coals in padded hands. She set down the tray and straightened, smiling at him. She no longer wore the costly trappings of the Court, a simple kirtle and bodice with lacings showed the gentle curve of pregnancy. *We could be brother and sister,* he thought, *so alike in colouring.* Her hair was so black it shone blue where it caught the light, caught back from her face to fall in ringlets on her shoulders, her long Byzantine eyes coal-black. Her white skin was transparently fine, the veins made a lilac tracery at temple and breast, her lips, like his own, were full and red. A plaid in the soft reds and greens of the Melville weave, pulled close about her shoulders, followed the lines of her straight narrow back.

"I heard the horses," she said. She poured the spiced wine, set the jug near the fire and went out calling for the boys.

The household cat, heavy with kit, opened one green eye where she lay by the fire and rolled over to display her spotted furry belly with its swollen nipples.

"Dear me," said Marlowe, "what a terrifyingly fecund place this is…" The cat got up with a trill and strolled over to twine round his ankles and strop her jaws against his boot. He reached down absently to tickle her. "And what copy shall I leave of myself, eh, puss? My plays, Nicholas would say. A barren thought. All very well for you, my lusty young friend, with two fine sons and another in the making." His hand stilled, and the cat, after a nudge or two, stalked off, tail erect and twitching. *I wonder what a brat of my breeding and talent would do,* he thought. *Foh! What a vain egotistical fool. Not could not, I would not. The issue of some bawd – no. There would be all the fatigue of choosing and courting – ugh! Damn you, Nicholas. God, I hate the Spring! Damn you.*

Nicholas walked in smelling of fresh air and the stables. He seemed to have forgiven Marlowe, he smiled and came to stand by his chair.

"Is it finished? You were inspired by this place, Kit, were you not?"

"Almost," said Marlowe, ambiguous as ever. "Tell me, Nicco, did you never want to play the lead? You have the voice for it, the presence – dammit, you even have shares!"

Nick laughed and shook his head. "Events have overtaken me, Kit. When would I ever have time – or be allowed?"

"You are an actor. It does not go away."

"No. I played Laertes well, I think."

"Burbage had a little too much bombast for my Hamlet. You could play him." He thought for a moment. "There is a new player come into the company, I see. He was the Player King and the Gravedigger—"

"Master Robert Armin. I didn't see it, but he played Touchstone to some acclaim, I believe."

"So, he can sing."

"Like a nightingale, sweet and sad. He has a deft touch with the lute."

"He could play Feste. I have been wondering—"

"Feste?"

Marlowe bent to rummage in his bulging bag of scrip.

"You whisked me away before I could think, Nick. I brought a play with me to London, a comedy – my best. I have been meaning to give it to you…"

Nick snatched at the manuscript. "A new comedy? All this time and you have not spoken of it? And here we are in Scotland!"

"You would have it so."

"Tuh! What is it called? *Twelfth Night*? For God's sake, Kit, Twelfth Night has been and gone!"

"There will be another. The world goes on turning… You forget, my hasty one, I was there in a new theatre, a wonderful new space, watching my play with another already growing in my head, an idea that came to life here in this wild country. I can't be expected to think of everything."

"What are we to do with it?"

Marlowe shrugged. "Send it to Tom Walsingham if you're in such a hurry. I see the lad I had in mind has grown a beard and swaggers it."

"Did you not think Gertrude was good? And Ophelia?"

"Very good, they have a rapport. It works. I shall make a few changes."

"Let me read it first."

"Your wife calls us to supper."

"Give it to me, you wretch. By God, Kit Marlowe, I should have left you to take your chances."

The story that night was short and the boys were packed off to bed early. Nicholas settled down to read the play while Marlowe lolled back in his chair. He read fast and presently was nodding and smiling and laughing to himself. He suddenly laughed aloud and looked up.

"'I was adored once, too,'" he said in a high mournful voice. "Oh, how I would play that part!"

"Why do actors always long to play the parts they are least suited to? Aguecheek is not for you, in fact there is no part for you, unless it be Malvolio."

"That pompous—"

"Read on."

Nick bent his head obediently and after a while said, "Ah."

"Yes. A part for a genuine actor. The groundlings will love to hate him."

"Perchance I should carry this myself. I need to speak to Will Shakespeare. He was getting a bit above himself with the Prince."

"His Ghost was passable."

"It was the best thing I have seen him do."

"Yes. You will understand I am loth to give him credit. Do you really wish to make the journey? Is it necessary? Surely young Trelawney may be trusted with it."

"Have you a copy?"

Marlowe shook his head and Nick sighed.

"Then that is the first task. I would trust Trelawney with the only copy, but not wind and weather. This is fine work, Kit. What if it were lost at sea like poor Viola and Sebastian? William might help with a few pages, he writes a good hand."

"I have more important things to do."

Nick glared at him and shuffled the pages together.

"Very well. A thing finished is over and done with you, I know that. I'll see what can be done. May I know what is this important thing?"

Marlowe hesitated. "It is a tale of jealousy," he said at last. "Jealousy both hot and cold. I need to rid myself of the green-eyed monster that has set a canker in my soul."

"You, jealous? What have you to be jealous of?"

"You, Nicholas, you. You, with that strength and beauty you will not share with me, you with your passion for Rosalyne, you with your wife and your fine sons. I do not imagine you would behave as does my Moor, I cannot see you infected with doubt and a terrible jealousy, but I know the heat of your love and what

88

it could turn to. I feel in myself the creeping cold envy, I am become nothing. I see another in my rightful place, with everything pleasant about him, 'sweet Master Shakespeare'. If I cannot pull him down, I can pull down others, the best of them, with sly insinuating manipulating words."

Shocked, Nicholas said, "For shame, Kit. This is not you. You are better, far greater than this."

Marlowe shrugged. "A playwright is all men. Presently, I am a petty man who cannot see his own failings, only that others pass him by and take what he knows should be his. He looks with spleen at his general in his splendour and his passion. Why should this alien creature have won a Venetian beauty and Iago be trapped in a barren loveless marriage? I am a meddler, a sour opportunist who cannot see further than the end of his nose. I improvise, I invent, I seize on the moment, I destroy, as a boy pulling off the wings of a butterfly, because I can. I revel in my secret power, and in the end I don't care. It has been worth it."

"How far have you got?"

"You shall see. Once it is written I am free of it. I shall enjoy you and your happiness and your children again. I shall be the greater for it."

Nick recognised the old obsession. Once in the white-hot grip of it there was no holding him, the fever must run its course before Kit Marlowe was himself once more. It was *Hamlet* all over again, the poet had found someone or something to identify with, delving deep into his own soul.

He got up to go and Marlowe stopped him, saying, "Do you never think of those men who were before you with Rosalyne, Nick? Mowbray, perhaps, and that second husband she deceived with your child? Do you never wonder what devious wiles she may practise on you? Or imagine how she enjoyed their paddling fingers at her neck—"

"Enough! You dare to speak to me so? If it were anyone else – do not experiment with me. I am not one of your helpless creatures to be pinned to your dissecting board. Is this how your villain sets about his schemes? Let him choose his victims better."

"You don't answer. Is there doubt, I wonder—"

"Be careful, Kit. Does it not matter to you what harm you may do in your cause? I would cry scorn on it if I did not know its value. But I had not looked for such cruelty from you."

"Then you *do* doubt."

"Of course I do!" shouted Nick. "And where I doubt, I love. I love every freckle and stippled mole in her nature, she is my other self. She lets my past and my imperfections lie, as I do hers and there's an end."

"A right true end. I salute you Niccolo. You almost jar me from my purpose."

"And what purpose is that, pray? To drive a wedge between me and Rose?"

"To finish my play, of course."

"'Poison in jest' is it? You drip poison in my ear and expect me to laugh it off? I cannot love you for this."

"I beg pardon, milor," mocked the poet. "I understood you to say—"

"To say is easy. Feelings go deeper."

Suddenly horrified at what he had done, Marlowe hastened to make amends.

"Nicholas, be easy. They are only words. Let the galled jade wince, it cannot hurt you. I should not have used you so, come, read what I have written. You will see it is all invention."

Nicholas had calmed a little. "You do not think that. You write truth even if you don't speak it."

"Then I shall tear it up."

"I know you will not. The words have been spoken. I will read your play when it is done. Rose and I will read it together. Something may come of it."

The door slammed behind him and Marlowe let him go. *It works,* he said to himself. *My point is proven. Shame, shame on you, Kit Marlowe, to do such a thing, and to your dearest friend. But if there is health in their love, it will stand. If not, better perhaps to know it.* And with that dubious piece of reasoning, he went back to work.

Nicholas changed his mind about taking the manuscript of *Twelfth Night* to London himself. With some help from an eager William, scribing with his tongue out and his eyes bright, he copied the manuscript of *Twelfth Night* ready to go to Edinburgh to meet with the *Snipe.* This labour was undertaken in what time he could spare from work on the estate and attendance on his wife, who was grown crotchety. It was not the labour of love it would have been. His relationship with Marlowe was strained to breaking point by what the poet had done. The words prickled in the back of his mind, they went with him as he rode out with the boys, he came near quarrelling with a Rose grown irritable. He came very close to taxing her with unforgiveable questions and had the sense to leave it alone.

If Rose was irritable, she had cause. Her husband seemed jumpy and short-tempered; when she made a gentle overture in bed he took her almost roughly, without speaking, and then tried to make amends. She put it down to worry over his impending departure to Edinburgh and, perhaps unwisely, refrained from asking him questions.

91

She sat heavy on their bed watching him pack his saddlebag. The sealed packet lay on the coverlet and she picked it up and weighed it in her hand.

"What is this? Must you burden yourself with it – it weighs heavy."

"It would weigh heavier on my conscience to leave it. Papers for London."

"Reports? Is this what you have been toiling over? And you are taking only Hob. What if—"

"Who knows but we two? Don't fret. I would rather travel fast and be back the sooner. Better by far to leave you well-guarded. I am looking to the future, Rose, when I return, we will talk."

Once in Edinburgh, waiting for news of the *Snipe*, he set about his secondary object, finding a good surveyor. Inevitably, word of his coming had reached the Court, and he was summoned. The King was on a Progress, a genuine one this time, it was the close season for hunting, and he met with Abercrombie in his chambers.

"You have had news?"

"No, my lord. Something may come with my ship. I have business in the city."

"Your business thrives, Nicholas. How does your lady?"

"Thriving also. I have a mind to explore the lands gifted to me and I am here seeking an experienced man to survey."

Abercrombie fixed him with a shrewd eye.

"Scotland seems to suit you, lad. You have no longing for the bustle of London?"

"Not at present. It looks like being a good harvest this year."

"Warned off, are you? I don't say you are not wise. There is trouble coming. But I don't see you as a farmer, Nicholas."

"Strathyre suits me."

"For how long, I wonder. I may know a man who would suit. Sit, and take a cup of wine, there have been developments."

Most of what Abercrombie had to tell him, Nick knew already from Tobias and the stream of encoded messages from Cecil, largely disregarded. He was concerned, however, by Abercrombie's suspicions that the king had involved himself with Essex.

"There has been a man about the Court, and letters – I know our James gives ear to them. Come back when you can, Nicholas, he may speak to you. He trusts you."

"I am honoured that you think so. These are weighty matters; he would do best to keep his own counsel."

"You would like to stay out of it. I cannot blame you but you may be drawn in whether you will or no. Watch your back, Nicholas, you have enemies here at Court, do not estrange yourself from our Jamie."

The surveyor recommended by Abercrombie was exactly the man Nick had expected to see as Abercrombie's protégé. Henry Wallace was a close-lipped Scot, short and hairy, with inquisitive brown eyes and tufty eyebrows. He reminded Nick of Butcher. He seemed eager to get on with the task and be gone, proposing to take his horse and ride to Cawdor, making observations on the way. Nick persuaded him to wait for Trelawney and the *Snipe*, mentioning the work Tim had seen going on along the cliffs by Loch Ness.

"Outcrop," said Wallace. "Worth a look."

The *Snipe* sailed in on a bustling wind, bringing a cargo of heavy cotton and canvas, iron and copper and a budget of news. Trelawney waved from the poop deck and concerned himself with the unlading. He seemed intent on fulfilling the sailor's dream of a girl in every port and disappeared after imparting the latest gossip, coming back at breakfast time to sit under the observing eye of Henry Wallace and answer questions.

"There is something you would wish to see, sir," he said. "I saw them when we loaded the cod. Salt pans. Would they be of interest?"

"They would indeed." Wallace turned to Nick. "You know, of course, the Campbells are the clan thereabouts. I'm wondering what they'll be thinking of another absentee landlord?"

"Their kinfolk came to our aid at Strathyre. I can send an escort with you if you're worried."

Wallace bristled. "Whether I'm worried depends on your intention, my lord."

"Offer them fair rents and fair pay for their labour. I'll have no slaves. If there is money to be made they shall share in it. Can I trust you, Master Wallace?"

The man scowled. "What do you think?"

"I think I shall. I look forward to your report."

"A fair landlord will be a novelty," said Wallace. "Can't wait."

When it came, the report confirmed Trelawney's observations. There were surface strata of coal, already being mined piecemeal by the local families and salt pans already being worked. Wallace proposed to stay and oversee developments and continue his search for minerals. Nick was itching to go and see for himself, but he was equally anxious to return home. He handed over Marlowe's manuscript with instructions that Tim was to guard it with his life and deliver it to Tom Walsingham in Kent, and rode back to Strathyre.

He found a warm and loving welcome from his wife, she was blooming, and to him more beautiful than ever. He had taken himself to task during his absence and succeeded in almost banishing Marlowe's words from his mind. He saw little of the poet, Kit was scribbling away in his quarters, forgetting to eat and Nick asked one of the maids to see he was looked after. Gone were the days when he would clear up after him himself.

Nicholas was gentle with his Rose, they made plans for the coming child, who would be born after the harvest.

"He will be born under your star sign, Nicholas, a little Scorpio. He will have your nature."

"God help *her*, then," said Nick.

The weather stayed fine, the boys had another spurt of growth. The only cloud was the continued lack of information about Mowbray, who seemed to have gone to ground.

Chapter Eleven

October 1600

The harvest was in, better than last year. The fruit crops were being gathered and preparations were afoot for the combined celebration of Young Colin's wedding and harvest home, an occasion for many lewd jokes and suggestions regarding fertility rites. Young Colin bore it all remarkably well, considering. Nick took pity on him and sent him off to take charge of the guard that still patrolled the boundaries. Once the ceremonies were over, Nicholas planned to take Rosalyne by easy stages to his cousin's home in Linlithgow where there was a well-regarded physician for her lying-in. This was on the advice of Anne Melville who did not like the way the babe had positioned itself.

For him, this was the only cloud on a perfect day. The sun was high and hot in the sky, his lands and his people were in good heart, joking and working and looking forward to broaching the barrel of ale at the end of the long barn. The good smell of apples and new bread drifted across from the cider press next to the bakehouse, and he whistled as he worked alongside all those who had come in to help. The only ones missing were his son William, who found the heat disagreeable, and Tom Percy, who had taken him up into the wooded hills to look for flowers and rabbits.

Rosalyne had taken to her bed in the cool of their chamber. Mistress Melville again.

Nicholas, bare-chested and sneezing, stuck about with flying chaff, helped to manhandle the barrel onto its trestles, and thought about her. Last night he had lain spooned against her narrow back, his hand on the swell of her belly, slippery with sweet oils, and felt his child turning.

"Impatient, my lord?"

"Yes – no, the time passes more easily for me; I have much to occupy me. It must hang heavy for you."

"Not long now."

Presently he said, "After the babe is born, I think we should go south for the winter – open up the house in Richmond for Christmas."

"There is something you must do?"

Half asleep, he muttered, "Always."

He had turned his hand to bringing in the planks for the tables when Jack came flying in, wildly excited.

"Father, there is a man come! With a banner!"

The man had been brought in under escort, blindfolded before coming through the fortifications. Nick was taking few chances these days. He wore Mowbray's livery of orange and sky-blue and carried a pennanted lance and a flag of truce. A mere caricature of chivalry, he was shabby and looked half-starved and frightened. He was brought to stand before Nicholas and the blindfold was removed. His eyes flickered round the room, taking in the men standing and staring, coming to rest on this man who was his master's professed enemy. He saw a young man in all the pride of his youth and strength, half-naked and calm. The herald bowed awkwardly, his heart was not in this errand.

"Well? Give me good reason not to run you off on a rail."

"I come as herald, my lord and claim privilege."

"Your master has forfeited knightly privilege. What does he want?"

"He challenges you in mortal combat, the choice of weapon yours."

Nicholas could not believe his ears. After all the man Mowbray had done, to assume the right to knightly usage? He was out of his senses.

"Take this man away," he said to d'Arblay. "See him fed, and his horse. I would like to speak to you at your leisure."

The two young men met in the stable yard, away from the house. D'Arblay had very strong views on the matter. "It's an insult. He has lost all claim to knightly conduct – if you trust him to stick to the rules you'll be as mad as he, Nicholas. Mark me, there's some foul scheme afoot."

"Forewarned is forearmed, as they say," said Nick. "I shall know where to find him at last. And I shall not go alone."

"Why fight him? Go to arrest him, let him stand trial."

"Where is the satisfaction in that? If he will face me for once—"

"Why now?" said d'Arblay. "He has crept about behind your back all this time, used others to try and kill you – why do this now? I say again, find where he is and send to arrest him."

Nicholas was thinking of the letter from Essex. Arrested and back in the Tower, Mowbray would still be dangerous, could and surely would do his best to implicate Nick and his family in treason. The man would have to be killed and if he could do it with some semblance of honour he must seize the chance. He could not explain, better his friends did not know. He assumed a stubborn look.

"I want it finished. I will meet him. Don't worry, I shall make sufficient safeguard."

D'Arblay shrugged. "Can't really blame you," he said. "Although I think a clean death is too good for him. I'll come with you if you permit. He wants a proper challenge – he'll get it."

Nicholas sent for the messenger to be brought to him again. With food and drink inside him, the man looked less pinched and frightened.

"Perform your office."

The man drew himself up. "My name is John Ratcliffe of Derby, herald to my lord Mowbray. He challenges you to a duel to the death, the weapons of your choosing, the field of combat, beside the loch."

He drew a crested gauntlet from his belt, the gold thread tarnished and the embroidery frayed, and threw it down in a travesty of knightly custom. Twisted round the cuff of the gauntlet was a tasselled girdle of powder blue and silver, the lady Rosalyne's girdle. Worn the day of Nick's first meeting with her.

"Do you accept, my lord?"

If anything would make sure of acceptance, the girdle was it. Nicholas could hardly speak for the rising tide of fury.

"I accept. Tell your master I choose the sword."

Ratcliffe bowed. "I may leave?"

"With all speed. No-one will harm you. My Lord d'Arblay will arrange escort."

D'Arblay sent men with the herald and confronted Nicholas. "I don't like it, Nicholas. How does Mowbray propose to get past the guard? Where is the guard, by the way?"

"Young Colin must have him under watch. Hob, my sword."

"How do you know that? Listen, do not be in such a hurry – what will Rosalyne say?"

"She knows my mind in this. I have wanted to deal with him on my own ground in my own way and here he is on the killing field. Throwing down the gauntlet was a last foolish gesture – you saw the pitiful parody," he said. *And I saw the insult.*

"Nick, the man has tried every stratagem bar this to have you killed. Never yet by his own hand. Why this? Why now, here? Take thought, for God's sake, make provision. There may be some trick—"

"I have to meet him. I have accepted the challenge. I cannot just murder the man, it must be in battle or fair fight – send out another patrol if you feel you must."

"You are not honour-bound to do this. If you scruple to murder him there are others not so fussy. I'd do it myself with pleasure."

"Not as much as I will."

D'Arblay tried once more. "Don't you see, Nick? *He* has chosen the killing field – his time, his place. Does that not tell you something?"

"It tells me he is here." Nick's brows met in an implacable line. "'The readiness is all.'"

D'Arblay turned and strode off. "Arrogant, bloody-minded…" he muttered. He did not know the significance of the tasselled girdle – how could he – but he could see that a studied taunt and insult had been cleverly calculated to get under Nick's guard. He summoned Marlowe and the MacNab and with them made what dispositions they could in the time.

Shown the gauntlet with its dangling ornament, Marlowe drew in his breath with a hiss. He himself had jogged Nick's memory and relit this particular fuse.

"He must be stopped."

"There is no stopping him."

"Then double the guard."

"All the reserves are at the harvest."

Marlowe stared at him. "Then if you have a god, pray. This has been planned well. Jock, you had best stay here, two esquires will be enough. We'll take an escort." *If I helped to bring this about, he thought, I shall at least be there.*

Chapter Twelve

The Reckoning

The field Mowbray had chosen was the length of a jousting arena beside the loch. Wary, Nicholas rode forward, his eyes fixed on the small group at the end of the field. Mowbray stood there, in full jousting panoply, his sword tip to the ground, his helm with its three draggled plumes under his arm. Behind him stood his two squires with the horses, an unhandy-looking pair, no tabards, no heraldry, no pennanted lance. Where were all his men? Had the lordly Mowbray come to this?

The men who had escorted the herald reported no men beside these. There seemed no more to do than get on with it.

Behind Nicholas, d'Arblay, Marlowe and the few men of the escort halted and stood in line. Nicholas dismounted and walked forward, the scars on his chest prickling. He had only his fighting jack and a cuirass of chain mail to protect him, and carried a simple round helmet. As he drew nearer, Nicholas saw a diminished Mowbray, no longer the full-fleshed choleric man of the tourney: he seemed to have shrunk inside his elaborate armour. His expression had not changed, however. Hateful and arrogant as ever, he sneered as Nick approached the line scored in the dust.

"Come to pay the reckoning, my lord?"

D'arblay and Marlowe ranged themselves behind Nicholas. Nick drew his sword, unbuckled the sword belt and let it fall. He put on his helmet. Ratcliffe came up to the mark and beckoned the combatants forward. Mowbray handed his helm to his other henchman for it to be lowered over his head. He snapped down his beaver and drew his sword. Ratcliffe raised his arm and withdrew.

The fight began.

This was not the duel Nick had expected, even been looking forward to, flailing, not dancing. The monotonous clang of their swords had the comfortable sound of the smithy. Sweep up, across, down and forward, the tip of his broadsword seeking always the gap between visor and breastplate or the vulnerable spot under an upraised arm. Up, across, down and forward. From the outset Mowbray was slow and heavy, slipping and sliding, giving ground, his breathing laboured, every lift and lunge an effort. After Nick had beaten his sword down for the third time, he drew back, dropping his guard.

"I cannot fight this man," he said. "Arrest him." He turned away, and Mowbray lunged to take him in the back. Marlowe's poniard flew, too far to pierce armour at that distance, enough to send Mowbray staggering back to fall in a clatter of metal. His men ran to heave him up and Marlowe was at Nick's side. Mowbray put up both hands to take off his helm. He was smiling, an unholy light of madness in his eyes.

"What of home, my lord?" he said. "A fox in the coop. All your pretty chickens and their dam – the treacherous scheming bitch will betray no more men – what do you think my men are doing now?" He laughed, and Nicholas in a red rising tide of terror and rage, lifted his sword and swept it round in a whistling arc to take

Mowbray's head clean off his shoulders. It bounced along the ground in a red trail on the grass and a fountain of blood sprayed Nick from head to foot as the armoured figure swayed and slowly toppled, to lie, a headless heap of metal at his feet. Nicholas did not pause, he turned and ran for home.

Far-sighted William, up on Fairy Mountain with Tom Percy, spotted the cloud set up by a large body of horsemen coming from the north. As he watched, the riders spread out and gathered speed, closing in on the steading. He could see his father out in the field, a tiny figure confronting a man in armour. They were fighting.

Tom had climbed further up the bluff to look at a clump of wild gentians and William wasted no time. He leapt on Tom's horse – his pony was too slow – and lashed him to a reckless speed, slithering and bouncing in the saddle, downhill to the tower. The bell-rope was twisted up out of the reach of children, and he ran up the spiral stair to launch himself at it. He clung to it and swung like a monkey, deafened as it pealed out the alarm. He knew a guard had been set on the house, but they were too few. The bell rang on to summon in the other men and he hung on until he lost his grip and fell. He knew nothing of what happened next until Tom came to find him.

The bell was the signal for all those who had been standing watching the combat from a distance to run for their weapons. A shot rang out and there was a clash of arms from behind the keep. A scream, and Nick arrived in time to see Jack outside the house waving his small sword at the man with his foot in the door and an axe in his hand. Anne Melville was running towards him, another shot and she fell, taking Jack down with her. The axe man raised his weapon to kill the child and hesitated a fatal moment. Nick ran him through, spared a glance for Hob behind him bending over the boy and leapt for the stairs. A giant of a man had burst open the door of the bedchamber, and Nick, in a red rage and with no room on the stair to use his sword, took him in the back with his shoulder and bore him sprawling forward into the room. He stood on the man's arm and brought down his sword with both hands, turning in the same movement to defend the stair. He felled the first of the two coming up and the other, with Marlowe behind him, dropped his weapon.

"Fight, damn you!"

The man crouched and Marlowe downed him with the flat of his sword.

"Jack—?"

"Safe." Nick lowered his sword and went to his wife. She was sitting up, as white as her shift, eyes staring and her arms wrapped round her belly. He went to take her in his arms and realised he was covered with blood.

"You are hurt…"

"Not I. Lie down, sweet, it's all over. The boys are safe, lie quiet."

"Anne—"

"Hob is with her, she will come to you presently." He gave her a sip of water and drew up the coverlet. "Promise you will lie quiet, there are things to do."

She managed a faint smile. "As always, Nicco. Come to me when you do not reek of battle and sudden death. Why do I feel I am part of one of your bloodthirsty plays?" A little reassured he nodded and turned to the first task. MacNab had appeared and between them they dragged the giant carcase out of the room.

"Stand guard, Tom."

"No need. It'll be just the tidying up."

Nick gave his short nod. "Who is the goodwife who tends the women hereabouts?"

"That will be Long Bessie. She's on her way. I'm sorry, Nicholas. Mistress Melville is dead. She took the ball meant for the boy."

Nick stood still. *Oh God,* he thought. *Not sweet sensible Anne Melville. She is our rock – invincible. No.* Aloud he said, "She will be missed. Come with me then, Tom. There must be a reckoning."

They stepped carefully down steps slippery with blood, and the MacNab observed in conversational tones, "The priest is come for the wedding. Young Colin will come, if he comes at all, on a litter. The only other is William. He broke his arm falling off the bell-rope. Two brave lads you have there, Nick."

"Mm," said Nick, his mind still on Anne Melville.

"So," said Marlowe, falling in beside them. "The wedding breakfast will furnish forth the funeral meats. Strange reversal."

Nick rounded on him with a snarl. "You cynical devil – this is not a play!"

"We all have our ways, Niccolo. Mistress Melville was kind to me, too."

It was a long time before Nicholas could return to his wife's bedside. William had knocked himself out in his fall and unfortunately came round before his arm could be set. Held tight in his father's arms, he tried hard to be brave and Nick said, "You have shown courage enough, Will. Don't fight it – you should have heard me when I squashed my fingers. I yelled the place down."

It was a clean break and soon over. More comfortable with it strapped and splinted, Will asked, "What happened to Jack?"

"A few cuts and bruises. He'll do. You both played your parts well, I'm proud of you."

"Mother is safe or you wouldn't be here." Nick saw he would have to break the news of Anne Melville's death and he did so as gently as he could. He held the boy while he sobbed, not far from tears himself.

Jack was a different matter. He had lost the woman who had raised him from a baby, and been a real mother to him. He had taken all his changing circumstances in his stride as long as Anne Melville was there, and now, as Nicholas feared he would, he held his father to blame. He stood there, his face scarlet with rage and grief, blubbered with tears and yelled, "You let it happen! Why did you go off and leave us – you are always leaving us! It would serve you right if—"

Half out of his mind with worry for Rosalyne, Nick took a step towards him and MacNab intervened.

He picked the boy up and rocked him in strong arms, muffling his cries and nodded to Nicholas over his head.

"I'll be seeing to him. Do you go to your lady, she'll be needing you the most."

Nicholas had other cause for grief. Young Colin and the patrol had been north of the steading and caught in the path of Mowbray's raiders. He had taken that first shot in the shoulder, and fighting desperately on, had been badly wounded in the leg. He lay in the keep, being attended to by Hob.

All the attackers were dead, save the herald. Before Nick could stop them, the enraged clansmen had hanged the survivors from the nearest tree. Tom Percy had come down at a run from the mountain, leading Will's pony, marvelling at the boy's daring ride and lamenting having missed the fight. Nick put him in charge of the burial party. Unwilling to labour over a hole big enough they built a pyre and, still angry, flung the bodies on that, topping it off with Mowbray's severed head. The luckless herald protested.

"My lord Rokesby, this is not seemly. My lord Mowbray was a knight—"

"He was a coward and a poltroon. He head belongs on a spike on Traitor's Gate. You may join him if you wish."

"No—"

"Then get out of my sight. Carry a true tale back to Court. Go quickly before I change my mind."

The priest spoke a few hasty words for the dead and the MacNab muttered, "What use prayers for those black souls? That woman was a jewel."

Anne Melville lay in state in the tiny chapel, covered in the flowers gathered for the wedding, and Rosalyne went into labour.

Nicholas stood vigil over the woman his wife was screaming for, alternately pacing and sitting, thoughts and feelings in turmoil. William's arm was giving cause for anxiety, Young Colin was fighting a desperate battle for life and limb, and worse than these, Nicholas could not yet face the white and furious gaze of his first-born son.

It was a long hard labour. Rosalyne cried out for Mistress Melville in her agony and for the next two days Nicholas feared he would lose her too. On the day they buried Anne Melville, his child was born – a daughter. She lived only a few hours. Nick cradled her in his arms for a while then covered her face and went down to lay her beside the woman who had so joyfully looked forward to her birth. He placed a little bunch of violets and rosemary on her breast and turned away.

"Her name is Flora," he said to the priest, "baptised or not."

The fight did not end there, for days more Rosalyne's life hung in the balance, and a distraught Nicholas was a helpless onlooker. The iron smell of blood was everywhere, in the bedchamber, on the hastily-scrubbed floor and on the stairs. The woman in the bed looked as if there was no blood left in her, she lay like an effigy, white and still. Blood was the only smell, the dreaded fever did not make an appearance, and slowly she began to mend. Nicholas sat with her as often as he was allowed, holding her hand and talking. How much she heard he did not know, she made no sign. When he was not there, he was at Young Colin's bedside, who seemed likely to lose his arm. The King's Physician came, sent with words of condolence by James, but Nicholas thought it was the sensible nursing of Long Bessie and Young Colin's betrothed that turned the tide.

There was little enough Kit Marlowe could do. He had watched as his beloved friend spoke quietly to William and a swollen-eyed Jack, trying to comfort and explain, kept vigil with him in the long hours of waiting. He had watched him weeping as he stood at the bedside with his tiny daughter in his arms and stood by him at the graveside to bury her beside her nurse. Nicholas had shed no more tears, took no part in the ceremony, only turning away as the first clods fell. Men had come from far around – Melvilles, Menzies, Campbells, Murrays – all those who had fought in the battle for this place. Seeing, perhaps, that for Nicholas, Strathyre and all it stood for was lost, they said little, their pipers played the lament and they left as quietly as they had come.

The boys took no part in either ceremony and Nick was moved to the tears he had not been able to shed before, at the way all those women his wife had befriended now came to their aid. No-one appeared to hold him to blame, except himself, all that kept him from black despair was his duty to his wife and his sons.

Rosalyne was slow to recover her strength and when two weeks later, Lord Abercrombie came to represent James, she kept to her bed. A second short and brutal memorial service was held. After the ceremony Abercrombie drew Nicholas aside.

"This is surely not the time, lad," he said. "I know it and the King knows it – none better. His own son Henry is sick. But this other matter will not wait. Essex—"

"The devil take Essex! I shall not leave my wife at this time, and she is hardly fit to travel. Find another—"

"This is not a request, my boy. A refusal will be taken as treason. Matters in London are coming to a head. His Majesty proposes that your lady be cared for at Court by the Queen's own Physician, until she is strong again. Then – we shall see."

Nicholas saw very well. Rosalyne had become a pawn in their game. To try and smuggle her away was to risk her life, to leave her at Court made of her a hostage for his own behaviour… He glanced out of the window and saw the escort Abercrombie had brought with him. It included the Queen's coach. They had everything planned. He looked into Abercrombie's face. The old statesman's eyes were sad.

"Either you give me time, my lord, or arrest me. I can think of nothing but brute force that could move me at present."

Abercrombie nodded. "I see that you are grievously wounded by this traitor Mowbray, my lord, and so it shall be given out. May your recovery be swift."

"No, my lord. The truth will suffice. I shall come when my wife is out of danger. My informants tell me matters in England are contained. The King need not fear for his position at present."

Abercrombie inclined his head. "I shall do what I can."

Chapter Thirteen

The first person Nick sought out after this interview was Marlowe. He was scribbling in his room as usual. When not at Nick's heels, Butcher liked to keep the poet company. The little dog sat propped on his short skittle-like forelegs, his head cocked to one side, one ear inside out and his brown eyes glazed with concentration. He seemed to like listening to Marlowe declaiming his words. His tongue, a pink tulip petal, hung out, dripping.

Marlowe looked up at Nick's step, caught sight of Butcher and burst out laughing. He laughed until his eyes watered and he started coughing. Butcher rose with comic dignity, shook himself and began to bark.

"Take him away," gasped Marlowe. "That animal will be the death of me – tell Master Shakespeare to put him in a play – no, I'll do it myself. How will that please you, Master Butcher?"

"He's a comedian," said Nick. "Just as well he can't talk."

"He has no need to." He looked at Nick's face and sobered. "What is it, Niccolo?"

The poet heard him out with a grave face. "They have you in the jaws of a nutcracker, my friend. If your lady were well I would spirit you all away with me, but—"

"You are leaving me too?" An echo from another time, another place.

"Needs must. Another winter here would kill me. I'm for warmer climes. I need to see the sun. I shall take ship from Carlisle, your agent in Venice will give safe transport for my plays. No argument. You can no longer be spared to fetch and carry." He added with a wicked smile, "It is beneath your dignity as a patriarch and embryo statesman."

"Careful, my friend. I am not in my middle years yet—"

"No, you should be spending your youth as is fitting, not clucking after me like a hen with one chick. You are grown a powerful and dangerous man, Nicholas, and you seem not to know it. You could move men and shake the established mould if you were free to do so. If I could help you, I would stay – as it is I am another millstone round your neck."

"I do not regard my family as a millstone."

Marlowe looked at him thoughtfully.

"No. I see you are not ready. If you have come for advice, I say do as they want. When your lady is recovered, there will be opportunity. You are a rich man, Niccolo – money buys all things."

"Except freedom, it seems."

"That too. Put money in your purse and wait your time. Even Robert Cecil may have his price."

"I'd as lief pick up a scorpion."

"I think you'll be a hard nut to crack, Niccolo."

Nick had been thinking.

"Money buys other things than people," he said. "Did you know that my lands of Cawdor sit on fields of coal and salt? And the fishing fleets put in at its estuary. Remember what Archimedes said about leverage…"

"Give me a place to stand," said Kit with a smile. "I see I have no need to worry about you. One promise."

"Yes."

"Use your talent. Speak my words onstage, even if only once."

"I will."

Silence, then Marlowe said with a stagy flourish, "Sweet prince, I have leave to go?"

"Not by my will. Mark me, if I have no word, I shall by indirection find direction out."

Marlowe clapped him on the shoulder. "Excellent! You have not lost the knack. My respectful love to your dame, Niccolo, may she give you what you want. If I can't have you… Take that dog and go! Send for me tomorrow and you will find me – gone."

A finger of cold raised the hair on Nick's head. He stepped forward to cup Marlowe's face in his hands and kissed him for the first time, on the lips.

"Look to yourself," he said roughly. "You have been the making of me."

Kit Marlowe watched him go, tears standing in his eyes. "Perhaps I might say the same…" he said.

Next day he was gone, taking Hotspur with him.

"The nerve of it," muttered Hob.

Christmas came and went before Nicholas would risk making the journey to Edinburgh. He had had disquieting news from Tobias and in all conscience could delay no longer. It was the very dead of winter and looked like being as fierce as the last. He juggled his options. If he left his family behind with his kinfolk there was every chance they might be cut off from help if anything went wrong. And he would not know. On the other hand, a carefully planned journey by easy stages was achievable. He decided to take a leaf out of Toby's book, the real brain behind the itineraries of the courier business, and sent scouts ahead to make reconnaissance. It was only a matter of some fifty miles, but he would take no chances. A coach might overturn, and he caused a sleigh to be built, like the drawings he had been shown on the voyage of the *Northern Star*, which meant of course that horses must made accustomed to it. As far as his children were concerned, he could have thought of nothing better. Both of them, even Jack, were brought out of their misery and entranced by the idea. The scouts brought back news of a small church and its manse that offered hospitality and a halfway house. Nicholas went to consult with Rosalyne. Still pale and listless, she hardly roused herself to answer him.

"Whatever you think best, my lord." Her apathy frightened him. He went to call on Long Bessie.

"She'll do no good pining here, my lord," said that wise woman. "It will take time and the company of others. This time o' year there's no' much visiting hereabouts. At Court she'll mebbe have no time to miss Anne Melville and brood. Best take her with you…we shall miss her."

Hob rode the lead horse and Nicholas drove carefully over the close-packed snow, a wary eye on the weather. In front of him, warmly packed among furs and baggage, Rosalyne regained some colour in her cheeks: it was hard not to respond with some lift of the spirit to the low sun sparkling on the white waste of the valleys and the ice-sculpture of the hills. The smooth runners hissed and sent up plumes of snow-mist, the boys whooped and yelled, dangling on behind or scrambling over Rosalyne to ride in front, where Hob had put bells. The armed escort was hard put to keep up, ranging on the high ground where the snow lay less deep.

Nicholas, balancing at the back, the reins of his three horses

114

harnessed in tricorne in his hands, yelled too, exhilarated by the cold wind in his face and the speed of their progress. They hardly needed their halfway stop but out of courtesy and consideration for his hosts, his escort and the horses, Nick pulled up and helped Rosalyne to alight. Her eyes had found some of their sparkle and she smiled.

"One of your better notions, Nicholas."

This was balm to his soul and he set off next day with high hopes. Nor did anything untoward happen to dash them and they arrived in fine style, skimming up the hill towards the castle to a cheering mob come out to see. That was almost the last he saw of his family before he left for England. They were swallowed up in the Queen's apartments while Nicholas sought audience with an agitated James. It was some time before the King could be brought to the crux of the matter, and at last Nick put the blunt question.

"What do you wish of me, your Majesty?"

James would not meet his eye. He motioned for the other courtiers to leave the room, and when Johnnie Mar seemed reluctant, stamped his foot. Once they were alone, he turned to the small chest by his side and unlocked it. Nick's heart sank as he saw the familiar coded letters from Cecil, and what was more worrying, several papers covered in the hand of Robert Devereux. James handed him the first of these.

…believe the time has come to stop the malice, the wickedness and madness of these men—

Nick looked up. "These men?"

"My lord Cecil and the rest," muttered James. Nick nodded and went on reading.

...and to relieve my poor country which groans under her burden. This, my action, will be in the best interest of the Queen, for if she continue in believing none nor hearing none but what they direct, she must be led blindfold into her own extreme danger. Do you my lord, send an ambassador to England...

The idea seemed to be that once Essex had achieved his coup d'etat, this ambassador would complain of the men in whom Elizabeth trusted, and she would take proceedings against them. This seemed to Nicholas so far-fetched and so typical of all Devereux' strategies, that he could find nothing to say. He looked up to see James staring at him with a hangdog expression. Surely he hadn't—

"Your Majesty, did you honour this with an answer?" The silence lengthened. "Your Majesty, may I know your reply?"

James levered himself out of his chair and went to stand at the window, gnawing at a nail. Presently he said, "There is a man here about the Court... He brings word from Ireland..." His voice trailed off. Nick knew of this development from Tobias, who had his ear to the ground in London. The time for an alliance between Tyrone and Mountjoy in Ireland and James' forces in Scotland was past. Devereux' sense of timing was, as ever, faulty.

"Your Majesty, that bird will not fly. Neither party will now take the risk." He waited. "What would your Majesty have me do? Have you spoken of this to your counsellors?"

James shook his head.

"To my lord Cecil, then?"

James hunched his back and shook his head again. It was like pulling teeth. Nicholas stood patiently and waited. He was not going to put words into this man's mouth. He was aware of a growing disappointment. He had thought James stronger than this, a fit man to unite the two kingdoms.

James stirred at last, straightened his back and spoke clearly. "If the man has been foolish enough to misconstrue my words and keep my letters for his own purposes, I would have them found and destroyed – if not by his will, then by mine."

As careful as the king to name no names, Nick said, "I believe the gentleman in question to be an honourable man."

James sniffed. "Have you not learned, my thane? Trust no-one."

"Your Majesty wishes to entrust this task to me?"

It'll be my head on the block, he thought. *If not worse.*

"You shall be rewarded," said James the Sixth of Scotland.

As he left, he caught sight of the thin elderly man who was once more the emissary of Essex. He didn't blame him for staying away from London. He found Tom Percy with d'Arblay and charged them to guard his family with their lives. He had no real fear that anything would befall them at Court, his main worry was his wife's health – apart from his own.

He was strapping up his baggage when a tap came at the door and Robert Carey walked in.

"You are among the great ones these days, Nicholas," he said. "Quite difficult to get past your guard."

"None of my contriving, I promise you," said Nick. "No sooner do I turn my hand to husbandry than I am sent for on some petty task."

"Not so petty, my friend. Much hangs in the balance. Elizabeth's Treasury is empty, paid out on these troublesome Irish. I should know: she has not a groat to spare for me. Her sweet Robin is still at his old tricks, suing for money and power. You should teach him the way of it, my lord of Strathyre and Cawdor." There was a note of rancour in his voice that Nick had not heard before. This was a friendship he would be sorry to lose.

"I am sent to London with goodwill messages any courier could deliver. I should be about my own business."

Always chronically short of money, Carey rubbed fretfully at his grievance. "Well for you. You should be in London, not feathering your nest here with James. Money breeds money – you have your rewards—"

"The earldom is an empty one," said Nicholas. "A name only. Strathyre is a money pit, it will take years to recover. I swear, Robert, I don't know why I am in demand – in the right place at the right time to abate a nuisance, I suppose."

Carey had cheered up. It was not in his nature to harbour a grudge. "Intelligent? Charming? Honest? Two out of three's not bad. Come for supper and a game of cards. We absent husbands must hang together."

"Hang together? I hope not. I pray you excuse me, my gambling takes place on the high seas."

"What a poltroon! Afraid to lose a little of your ill-gotten wealth?"

In the end, denied entry to his wife – "my lady is asleep" – Nick went, and watched Carey gamble away his stake, borrow more and win it all back on the turn of a card. He waved away the offer of repayment. "Let it pay for my entertainment."

"Put in a good word for me with my Queen-cousin, Nicholas."

"I value our friendship too much, find another pimp. But I will take a letter for Her Majesty, if you want. I leave at first light."

Carey clapped him on the shoulder. "'Tis almost that now. You shall have it – and a letter to my wife, if you will. And Nicholas, an honest man is a rare thing, to be found and courted." He could not resist a final sour dig. "Easy to be honest if you have means."

A packet came before he left, from Tobias.

My dear friend,
I pray your lady is recovered and you yourself in better frame. I have a report that may cheer you. Will has provided us with a miraculous new comedy, just the physic for this time of turmoil. The steward Malvolio has taken the town by storm and Feste's songs are sung and whistled in the streets. Master Armin has made the part his own and the Queen has commanded the play at Twelfth Night (the name of the play) at Whitehall. There is no part for you in it Nick and I rejoice at it, I would not have you seduced back to London at this time even for such a play as this. Will has excelled himself with his portrayal of a drunken saucy knight and such parts for our new boy players! I laughed 'til my sides ached at their predicament. I have had a copy made for you as you see. We have well and truly wiped the eye of our detractors.
   The report of our lost argosy was false, one ship foundered off the Goodwins...

The rest of the letter dealt with business and Nick set it aside to read later. The packet contained, of course, a fair copy of *Twelfth Night*. Nick knew it almost by heart, but he smiled and put it in his pack to cheer the journey.

On his way to bid farewell to Rosalyne, Nick thought of the many honest folk he numbered among his friends: Harry Munro and Young Colin, Hob and MacNab and d'Arblay, Tobias, Challoner – and Angelica. "I am fortunate indeed," he said.

Rosalyne was still asleep. He did not wake her, instead he wrote a loving note and placed it with a little nosegay on her pillow.

And so I avoid the pain of leavetaking, he thought. *Coward!*

Butcher, snuggled in the small of William's back, opened one eye and moved his tail. The scar across his skull like a raised eyebrow gave him a cynical look.

"No, my brave fellow, you will stay here and guard my treasure," said Nick softly. "London is not for you."

PART TWO

The readiness is all

Chapter Fourteen

On Nick's abrupt departure from the Globe with the mysterious visitor, all the plates he had been so industriously spinning in the air were passed as from one expert juggler to another, to Tobias. Tobias, the lanky tow-headed companion in most of Nick's early adventures, was used to this. A soldier of fortune himself, their business ventures had made him a rich man.

He even fielded the one connected with the playhouse, he knew the lines and the moves in the fight sequence as well as Nick. Something had happened in those months gone before. Tobias had caught the disease for which there is no cure. Stage fever.

Love of the theatre is a disease: once contracted there is no getting rid of it. It is not fatal, on the contrary, actors live long.

"Even so quickly may one catch the plague…" mused Tobias. In the play, Viola was talking of lovesickness – the stage-struck Toby hung around the Globe. He was no actor. His moment of glory was soon over, but he concerned himself with the machinery of backstage.

He did not neglect business, of course not, but every spare minute he was at the playhouse, content to be one of the invisible army without which no play would ever be put on. He had taken

Nick's place as fight manager and even saw his name on a playbill once, but apart from that he worked behind the scenes, making himself useful.

Without Nicholas and his family, the manor house at Richmond proved too big and empty for Tobias, and he negotiated with Tom Walsingham to purchase the snug little property in Deptford. Crosstrees had the advantage of being close to both the docks and the playhouse. He intended this to be just his London lodging, but when he paid a visit to the manor at Lower Rookham that Nick had offered him, he had been overawed by the magnificence of the building going up under the eye of Master Inigo Jones.

"Not for me," he muttered. "I've enough to do without this. Never fancied myself Lord Muck. Can't imagine Nick living here either. Rosalyne might have other ideas, of course. No, I'm suited with Crosstrees."

On arriving back, however, the place did seem a little cramped. *Easily remedied*, thought Tobias, and added the rebuilding of Crosstrees to his list of things to do. The weeks passed and he began to worry. Word had been brought by courier from Nicholas who was apparently in Scotland – no news of the ship he had left in. Young Trelawney should have been back by now.

All Saints' Day came and went, and on a frosty November morning a boy came running from the docks to say the *Snipe* had been sighted off Gravesend. Tobias slammed his papers together, snatched up his cloak and called for his horse.

He stood watching the ship come in. She was gaily bedizened with flags and seemed to ride low in the water. She had left London with only Nicholas and his party and precious little in the way of luggage – perhaps she was holed and taking on water…

Tim Trelawney was on the poop deck shouting orders and the ship came cleanly as a gull to her moorings. Trelawney caught sight of Tobias and a broad grin spread over his face. He waved and sprang down, calling for his skiff. Men were busy among the cranes as the holds were opened and bales, boxes and sacks started to appear. Tobias stared as the young man weaved towards him with the unsteady gait of a man long at sea.

"What in God's name—"

"A rich cargo, Master Fletcher, and more to come!"

"Did Lord Rokesby—"

"No – look, there is much to tell, come to the tavern. Bates can manage the unlading." This was a new Trelawney, filled out and weather-beaten, his blue eyes bright with the far-seeing gaze of a sailor, wearing the mantle of authority. He led the way without waiting for an answer and Toby found himself in the back parlour of the Spaniard's Head with a pint pot in his hand listening to Tim's tale of adventure.

"I didn't see the sense in coming back empty of all but ballast," he was saying. "The cod was in, and just up the coast there was the fishing fleet and the salt pans. I sold all I had and borrowed the rest to pay for it and sailed for Amsterdam. The floats and barges were in from Russia – great timing – salt cod for furs and timber and luxury goods – you should see the silver and the plate! I bought some bulbs as well – bit of a private speculation that. What I thought—"

"Just a moment. Who authorised you to do all this?"

Tim had the grace to look a little abashed.

"Well, no-one, sir. I used my initiative like Nick – I mean Lord Rokesby always says."

"Hmm. And the money?"

"If you'd like to come to the customs shed, I'll show you the manifest. I've sold ahead on the next cargo." Lost for words, Toby drained his pot and followed him to the dockside. What he saw there impressed him still more. Trelawney had not only made a healthy profit (net) but had set up a valuable trading link. He brought the young man back to Crosstrees – now to be known as 'Fletcher's Piece', and sat him down to a hearty supper.

"I congratulate you, Tim. I don't imagine you did all this from the kindness of your heart."

"I don't know what you mean, sir."

"I mean you had better stop 'sirring' me and take your fair share. Nicholas will be proud of you. But before we go into all that, what news from Scotland?"

Trelawney had called in at Edinburgh on his way to the Low Country for news of Nicholas and an extra cargo of scallops and oysters – "seemed a shame not to, we had salt and ice" – and it was late into the night before all the news was exchanged. In unconscious echo of Nick's words, Tobias said, "He seems to have gone from one hornet's nest to another. Of the two, he may have the best of it. I'll have a report for you to take back."

Chapter Fifteen

London. 1600

The celebrations for the dawn of a new century were rather muted. England was still at war with Spain, and there was fresh trouble in the Netherlands in spite of the entente with France. The Irish problem was compounded by the delays and inactivity on the part of the new Lord Lieutenant, the Earl of Essex. He had ennobled over a hundred new knights and the money granted him, together with the cannon (at a cost of £23,000) and the weaponry and clothing he had demanded, ran into tens of thousands. By the summer, his splendid army had dwindled from 1,400 horse and 16,000 foot to less than 11,000 men, decimated by ill-thought-out skirmishes and disease, the Irish ague and the Irish looseness, which referred not to the state of their morals but to an affliction of the bowels. The march which had begun with such a flourish at Richmond to the accompaniment of a violent thunderstorm had descended into ignominy and failure. The queen was furious at the waste of time and money, all spent with no result.

Tobias had not the inside information available to Nicholas regarding King James' part in Devereux' headstrong behaviour, and so he was as astonished as anyone else when Essex defied the Queen's express wish and returned to England on the twenty-eighth of September with his band of friends and new-made knights.

What happened next bade fair to divide the country. The charming, handsome Earl with his dashing ways and ready smile was much loved by the people, who knew little and cared less for politics and the proper conduct of wars. At Court and among the financiers and governors of the country, he was looked on as a loose cannon and a danger to himself and those around him. Toby thanked Providence and the good sense that had kept Nicholas from joining him all those years ago.

The news went round the town with the speed of a plague-carrying rat. My Lord Essex had burst in on the Queen in all the mud of his journey, before she had even got her wig on, and sued for favour! Rumour said it was a coup, Essex would take the throne; common sense held that Elizabeth would soon send him to the right about. Tobias had it third-hand from John Challoner that in her fear the Queen had first spoken her Robin fair, and once she was dressed, bewigged and protected had confined him to his room and denied him access. Toby learned more from a visit to Nick's uncle, Admiral Sir William Talbot, now a member of the Privy Council.

The Admiral received him in his study, a snug little room that resembled his cabin aboard ship, everything neatly stowed away, the brasswork shining and the wood polished. He poured ale for them both and sat Toby down by the fire. Tobias had news from Scotland and Sir William heard him out in silence.

"So," he said, "our Nicholas is grown powerful. Tell him to watch his back."

Everyone says that, thought Tobias.

"I mislike it that we have lost sight of his greatest enemy. I shall look to it. Now, Master Fletcher, this is for your ears and Nicholas' only. I take it you are in touch with him? Yes. He should know, if he does not know already, that the Council fears Essex is planning a rebellion. If this will involve James, we need to know. The unruly Earl has been twice before us already and is now confined to his room."

"On what charge?"

"No charge. That surprises you? If you want a list of his misdemeanours—" He held up a horny hand and counted his fingers. "The Queen is very angry. His conduct in Ireland, his defiance of her orders, the creation of all these impecunious knights who may form a cadre to stand with him against her – to my view, she is over-lenient. There are those of us – Ralegh and Cobham among them – who would like to see him either charged and under arrest or set free, but she cannot yet bring herself to a decision." He scratched his chin with the stem of his pipe and went on musingly, "Mind you, I would not trust Cobham a flea's jump. Too like his father – did you ever meet him?"

"I believe Nicholas did."

"This delay is damaging, Tobias. Devereux is the people's darling, the longer he is kept dangling, with no official charge, the more sympathy he gains. There are those bravos in the city who live by their wits and the sword, adventurers I say, who would make trouble. We have more information. It has come to the ears of Robert Cecil that Devereux met privately with Tyrone. This, at a time when he was expected to join battle with him. It is said that the Irishman will join with the King to invade England."

Tobias snorted in disbelief.

"You may shake your head, young man. What does Nicholas say?"

"Nothing. Nick keeps his cards close to his chest. If it comes necessary, he will act, not talk, that I *do* know. If the queen were to know of this, I warrant she will be spurred into doing something. It is treason, surely."

"No proof. Unless Nicholas–"

"As far as I know, Nicholas is minding his own business."

The Admiral sat back, his eyes twinkling. "Which is flourishing, I hear. God send us all such loyal friends as you, Tobias. You are right, stay out of it. This news of Tyrone will do the trick."

On the first of October, Essex was confined in York House under the eye of Sir Robert Egerton, the Lord Keeper. Feeling against Cecil began to run high, it was thought that he had inflamed the Queen against Essex, and soon he was obliged to take a bodyguard whenever he ventured out. It was useless for the justices and government ministers to proclaim publicly the many failings that had angered and disappointed the queen. Those swaggerers and troublemakers foreseen by the Admiral put it about that, "this was to condemn a man unheard and to stab him in the back, leaving Justice her sword and taking away her balance, which consisted of an accusation and a defence."

To make matters worse, Essex fell ill. The dysentery he had brought back from Ireland grew dangerous and by Christmas he was so debilitated he was said to be like to die. Elizabeth sent her own physicians to care for him and was then further affronted when a number of eminent churchmen led the public in prayers for him. Whichever of these remedies worked, he was much recovered in the new year, enough for a date to be set for his trial in the Star Chamber.

"We did think we had him," sighed the Admiral. "But no, the cozening rascal has written to her Majesty pleading his cause and she has cancelled the hearing. Had he come before us, I have no doubt it would have been a hefty fine and the Tower for him. She has even allowed him back to his own home. Treason it may be, Tobias, but sometimes I despair of being ruled by a woman."

Essex went back to a house stripped of his own servants and still under strict guard, this time in the custody of Sir Richard Berkley. The Admiral's soft-hearted wife was sorry for him.

"Such a pity, Tobias," she said. "Such a handsome young man as he was, and the Queen will not even allow him the comfort of his family, only his wife by day. To be so at her age—"

"Quiet, my dear," said her husband. "You are not fully informed. Such a gaggle as formed to celebrate his release – premature to say the least. Her majesty has much to bear – and fear – from him."

The tragedy of Robert, Earl of Essex continued to unfold, to the detriment of trade and foreign affairs. In June, Tobias wrote to Nicholas to tell him that Essex had been called before a tribunal and stripped of all office save Master of the Horse.

Matters go from bad to worse, Nick, he wrote. *All the talk on 'Change is of the growing support he draws about him. Men like Southampton and Rutland, Mounteagle and Cromwell gather to him and I hear even in the taverns that plans are afoot. It is said he rails at the Queen like a madman. "As ugly in her mind as in her carcase!" Those first two are men of straw, but there are others more dangerous. He has hanging about him a man called Cuffe – calls himself a secretary and encourages him with foolish talk. All this unrest is bad for business and I am taking steps accordingly.*

He wrote again just after Christmas to warn Nicholas once again to stay away.

His lordship throws open his doors to all comers, bold confident fellows, men of broken fortune, all the rag tag and bobtail you would expect, discontented and hopeful of trouble. You have sore troubles of your own, for which I am truly sorry, my friend, you were best stay where you are.

By the time this message was delivered, Nicholas was on his way south.

Chapter Sixteen

London. February 5. 1601
The play's the thing

Nicholas arrived back in London to a strange sense of unease. That sensitive organ, his nose, detected the reek of the city in its brown fume of smoke as far out as the village of Highgate, where he was stopped for the tolls. As he rode on into the city, Hob behind him with their spare horses, he noticed the knots of men gathered on street-corners, who fell silent at his approach. He might be dressed in plain and humble fashion, but there was no denying the quality of his horses and the jewelled hilt of the sword strapped to his saddle. There were more watchmen and men-at-arms than usual patrolling the main thoroughfares: surely the number of beggars had multiplied. Pamphlets were nailed up and as swiftly pulled down, the taverns oddly quiet. This impression was to be strengthened in the next day or two. He decided to rack up at the Elephant, and left Hob there to take his rest while he went to seek out Tobias.

He found him at last at the Globe, sitting on the edge of the stage with a script in his hand, hearing Burbage's lines. They were putting on the *Merchant* again. It was becoming increasingly difficult to find a play with no sensitive political overtones.

"Can't even do the Roman play," complained Burbage. "Or Henry Four and as for Dick Two – don't talk to me about that, mustn't mention the U-word, no crown-snatching if you please. Yet I was pestered to death by those out for trouble and wanted it played! Of course we did it in the end – tell you about that in a minute – and there's Marlowe's old piece about a king with a skewer up his arse – well! Might as well take up pantomime."

"Assassination out then," said Nick, thinking of the dark play in his satchel.

"Oh, hush! Don't say the word. I told you, not even *Julius Caesar*. My life is hell and Will was at his wit's end. They were saying he'd written himself out until he produced that new comedy. We played it for the Queen at Twelfth Night. It's still running. And that last one – oh yes, that's still good box-office." Here he found a fresh grievance. "What the hell did you think you were doing, you runagate – pissing off without a by your leave? Young Thomas nearly had a seizure."

"He knew the parts," said Nick, unrepentant. "His finest hour. And I hear Toby saved the day. Are you telling me receipts are down?" Nick had shares in the Globe, taken to protect Marlowe's interest. He had a voice in what plays were performed.

"No, no, we've hardly lost a day even in the cold weather. Come and have a sup and I'll tell you."

"Have a heart, Dick, the man's just arrived. What he wants is a meal and a bed," said Tobias.

"I shall find Richmond a haven of peace after Strathyre."

"You would indeed, living among the dust-sheets. I closed the place up. You see before you a man of property, Nick. Crosstrees is mine and I am a-building. Ask the price of masonry and timber and I'm your man."

Nicholas smiled and did not answer the unspoken question. *Twelfth Night* was having the success it deserved. Good. *Macbeth* could wait.

"You've room for a lodger, then," he said as they left the playhouse and turned toward Deptford.

"Richmond can be ready in a trice. Deptford is no place for a family."

"Rosalyne stays in Edinburgh for the nonce. The business with Mowbray hit her hard. She and the boys are safe at the palace – I have things to do – it's complicated."

Sobered, Toby looked at him.

"It was a sad loss, Nicholas. And you, how do you find yourself – glad to be back?"

"I am to be kept busy, it seems. No time to mourn a grievous lack of judgement. Mother of God, is that Crosstrees?"

Warned off, Toby said lightly, "Fletcher's Piece, if you please. Oh, I have thrown out a wing here, added a room or two there. You won't suffer any loss of dignity, I promise you."

"Less talk of my dignity, I thank you. I didn't notice Burbage paying it much heed."

"You know yourself, Nick, we players spend too much time aping our betters to afford them any respect."

Nick laughed at that. "We players, is it? Lead me to a dinner of Alice's making, and we'll talk… May I send for Hob?"

"My house is yours – seeing as it was yours in the first place."

After a comfortable dinner, the two young men established themselves in their old-accustomed seats either side of a roaring fire and Toby took down his pipe. Nicholas surveyed the room, noting the new frieze of painted and gilded leather above the panelling.

"So," he said, stretching stockinged feet to the blaze, "your courtship prospers?"

"Ah, you are like all married folk, you want every man to put his head in the noose. No, my lady Caroline grew tired of waiting for me to make my fortune. She married in the autumn, did I not tell you? A paltry fellow, but there, she has her title."

"Sour grapes!"

"Not a whit. I should never make a good husband."

"And what of Trelawney?"

"That young dog? I keep him a room here, but he is seldom in it. When he's not wenching, he has a good head on his shoulders, does Tim."

"That reminds me. I've a mind to develop what he found in Cawdor…" The talk strayed into business matters, until Toby leaned forward and knocked out his pipe.

"You are not here on matters of trade, Nick. Is it to do with my lord Essex? Or shouldn't I ask?"

"There are some things you are better off not knowing. But yes, in a way. It has been forcibly brought to my attention – by those I trust, I should add – that like it or not, I seem to be in a position of – shall we say…influence? I am urged to put money in my purse and look to my affairs. At the moment, Rosalyne is an earnest of my good behaviour. I cannot like it." He got up restlessly and poured them wine. "I am no Essex, Toby, you know that, but I have been blind to what has come about."

"You have indeed," said Toby drily. "A trifle naive, in fact. You have been a little like a blinkered horse, taking each fence as it comes. Time to take off those blinkers and take a look at what you have done. Raise your horizon, Nick." He sat back and leisurely filled his pipe from a handsome tobacco jar. "I am one of the beneficiaries, if you have not noticed."

"I had noticed, and you have earned every groat yourself."

Toby shook his head. "The difference between us, my friend, is that I have done what I have done with my eyes wide open. To you it seems incidental, a sideshow to the main event." He reached for the tongs and took a coal from the slumbering fire. He paused a moment. "This coal could start a conflagration," he said, "were it set to tinder. Like you. Listen, Nick. Men fear you. They fear what you could do – if you chose. No, hear me out. The business is making money hand over fist. You have been given an earldom, lands – and with the devil's own luck, some of those lands sit on a raft of money. Was it luck that you found it out? No, you used your wits and found a surveyor. Trelawney used his, he saw an opportunity for further trade. You gave him his head, Nick, and you are repaid. To deal with the scourge of the MacGregor you raised a small army of men and trained them. They would come at your call. This is what men seeking power fear. They do not know you as I do."

This was so like what Marlowe had said to him, and Essex had written, that Nick could only stare at his friend. Toby calmly applied the coal to his pipe and got it drawing.

"You were wise not to argue about leaving Rosalyne if she was unwell. And you are right – she is a hostage to fortune. If you want my advice you will persuade Elizabeth to send for her – I take it you will have audience with her gracious Majesty? She will send, I've no doubt."

"There is something I must do first."

"Be quick about it, then, things are coming to a head. Much depends on Devereux' next move," said Toby. "I wish to God he'd do something, the markets are down."

Nick stood up. "I'm going to bed," he said.

He dropped his clothes on the floor and lay down in his bed, but tired as he was, he did not fall asleep at once. He lay there, mulling over what Toby had said.

It had been a long hard ride from Edinburgh. They had got through the border lands unscathed, thanks to Robert Carey's escort and his own reputation, but the snows of Northumberland and the north country had been uncomfortable, and the driving rain that followed. Further south conditions had been kinder, but he had not reckoned on Toby's dissertation that night. He seemed to have underestimated his partner. He had had plenty of time to think on the journey and he knew what Tobias had said was true. Marlowe had seen it, and in those last days at court he had understood for himself what a weapon he had forged if he chose to use it. It seemed to Nicholas that he had been following a path mapped out for him, guiding him through a minefield, all unknowing. Now the blindfold was off. It was time to take his destiny in his own hands.

He slept.

Chapter Seventeen

London. February 6th. 1601

When he woke in the morning, Nick did not immediately get out of bed. He lay for a while going over what had happened. There was more trouble ahead. Time to make plans perhaps.

He threw off the covers and went to stand shivering and naked at the window, scratching at the scars on his chest. Hob was in the yard pumping water into a bucket for Alice. They were laughing and Nick smiled to himself. Hob had lost no time there.

It was a fine day. A day to find out what was afoot in the city.

Hob had been busy. A suit of clothes had been laid out for him, there were warm water and cloths and a tray of bread and honey and small beer.

Dressed in a style become unfamiliar to him, black figured brocade slashed with silver and tailored to fit a brawnier figure than he was now, he ran down to find Toby at a late breakfast.

"Greetings, friend. What news on the Rialto!"

"We are about to go and find out, my play-acting friend. You've lost weight."

"Pass me the ham. I see Hob has made himself a niche in the household."

"A welcome addition. I'll be in the stables when you've finished, Nick. I had it in mind to visit 'Change, there may be news."

Visiting the Exchange with Tobias, he found that in spite of the opening up of new trade in the Baltic, the atmosphere was subdued. They learned that two of their ships had been sighted off Gravesend. One was from Genoa, and Nick hoped she brought among her cargo a suitable present for the Queen – he could not go empty-handed. He wandered around, listening to gossip and the rather guarded talk of the older men of business, finding his views canvassed and listened to. They took their meat with John Challoner and went down to the docks to see their ships come safely in. Anchoring out in the broads, Captain Tim Trelawney was much in evidence, a man of authority. The young man had the air of a seasoned mariner. He caught sight of Nick and called for a boat. The three men had a lot to catch up on, and it was late in the afternoon before Nick could embark on the next part of his programme. His uncle, Sir William Talbot was a member of the Council now, and Nicholas wanted the latest news of Essex.

The Admiral was in the middle of a fine dinner and rose to welcome him with open arms. He sat Nicholas down between his two elder daughters and sent for an extra trencher and a goblet of fine wine. They ate and talked of everything but the matter occupying their thoughts until the board was cleared and the womenfolk gone. In the quiet that followed, he took his seat by the fire and motioned Nick to the one opposite. He looked more careworn than when Nick had last seen him. He took some time getting his pipe to draw to his satisfaction and at last said, "We grieve for you Nicholas. And for Rosalyne… Is Jack with you? We look forward to taking him into our household – an honour to be asked. How does your lady?"

"Better, I thank you. Both the boys are still with her in Scotland."

"It will take a while. I remember my Joan… These things happen, lad. Be patient."

Nicholas gave his short nod and said nothing.

The Admiral cleared his throat. "And what brings you here? Sent for, or on James' business?"

"A little of each, uncle. The matter was urgent or I would not have left Rose. I don't like the feel of things."

William Talbot burst out, "He should never have been sent to Ireland! The silly man's nursed his grievances and ambitions until his wits are quite turned. The arrogance of it – to burst in upon the queen as he did! Did he imagine she would swoon into his arms and grant his every wish? The spoilt darling—"

"Yes," said Nick. "He has been spoiled. Led on and worked upon by those he thought his friends. It could have been very different."

"You are too generous, Nicholas. Nature will out. Have you seen him?"

"No. But from what I heard in Edinburgh, there is no turning back in him."

The Admiral got up to stamp about the room. "His own actions speak against him. Making so many idle knights in Ireland, spending the Queen's money like a drunken sailor – or so she says – 'it's muddy, it's wet, we have the sickness, can't find Tyrone in these sodden Irish bogs' – tchah! Excuses, excuses…"

This came from a man for whom conduct on board ship brooked no excuse and Nicholas held his tongue. The tempest blew itself out and Sir William settled down to give Nick a statesmanlike report. Essex had borne himself well at the first meeting of the Council. "Stood quiet and sensible – hard to tell if he realised he'd missed the boat. If he'd pushed on then, when he had the Queen at his mercy, his supporters would have followed him – the coup would have succeeded."

"His supporters?"

"Worcester and Rutland, Mountjoy, Rich, and Henry Howard – the usual hangers-on. That man Cuffe – you speak of leading on…he is at Devereux' elbow night and morn, feeding him nonsense. Her majesty delayed three days – listening to Cecil of course – and finally committed him to the charge of Lord Keeper Egerton in York House. If you had seen him, Nicholas, you would know the change in him. It was a bad time. He seemed to be prey to melancholy and the sickness he brought with him from Ireland grew worse. Half the troops had the dysentery, he wasn't exaggerating there. We did our best for him, asked for him to be set at liberty – he had failed, after all, but her Majesty was angry. This is the danger, Nicholas. The town is full of his men, those that followed him from Ireland, he is the people's favourite and the longer she delayed a decision the more feeling rose against her. It wasn't until the end of November we all met again. Then, of course, it all came out and she was seen to be justified… Poor Devereux, stripped of his household, he grew worse, seemed like to die at one point, the bell was tolled for him on the tenth. Did you hear any of this?"

Not knowing how much his kinsman had seen of Tobias, Nick shook his head.

"He was still corresponding with James, the last I heard. And Mountjoy…" The Admiral paused and sighed, and called for more wine. "Thirsty work, this." He waited until the wine was brought, and stood with his back to Nicholas, pouring it. "Poor, foolish young man," he said quietly. "He'll hang for a traitor yet – it will break the Queen's heart."

"Will she not see him?"

"Not she. Whether she fears him, or his beguiling ways, I cannot tell, but she is angry. Go and see her, Nicholas, if anyone can pry your Rosalyne away from Scotland, she can."

Yes, thought Nick as he rode away. He wanted his wife back. He needed to see the Queen.

Chapter Eighteen

The Audience

He rose next day determined to seek audience and dressed accordingly. His Court clothes had suffered in the many journeys and the finely-tailored doublet seemed to hang on him rather. He slung the gold chains of his Orders across his shoulders to make up for the deficiency. From Genoa had come fine goldsmith's work, and Nick chose for the Queen's gift a hair ornament in the shape of a galleon, with sails of diamonds floating on a sapphire sea. He could hardly go wrong with that. He packed it in a small box finely wrought with enamels, picked up his cloak and went downstairs. Toby whistled at sight of him.

"Off to see the Queen, I take it. You certainly pick your moment. Bad timing, friend."

"Things can only get worse, I fear. No point in delay."

Signs of his change in status appeared in his reception at Court. He was not left to kick his heels with the other supplicants to her Majesty, but was conducted to the antechamber where he did not have to wait above two hours before being summoned to her presence.

The signs of mortality were in her face. Broad shafts of sunlight slanted across the room, turning to gold dust the motes that fell everlasting. They fell on the hands twisting in her lap, roped with veins, a collection of roots held together with rings that flashed as they moved. As usual she was elaborately dressed in a stiff farthingale of velvet over an under-dress of satin, tawny over tangerine, all embroidered with topaz and pearls. His ornament had been delivered and she wore it in her hair – she had on a crimson wig today. The clear February sunlight was not kind…

A rich carpet covered the floor these days, softer to the knees of aging courtiers. She dismissed her lady-in-waiting and pointed to a spot where the sun shone brightest.

Nicholas went to kneel.

"No!" she said sharply. "Stand there where I can see you." She stared at him for a long time, from top to toe. He made himself relax and without realising it, fell into the pose that he had been taught for the stage, right knee bent and the toe slightly turned in, to give the best line for the leg. The pause lengthened. At last, Elizabeth sighed, the breath rattling in her chest.

"You could have risen high in our Court, Rokesby," she said. "You chose to serve our cousin in Scotland and he has honoured you. Perhaps you do well to stay away. I kill where most I love." She turned her head away, but not before he had caught the sparkle of tears. In the silence, Nicholas could clearly hear the shouts of the wherrymen and the scuttle of a mouse. She was looking back down the years at the procession of handsome, vain and ambitious young men that had passed through her hands, some self-seeking and foolish, some of them lovers, all lost. This man was different. She looked at him standing there, the bright sunshine burnishing his hair, one long-fingered hand on his sword-hilt, the other idly brushing his cap-feather against his leg.

"I lost the toy you gave me," she said abruptly. "Have you another?"

"Not about me, your Majesty. I gave one to my boy."

"Hah! He grows more like his true father – you, Rokesby – every day, I'm told. Does he know his parentage?"

"Yes, your Majesty."

"Why have you left them in Scotland?"

Nicholas looked her in the eye. His chance had come sooner than expected.

"They are kept in fee for my good conduct, my queen. If your Majesty would but send for them, my hands would be free."

"To do what?"

"To serve my country."

The shrewd old eyes, still bright, considered him.

"You could have power, my lord. What would you? A seat on the Council? The Privy Seal?" She slammed her palm on the arm of her chair. "Ask, damn you!"

"I ask only that my wife and children be restored to me."

"And is that your condition for your service, my lord?"

This was dangerous ground.

"No, your Majesty. That is yours without condition, best done without further reward."

"How do you propose to set about it?"

"In the marketplace, perhaps—"

"A tradesman!"

"More an ambassador for trade, your Majesty. New worlds are opening up, sea routes, the links with Scotland and Russia—"

"You will not take up arms for us? The Spanish are still snapping at my heels and the Irish are troublesome as ever."

"Your Majesty has a good commander in Mountjoy and if there must be war in Europe, it must be paid for."

"And you would provide the sinews of war, my lord?"

146

"I should prefer to address the troubles at home."

"In your own way, no doubt." She thought for a moment, and indicated the stool at her feet. "Very well, Nicholas. You have never been a courtier, to fawn and feign love or seek to buy favour, and plot in corners…you would be up and doing. The favour is granted. Now tell me, what do they say of me, what is my legacy? I know I shall hear truth from you."

Nick thought for a moment, choosing his words. He went on one knee.

"You have spoken often, and in public, your Majesty, of your love for your people. Fine, stirring speeches, to bind them to you. How do you see these people of yours? The common people, who fight your wars and pay their taxes, bring in the harvest and tend their beasts, Englishmen and women who grumble and laugh and go about their daily business. They may not see England, as the poet sees her – 'a precious stone set in a silver sea' – but they love their land and all that's in her and would fight to a standstill to keep her safe. They look to you and wise counsellors to govern and help them. Do you see these people or the nest of self-seeking warring men, powerful men squabbling for preferment? If it be the first, as it should be, how are they served, who serve you well and faithfully? Are they rewarded, enfranchised? And their women, who are given no voice, what of them?" He took a breath.

"We have gone far towards enlightenment in your time, my Queen, great thinkers and poets and explorers, new lands, new hope for freedom. If you look for a legacy, these will speak for you."

He stopped, his face burning. Men had been killed for less. She was staring at him, the spots of rouge standing out on her raddled cheeks.

She gave a sudden cackle.

"What a boy you are still. Take your speech to Master Shakespeare, it lacks polish. Freedom! Enfranchisement? That sounds like treason. Be careful what you wish for. You are a dangerous man, Nicholas Talbot, but not, I think, to me. If you speak from the heart, you may be forgiven. If not, if you yourself seek preferment and mean to teach us our business, you may be punished. Which is it, I wonder?"

"Your Majesty may judge."

"She may indeed. And I judge you honest. Thank your guardian angel, Rokesby, that I am an old and feeble woman who would not send you to the gallows for the hangman and the hook. Be advised, keep these words to yourself, they come too soon or too late. You cry for the moon, young man. Give the people freedom and they would not know what to do with it. Anarchy, rioting in the streets. Like you, they are children yet, they must learn. Go your ways, make your fortune and pay your taxes. We will not bind you." She tired suddenly, resting her head on her hand. "Leave us. Bring a new play like the last to amuse us."

"Majesty." He rose. "They will say you are without equal, my Queen. A player would say a hard act to follow."

"Off with you. Do your playacting in the proper place. Or do I wrong you? You never sought to flatter."

"Nor do I. I never forget that you found me my bride."

"Hah! Call yourself a hard-headed businessman? You are a romantic fool, Rokesby."

Nick laughed. "I am an Elizabethan, your Majesty, I can be both."

"At least your sayings are more beguiling than most. Wear this for me." She wrestled a ring over her bony knuckle and held out her hand for his. As she slid the ruby onto his finger, he caught a glimpse of the young girl she had been. He would have fallen in love with her himself. *And gone the way of Leicester and Essex*, he thought. He kissed her hand and she waved him away.

"Bring the players. I would see you play your part."

He bowed himself out and ran the gauntlet of envious stares from those waiting outside. The ring he kept hidden as he made his way through the familiar warren of passages to Robert Cecil's office, conscious that in all his talk with Elizabeth no mention had been made of Robert Devereux, Earl of Essex.

"It would seem there is likely to be a vacancy among the Knights of the Garter," said Cecil with a sour smile. "I believe her Majesty has it mind for you – when the time comes." Nicholas just stopped himself saying, "She didn't mention it," in time. He had decided to keep his audience with the queen to himself. Cecil would find out soon enough. He felt a cold breath on the back of his neck as he understood whose boots he would fill. Elizabeth might be old, but, clear-sighted as ever, she could face facts, however painful. Her Robin had betrayed her twice over, as a woman and as his monarch, and Nicholas was well aware of her grief.

Cecil, the Queen's little elf, had never made any secret of his hatred for Essex. After his recent hypocritical announcement that he would not speak against him, he had turned on him once more. He must be grinding his teeth to think of Nick honoured in his place. But the man was not dead yet, nor had he committed the ultimate folly. Clearly, Cecil hoped to push him into it.

"Well?" Cecil's voice was waspish.

"My lord?"

"What do you say to that?"

"Always a mistake to count one's chickens…" This ambiguous reply drove the angry blood into the Secretary's cheeks. He was not to be lured into indiscretion, however.

"You have a message from James? A task, perhaps?" The familiarity did not bode well for future relations with Scotland's king.

"Greetings from one prince to another, is all."

The little hunch-backed spymaster bounced in his chair.

"Listen to me, Rokesby—"

Nicholas stood up. "Should we not continue to observe the courtesies, my lord? The position is somewhat altered. I serve the monarchy in whatever way will benefit my country…as do you. Can we not work together for the common weal?"

"Fine words for a jumped-up play actor!"

"Thank you my lord. You show me where I stand with you. As you once told me, we live in interesting times." He picked up his cap and gloves and turned to leave.

The infuriated Cecil knew better than to let him go.

"A moment, my lord. You were not wont to be so hasty. Where is that elusive devil Marlowe – or have you been too busy about your own affairs?"

You can't beat me with that stick any more, thought Nick. *You taught me to lie, why stop now?*

Aloud, he said, "Christopher Marlowe is dead, my lord."

"Dead! How is he dead?"

"Of the plague."

Cecil hastily crossed himself. "Mercy on his soul," he muttered. "Much good his escape did us. Except of course, to bring you into our service, young man. You have rid yourself of Mowbray at last, I hear. I am told he was a tool of my lord Essex. Do you know anything of this, Nicholas?"

The wheedling tone tickled Nick and he smiled. He had long suspected that Cecil had a hand in Mowbray's escape.

"You find me amusing?"

"What could I know, my lord, I have been in Scotland."

"My meaning exactly. Well?"

"Her majesty must be much distressed. Her favourite is arraigned for treason. Why add to her burden with idle muckraking?"

Cecil looked fit to burst. "My task is to safeguard her kingdom, sirrah! I do not regard it as muck-raking. Be careful, young man, you go too far."

"There is a saying, 'Who touches pitch...' I am defiled myself, I cast no stone, I assure you. As far as I can see, James is now a safe bet, one task at least is done. Should we not be looking at the state of the country's coffers? These Irish wars, the threat from Spain still with us – unless of course, you still have ideas of a Spanish claimant for the throne – all these threaten the stability of the markets. And what of our navy? We need ships."

"I had forgot," said Cecil, "that you are a merchant these days." He almost spat the word. "Are you seeking a seat on the Council? I warn you there will be a great deal of opposition." He sat back and laced his fingers over his little pot belly. "I see you have learned one thing from me. Never answer a straight question with a straight answer. You will make a politician yet. Very well my lord Rokesby, keep your counsel, you are no more use to me."

"No?" said Nicholas. "I may yet be of use to you, while you still hold the reins of government – who knows? It may even be that our aims are the same. Good day to you, my lord."

Chapter Nineteen

The Globe

Lord and master of four handsome properties, without his wife and children Nicholas was as homeless and rootless as if he had none. Strathyre had become to him a place accursed, haunted by witches and murder and guilt, scene of the worst mistake he had ever made. He turned his back on it and the empty echoing rooms of Richmond and went to find his other family, the players.

He found them in the middle of an informal meeting. Comfortably sprawled on a hamper in the tiring room with a mug of ale in his fist, Burbage expounded, "As I said, Will's tearing what hair he has left. Back in February last year it started, I took no heed of it then. John Hayward brought out a book and dedicated it to my lord Essex, God rest his soul… Guess what it was about?"

Nick shook his head, not wanting to spoil the actor's punchline.

"Henry Four, that's what. You mind Bolingbroke in Dick Two turfing King Richard off the throne? Can't miss the connection with poor Essex, can you? We were asked over and over to play Dick Two – without the deposition speech, mark you – and I did it in the end, but the trouble it caused! We haven't seen the end of it yet – Hayward's book has been printed with and without the

Essex letter – first edition sold out, never mind the ban! Well, deserve it or not, the poor fellow's paid the price. I say to you, Nick, it's bad for business, us players shouldn't mess with politics. Act it, don't do it. And those little monkeys in the Children's Company stealing our audience – nothing new from Will since the comedy neither."

Nicholas sat relaxed in the gilt property throne, booted legs thrust out before him, Caesar's laurel wreath askew on his head, and let the familiar tide of gossip flow over him. He breathed in the smell of glue-size, wood shavings, sweaty costumes and paint, and smiled.

It was good to be back. He had decided to place a literal interpretation on Elizabeth's words, and if he had known it, this was precisely what she intended. He was no use to her in his present state except in the ways he had spoken of: kept hanging about the Court among the younger element he might even be a danger with his seductive ideas. Rokesby had always been her wild card and for the moment she let him go. She still had need of him and Rosalyne was the ace up her sleeve. She would play it when she was ready.

Tobias was busy at the table constructing something complicated, and listening. It seemed that Ben Jonson was the talk of the town and the company at the Rose was at odds with that of the Globe, stealing their best players and pirating their material. Burbage went on, "By the way, Nick, can you give us your Mercutio next week? Orlando plays Romeo, our new pair of lads for the women."

Nick shook his head. "Perhaps. Go on about Hayward."

"Not much more to tell. Now you're back, Nick, we'll have a proper meeting. The other shareholders are getting worried. And listen, you won't believe this, regarding the Hayward affair, Lord Bacon laid claim to writing Dick Two! In public! Only a rumour mind, but I heard he wouldn't dispute poor Hayward's writings and the play because – listen to this – he would be denying his own work. How about that? Will was hopping."

As well he might be, thought Nick. Marlowe's additions had been skilfully joined to what Nick had thought to be Shakespeare's own work. If Will had yet another writer using him as a conduit he must be as nervous as ten cats in a bag. *Better go and see him*, thought Nick. *Francis Bacon, eh? I thought perhaps Southampton…*

Burbage was still talking, coaxing. "Are you sure you can't play, Nick? We're damnably short and the Earl of – whatever you're called – would bring 'em in."

"You're always short. It's a new play you need to get them by the ears."

"Will's been writing something, but he says it's not ready."

No, Macbeth still won't do, thought Nick. Now he came to think of it, Marlowe had until recently always favoured themes of discord among the great. Of course he did, it was the stuff of play-making. He was never happier than when stirring the pot, holding up a mirror for others to see themselves. Not so important perhaps if they were not written in such unforgettable words. This play *Macbeth* was a strange marriage of his new domestic concern and the old blood and carnage. *Twelfth Night is doing well*, he thought. *Let it run a little longer*.

"Our ineffable Ben seems to be getting away with murder," he observed. "I marvel at it, after the *Isle of Dogs*. You'd think after that scurrilous piece of nonsense, a spell in jail would have taught him a lesson."

"Not him. Satire is the new comedy," said Burbage. "The young bloods have taken to it. And no kings and queens you see, he's a man of the people, taken a leaf out of Will's book there."

"Get him to write one for us. Or what about a nice dose of the horrors? I hear young Webster's written a piece or two. How does he these days? I remember him always behind doors. I swear he knew the length of every prick in the company."

"It's an idea. You don't think it would be selling out? Will's work is head and shoulders above theirs."

"A revival then, a comedy—"

"I doubt we'd even be allowed to put on the *Shrew* lest it be seen as a caricature of Elizabeth with no-one to tame her." He paused, shaking his head. "Although Time tames us all in the end."

"I wouldn't bet my boots on it. Look, if you're really stuck, bring back the *Dream* and I'll play Oberon or Bottom – so disguised my wife wouldn't know me."

You'll be hard pressed to disguise your voice, thought Toby.

Burbage jumped at the offer. "Oberon it is," he shouted. "And Tobias, you shall have your wish – it shall be as fantastical as you please, show Master Jones we know a thing or two!"

Nick stayed on to watch that day's performance of *Hamlet*. Moved as ever, he dried his eyes and went backstage to find fault with Laertes' footwork. He caught Will Shakespeare's eye as the playwright took off his Ghost's armour and arranged to meet him at the Mermaid. The boatman who took him across to Salt Wharf steps recognised him, and said, "Back for the fireworks? Trouble brewing and no mistake, Nick. M'lord, I should say – you've gone up in the world."

"Not really," said Nick, ignoring the fireworks. "Same leopard, same spots. Keep the change."

"I knew it," said the boatman, watching him bounding up the steps. He spat on the silver coin and stowed it away. "Trouble. Ah well, good luck to him."

The Mermaid was crowded as usual and as usual Ben Jonson was filibustering centre stage. In spite of the huge chip on the man's shoulder, Nick could not dislike him. He shared with the man a healthy fear of Topcliffe and the Tower, and appreciated his brand of humour. He could see the playwright irritated Will Shakespeare. Under the pleasant easy-going facade Will presented to the world, lay an ambitious man careful with his money, hoping for the title of Gentleman, who never looked for trouble – save that which he might bring upon himself, fronting for the work of another, unknown gentleman. Fortunately, the likely candidates – Bacon, Oxford, Southampton – were out of his social sphere, or Nick felt sure he would be asking awkward questions. Kit Marlowe, of course, was safe, being dead.

"Ben still on his 'purity of language' rant, I see," he observed to Shakespeare when he arrived. "Get on well with him, do you?"

"Hates me one minute, embraces me the next," said Will, sitting down. "No pleasing him. What have you brought me?"

"Don't be greedy, Will. The Dane is still pulling them in, and will do so 'til the crack of doom. The comedy will do well – plenty of time."

The poet's face fell. "There's more competition these days, you don't realise. Professional hacks, those wretched children—"

"There will be more at the right time, stuff to get our teeth into."

"*Our* teeth? You're coming back into the company?"

"Playing in the *Dream*, I believe. Tobias is contriving—"

"Contrivances! Engines! Inigo Jones and his moving scenery – gods descending on chariots—"

"Come, Will, I hear you contributed to his masques yourself."

Shakespeare flushed. "I have to earn a living. We do not all have the Midas touch, like you."

"You think so? Could it not be that 'there is a tide in the affairs of men—'"

"'That taken at the flood leads on to fortune.' Yes, yes, yes, I know. And who speaks the line? The thing is, you have the luck of the devil Nick, and you seem to know all the right people."

"Is that how you choose your friends? Let us not fall out, Will. Toby will whistle you up a storm for *Twelfth Night*."

"What need of contrivance? My words are enough—"

Nick raised an eyebrow and Shakespeare's eyes fell.

"I must think of them as mine, or I am lost," he muttered.

"They are enacted, that is what matters. The play's the thing, Will, leave your conscience out of it."

"And there will be more? Ben Jonson—"

"Let Master Jonson rail as he will, return to classic forms if he must. What we have is meat and drink to the soul. Power to his pen, he cannot harm us."

"He has a following."

"So do you, Master Shakespeare of the honey tongue. The work stands repetition, not like these twopenny hacks…"

"The crowd bays for novelty."

"And they like to see old favourites. I wager fat Falstaff still brings them in." "'Twas a pity he was killed off, he could have appeared again."

"Write it yourself, Will." Nick drained his cup. "I like the two new youngsters," he said. "Especially the Gertrude."

"Nathaniel and Dick? Yes, if we can keep them. Are there parts for them in the next one?"

157

"How should I know? I'm only the messenger."

Shakespeare looked at him out of the corner of his eye. "Are you sure you do not write them yourself? You have a turn of phrase sometimes—"

Startled, Nick laughed. "I am an actor, Will. It rubs off, the words sing in the blood."

"I think you are a better actor than you know."

The noise had grown intolerable and Nick rose to go. "You can judge of my Oberon, if I have not lost the touch. By the way, your Ghost is your best thing yet." He pulled on his cap with a flourish, and left.

Chapter Twenty

February 7th 1601
'...the sticking place'

Before the first crowing of the cock, Nicholas rose and dressed in the suit of plain black worsted Hob had laid out for him. Swinging on a hooded cloak, he opened the door with his boots in his hand and almost fell over Hob rolled in a blanket on the floor. The little man scrambled up.

"You weren't going out without me, my lord?"

"Sorry to disappoint you, Hob. This little outing is not for you."

"Who's going to mind your back and hold your horse? If 'tis a woman, I'll bide and no word said, but otherwise I'll follow you, say what you will."

Nick looked at the obstinate nutcracker face and shrugged. The man was right, of course. He would need a trusted ally. *I've delayed too long over this*, he thought. He had an uneasy feeling something cataclysmic was about to happen. *If Essex has kept the King's letters – and why would he not? – there will be the devil to pay and no pitch hot. James can kiss goodbye to the English throne.*

"Come then and stay quiet."

Hob had Oberon and his own pony saddled and ready and in the predawn murk they made their way in silence through the fields, past the shipyards and over the bridge. The city of London never slept, dark shapes moved and muttered as they passed, a solitary watchman called the hour: "Four of the clock and all's well!" They trotted quietly along Thames Street, past the mansion where Nick had been married and up St Andrew's Hill into Blackfriars. Here they skirted the City wall and crossed over Bridewell Bridge and the river Fleet into Fleet Street and on into the Strand. Essex House sat back from the bend in the river, with its gardens sweeping down to the bank, almost opposite the Globe on the other side of the Thames. Nick paused here a moment reasoning it out. The kitchens would be at the back and would soon be stirring. He knew there was a tunnel on the west side of the building between two substantial houses, leading to the main entrance and a climbable wall. On the east side there was Strand Lane and a grassy mound. *Essex would have his private quarters away from the principal rooms*, he thought. *Try the lane.*

He left Hob with the horses and orders to get away fast if he heard trouble, shinned a low wall and scrambled over the long mound. The mortar in the wall at the bottom was crumbling and it was an easy climb to drop into the garden behind. Signs of neglect were everywhere, the grass unscythed and the formal flowerbeds overgrown. Since his fall from grace Essex no longer had thought or money for outward show. Nick avoided the weedy gravel and crept towards the house with its twin towers. There seemed to be no guard set and a broken window gave easy access. He climbed down into a small chamber empty of furniture, lifted the latch and stood listening. No sound. Four large rooms opened off the passage, with their tall leaded windows and dusty wainscotting, the last with an overturned chair and last night's ashes cold in the grate. A small door was cut in the panelling and Nick opened it. This seemed a likely place. It was a narrow room stolen from the one next to it, light coming from a corner window. Under the window stood a desk littered with papers, a tray of half-eaten food pushed to one side. A cold brazier stood beside it. The smell of defeat hung in the air and Nick was seized with revulsion for this task he had been set. Not like this. He would wait and see the man face to face.

Nevertheless, some of Robert Cecil's guile had rubbed off on him. The papers were there. He had Devereux' letter to Mowbray tucked inside his doublet, further proof of the man's duplicity. He walked across and began to sift through them. The top ones seemed to be notes made by Devereux to speak in his defence. There was a crumpled-up draft of a letter to the Queen and another intended for Mountjoy asking for his aid. Nick found what he had come for thrust into a drawer – the letters from James. They were all there save one – the vital compromising promise, vague but dynamite. He sat down to wait, hoping the faithful Hob would do the same.

It was growing light by now and before long he heard footsteps in the room beyond. He stood as Robert Devereux entered the room speaking to someone over his shoulder. Devereux closed the door, turned his head and stopped dead at sight of Nicholas. Nick was shocked by the change in the man. Gone was the careless elegance, his recent illness had told on him, his eyes were dark-ringed and dull from sleepless nights. He stood for an instant, then advanced with arms outstretched, the famous charm well in evidence.

"My lord Rokesby! Come to join with me at last – or was it to rejoice at my trial?"

Nick held up the sheaf of letters. "No, my lord. To help you, yes, but not to join with you."

Anger flared in the other man's face, his arms dropped to his sides. "You dare come here – how came you in? I can have you killed—"

"I come to offer sensible advice, my lord. You stand in mortal danger. These letters are enough to damn you for treason." He could see that Devereux was beyond reasoning, but he persevered. "The King asked me to come," he said. "He fears he may have been indiscreet. I am to tell you he has no intention of following your plan to join forces with Mountjoy and attack England. I can tell you, too, that Mountjoy is making a success of his task in Ireland and is too much concerned these days with his own career to risk it for loyalty and a forlorn hope. It is not too late to make your peace with her Majesty."

"She has cast me off as she does anyone who threatens her throne. She murdered Mary and she will murder me—"

"Not by her will in either case. But if by chance she should see these—"

"You threaten me Rokesby? What do you want – money? Have you not amassed enough yet?"

Ignoring the insult, Nick said calmly, "I suggest you rid yourself of these and any other thing you may have from James." He saw Devereux' hand go to the black silk bag at his throat. "Your go-between was foolish enough to return here to Court. He is arrested and under the question. Without proofs you may still be safe." He held out the letters.

"And what do you hope to gain, Rokesby? Creeping round the throne, loaded with Scottish honours—"

"I want nothing. I shall not return to Scotland and a life such as yours does not appeal. Given a chance, James will rule well—"

"He is weak and ill-advised. He can barely run his own country, let alone two—"

"And you think you can do better? You can't even run a campaign."

The silence stretched out, Nick's words echoing in the room. Essex looked stricken, he seemed to have shrunk inside his clothes, the red flare of anger burned out, leaving his cheeks grey. Presently he drew close and held out his hand for the letters.

"Together we might have done it, you and I," he said. "You should have come to me."

"As you said to Mowbray? Oh yes, Devereux, if I thought you had set him on, you would be drowning in your blood at my feet."

Essex flinched and made a snatch for the letters. Nick held them out of his reach. He had begun to feel pity for this man, flown like Icarus too near the sun, defeated by his own wild fantasies and vaulting ambition and his inability to understand his Queen. Elizabeth would always put her England before all else.

"Shall we burn them?" he said.

"Give them to me, I will do it."

Nick hesitated, then handed them over. Devereux put the letters in the brazier, found his tinderbox and set fire to them.

"All of them," said Nick. Devereux snatched the black bag from round his neck and tossed it after the letters curling and blackening in the flames.

"A monarch's promises are as worthless as dog turds," he said. "I would have kept my word to you."

Without a word, Nick pulled the letter to Mowbray out of his doublet and showed it to him before throwing it after the others onto the fire. Essex flushed and seemed about to speak. Nick shook his head.

163

"No more to say. You sent me a ring once. I return it, having had no use for it." He set it carefully on the desk, where it winked spitefully in the growing light. "The people still love you," he said. "The longer the Queen delays and shows her anger to you, the more they grow restive. Make your peace with her, she has troubles enough."

"Take your advice and your presumption and go, my lord Rokesby," snarled Devereux. "Before I have you thrown out." Nick shrugged, pushed open the casement and flung a leg over the sill. He looked back into the room. Essex was at the desk, rummaging among the papers.

Nicholas left him to it.

As he clambered out of the window, he almost bumped into the guard belatedly patrolling outside, but from Nick's dress and demeanour, the man could hardly distinguish him from the other men pouring into the courtyard. Things were on the move. He found Hob on the verge of defying orders and coming after him.

Nicholas thought for a moment. "Stay here, Hob, and keep watch. I am going to Whitehall; I don't like the look of things."

He mounted up and rode back the way he had come, through a gathering crowd of noisy townsfolk. He was worried by what he had seen. He had done what he came to do, but it seemed to him that Essex was on the brink of doing something fatally foolish. He had missed two opportunities already, with his customary lack of foresight and judgement, and his followers might yet goad him into an outright attack on the throne. As he trotted up Fleet Street, he met an official-looking deputation making their stately way towards Essex House: the Lord Keeper of the Seal and his page, the Lord Chief Justice Popham, Worcester and Sir William Knollys, followed by their servants. Nicholas drew aside to give room, and Knollys reined up.

"Are you come from my lord Essex, Nicholas?"

"If you are bound to see him, I should warn you there is a gathering of his friends—"

At this point, a rabble of citizens rounded the corner and pulled up at sight of the group of horsemen. "I am for Whitehall," said Nick. "My lord, we should lose no time."

"We come from the Queen to see Essex, to enquire into the cause of this gathering and see justice done. The matter is in hand."

"I trust you are right." Nick reined aside and Knollys trotted on to catch up with the others. Nick eased his sword in its scabbard and turned Oberon's head towards the men crowding the street. He was recognised by some of them and they parted to let him through, one or two doffing their caps and calling his name. He made for that part of Whitehall where his kinsman had his office, and met his uncle coming out, buckling on his sword and calling for his horse.

"Hurry, man, there's trouble brewing – her Majesty has sent a deputation–"

"I met them. There are men gathering at Essex House."

"Then we must make haste."

The Admiral scrambled into the saddle and led the way back towards the City. They were halted by a barricade of coaches set up across the broad road to Charing Cross, and the Admiral angled off to the right towards Westminster. Nicholas, about to follow, heard Hob shouting his name above the clamour.

"They are making for the City, sir – Ludgate! They expect to raise a thousand men—"

"Go, Nicholas!" shouted the Admiral, wheeling his horse. "I am for the Queen—"

"Wait, sir! Hob, what of the deputation? I passed them—"

"Imprisoned, my lord. I saw them taken in and my lord Essex come out with his friends – there's a mob, sir, all cheering. He's headed for the City."

Nick turned Oberon and spurred towards Essex House, Hob close on his heels, leaving the Admiral to turn back to Whitehall with the news. As they passed under the city walls Nicholas saw bands of men in the crimson livery of the Lord Mayor, and the man himself, Sir William Ryder, middle-aged and fit-looking, directing them. Around Ludgate, which seemed the centre of commotion, things were in hand. Cumberland was there with Richard Bancroft, Bishop of London, gathering men, mostly armoured servants wearing the Bishop's own badge. Cumberland and Bancroft were in consultation with a grizzled soldierly man and when Nick approached they turned to him. Nicholas recognised the older man; he had met him at his uncle's dining table, an experienced commander called Leveson.

"Glad to see you come, my lord. We need some order here."

Nick spotted a likely looking pair of veterans and set them to work to organise the company. The streets were strangely quiet, the usual crowd of inquisitive city folk conspicuous by their absence. Under the arch were the posts and chains of the Gate that closed the City within the city at nightfall. They stretched them across and made a barricade behind of piled shot and wagons. In front of this, Nick placed pikemen and behind them the few that had firing-pieces. They settled in place and waited. And waited. In front of them the top-heavy houses of London town leaned together and waited silently with them: behind and along the river stood the great buildings of Westminster and Whitehall inside the City walls, beginning to buzz with activity.

It was getting on for noon by now, and Nick began to think Essex had chosen a different way. He sent Hob back to Essex House to see how the land lay. He was back in no time.

"My lord, they had no luck with raising the Sherrif's men and they are back. His lordship is at his dinner."

"At his dinner!" This was so much the pattern of Devereux' method of running a campaign that Nick despaired of him. He was in no doubt which side he himself was on, but the sheer inefficiency pained him.

The men were growing restive and, conferring with Leveson, he sent to the nearest tavern for bread and a cask of ale. "If his lordship has leisure to eat and drink, so have we." This raised a cheer and the food was passed round to the men as they kept their posts. Nick drained his tankard and found Hob at his elbow again.

"My lord, he's having a go himself at the Sherif – but it's my belief he's flogging a dead horse there. He won't find any to follow him in Gracechurch Street."

Nick turned aside to confer with those in command and came back to speak to Hob.

"They can't make up their minds. Don't know who to trust, it seems. Take Oberon and see if you can find my uncle, we may need reinforcements."

Still nothing happened and Hob came back with the news that any available man was being mustered against a possible attack on the Palace. No more could be done and Nick concentrated on keeping up morale, the long wait was beginning to tell.

At about two o'clock in the afternoon, all of a piece with Essex' dilatory style, they heard the clatter of hooves down from St Paul's Churchyard.

Essex was at the head of a band of followers, some two hundred of them, Blount and Southampton among them. They halted in surprise four pikes' length away and after a moment Essex cried, "Who commands here?"

"My lord of Cumberland."

Essex spotted Leveson, a man he knew well, and sent a messenger asking to be allowed to pass. He was refused. Three times he sent, while the pikemen stood steady in their ranks, their weapons levelled. Losing patience, some of Devereux' company ran out and fired their pistols. Essex drew his sword and shouted for Blount to set on. The man hesitated a moment then drove forward bravely with a section of his men. Nick surged forward with the pikemen, their points aimed high, and in the short sharp skirmish, Blount fell with a scream, gored in the face. This seemed to be enough for Essex, he immediately called off his men and retreated, clattering off towards the river, leaving Blount behind on the cobbles, groaning. Nick flung up his hand to stop the men anxious to follow.

"Enough! See to your wounded." Essex' page lay dead, shot through the heart, and two townsfolk, mortally wounded. Of Nick's party, the veteran Waite had been killed in his engagement with Blount, who was lying with his hands clasped to his face, blood running between his fingers, abandoned by his commander. Horses were plunging and running free, their unhorsed riders either lying still on the bloody ground or sitting dazed where they had fallen. One poor animal was standing with his entrails trailing to the cobblestones, and Nick seized a pistol from the man standing beside him, gazing open-mouthed at the troop disappearing towards Essex House. Hob was before him with a merciful knife.

Nicholas turned away, raising a hand in thanks. This whole affair nauseated him. He had never been attracted to the glamorous Earl of Essex and this disgraceful exhibition sickened him.

Call yourself a knight! he thought. *A leader of men – tuh! Beheading is too good for you…* The short-lived rebellion had been doomed from the start, mistimed and mismanaged. Devereux could not hope to hold Essex House. Nick had no desire to be in at the kill. He had not the stomach to see more lives pointlessly wasted on this man's stubborn vainglory. His thoughts with the Queen, he turned his frustration to clearing up the mess.

He met with his uncle at supper and heard the rest of the story. The old man looked tired and sick at heart.

"There was a deal of sword-waving on the roof, and talk," said the Admiral. "Two men killed getting into the courtyard. Amazing how soon it was over once the cannon were in place. A lot of argy-bargy – face-saving, pah! A good clean fight is one thing, but this! A disgrace."

"What will happen now?"

"All the expense of a trial. I only hope they hurry it up – the mood of the people is uncertain. We have to get it all in the open. I shall have to be there," he added gloomily. "You too, perhaps, as one of his peers."

Nick shook his head, thinking, *I know too much.*

"I have been too long away, Uncle. I am in no position to sit in judgement. Lord Cecil will excuse me." *He'd better*, he thought.

The wheels turned quickly for once. In a week the examinations began; in a fortnight Essex and Southampton were brought to trial. Nicholas was excused from taking his place among the peers by a timely attack of the flux. He spent the time with the players.

Chapter Twenty-One

A black comedy

A curled and scented equerry came to Fletcher's Piece to request a play for the Shrovetide festivities. This was unusual, Burbage or Shakespeare were always sent for by the Master of the Revels.

Sir Henry Frobisher, Handsome Harry to his friends, sat in the newly panelled hall with one elegant leg crossed over the other, drawing a perfumed handkerchief between his fingers. *Perfum'd like a milliner*, thought Nick. *About as much use as a rose on a battlefield.*

Frobisher was saying, "Her Majesty wishes the customary play for Shrove Tuesday. In the circumstances she feels it is too delicate a matter to entrust to a mere player – the choice must be a careful one, you understand, Rokesby."

"Why did she not send for me?"

"She will not grant you an interview at this time. You have been something of a favourite, my dear fellow, have you not? She no longer wishes you singled out."

"Her favourites do have a nasty habit of coming to a sticky end," muttered Toby where he sat on the window seat whittling at something. Frobisher flicked at his knee with his handkerchief, releasing a cloud of scent, and looked down his nose.

"I must say, Rokesby," he complained, "it is unheard of. Her Majesty grants a request of yours, I gather, and desires you to play a part. It is not seemly – a peer of the realm performing like a mountebank! I've no wish to insult you, Nicholas, but I pray you, observe a little dignity."

"At all times, of course."

"No clowning or jigging."

"She wants a comedy?"

"All is to be as usual. You may as well stay the night; you will have to be up betimes. There is no possibility she can change her mind. The warrant will be signed."

Toby looked up. Nicholas appeared unmoved. He knew already from his uncle that his presence was ordered among his peers for the execution. He would have to have the plague at least to get him out of this one. Elizabeth was making a point.

Frobisher took his leave and Toby opened a window.

"Do you mean to tell me she will watch a play one day and see Essex executed the next?"

"Ruling a kingdom is hard. She must send the right message to her people. Is the whole court to go in mourning for a proven traitor?"

"Those of her people who still love Essex will not revere her for this."

Nick shrugged. "It's a harsh world. They'll get over it. They'll soon find another favourite to cheer."

"Just make sure it's not you."

In this unsettled time, no play had been put forward for the traditional festivities. Burbage almost echoed Toby's words.

"All as usual! With Essex and Southampton in the Tower and Blount and Danvers to be executed? My God, it's almost blasphemous! A comedy? Fiddling while Rome burns is what it is. What play, for pity's sake? And you are commanded to play in it? My God!"

"I thought perhaps *As You Like It*. The title is apt at least and it is rehearsed. I would play Jacques and Charles the wrestler, if Thomas would not mind. Nothing there to touch a nerve. I could throw away the last couplet of the 'seven ages' speech or we could cover it with a laugh. Robert Armin could give us his Touchstone, Will for old Adam and a chance for those two youngsters to shine."

"That should bind them to us – a court appearance. Young Orlando can play his namesake, I'm getting too old for juvenile leads. I'll play the Duke." No need to ask which one. "Trees?"

"Ask Tobias."

"Settled then. We'd better get on with it."

February 24th 1601 Shrove Tuesday. Whitehall.

If a shadow hung over the festivities it was not acknowledged. That same day the order for Essex' execution had gone forth and the Queen had countermanded it. The players were ready and waiting and after the feast the play began. The performance was remarkable for the sparkling rapport between Rosalind and Orlando, and for the Queen calling out "Rise up, sir, rise up, for shame!" when Nicholas as Charles took a spectacular fall at the end of a well-choreographed bout of wrestling. The melancholy Jacques chimed well with his mood of the moment, and he turned in a sharp and witty performance in spite of some early heckling by some members of the Court.

After the play, Elizabeth retired, and word went round that no special plea had come from Essex, and Darcy had been sent with the warrant to the Tower. Nick had no stomach for the rather forced merrymaking, and followed her Majesty's example by retiring early, to wait out the slow hours before dawn.

Four o'clock found the chosen peers dressed and ready in the courtyard of the Tower, with its steps and straw, scaffold and block. A bench had been set for the more senior among them – Cumberland, Morley, Lord Thomas Howard – and Nicholas stood behind with the rest, wearing, like them, the full court dress of his Orders. Ralegh joined them for a while, changed his mind and decided to watch from the Armoury. He could be seen watching from a window.

"Five of the clock and all's well…" floated in from the quiet streets.

The cold struck up through Nick's boots from the stones; his mind felt frozen. This was another day of reckoning. He had sailed uncomfortably close himself to this same fate and he found he was trembling. The Queen had been merciful and her favourite did not face the horrors of the gallows and the hook, the traitor's punishment. It would be a clean stroke, if they didn't botch it.

The two executioners stood masked and ready – two in case one failed in his purpose. A whisper passed among the assembled peers. The procession was coming.

Devereux had chosen to wear black, a gown of wrought velvet and a suit of satin. He mounted the steps and turned to speak. Nicholas had heard that Essex had turned to his religion for support and he listened as patiently as he could to the long prayerful speech. He had to admire the fortitude of a man who could speak so long and lucidly on the scaffold. He seemed in no hurry to get it over. Essex removed his gown and ruff, handed

173

them to one of the priests at his side and knelt. Even kneeling he spoke on. He rose once more to take off his handsome doublet and in a scarlet waistcoat that was somehow shocking, knelt again to embrace the block.

"Six of the clock and all's well…"

Essex was still speaking when the axe fell and his head bounced into the straw. Blood sprayed and Nicholas thought of Mowbray.

Slowly, in twos and threes, the witnesses walked away through Tower Gate, and passed through the silent crowds. Robert Devereux, the people's darling, was dead. The rebellion was over.

But it was not over, not entirely. Feeling still ran high on both sides. Cecil's reputation was damaged and Bacon's part in the prosecution criticised. The Queen kept to her chamber and men hung about in groups in the passages, speculating.

Nicholas began to feel he had walked into a cobweb, damp sticky filaments covering eyes, nose, mouth, a thousand invisible spiders weaving their webs around him. He wrote every day to Rosalyne in the form of his journal and a regular packet went off to Scotland by Rokesby courier. His declarations of love rang false in his own ears, how must they sound to her? Would she think him faithless? God only knew there were temptations enough. It took all his will-power not to say, with no grounds at all, "sauce for the goose…" Damn Marlowe and his play and his poisonous words. Her letters to him were few and factual, his only real news came from William – *Mother is well and takes part in the doings at Court here but she still seems sad…* This was no life. And what were these *'doings at Court'*?

He stepped up the volume of work until even Toby began to complain.

"Get yourself a woman, Nick, for God's sake!"

"Who?"

"Bess Hamilton of the Queen's ladies has had her eye on you since the play, I'm told."

"The Queen keeps close guard on her ladies-in-waiting."

"Bess would find a way."

"She has breath like a lion."

"Eliza in the wardrobe then."

"Her front teeth lie across."

Toby sighed. "Very well, go to Scotland."

"If her Majesty does not send soon, I will." He put down the papers in his hand and dropped into a chair. "I am weighed down with all this, Tobias. You were right, wealth brings power and power brings trouble. I am seen as a threat to those who covet it and Rose is brought into danger. Something must be done. Will you come with me to Rokesby? These lands and estates hang on me like those chains in the Tower. It is not to be borne. Will you come? I would have your advice, it concerns you."

"Surely you don't mean to strip yourself of all you have worked for?"

"A little re-arrangement is all."

Chapter Twenty-Two

Under the leadership of Sergeant Ponsonby and the self-styled Captain O'Dowd, Rokesby resembled nothing so much as an army camp. The burned-out shell of the house had given place to a plain workmanlike structure of herring-boned bricks and mortar, with sturdy beams and diamond-paned windows. The big barn had been turned into a refectory and the fields surrounding it were now training grounds and exercise yards.

When Nick and Toby arrived, Ponsonby and O'Dowd were out in the fields, drilling a smart body of men, and Ponsonby's wife – she of the shrewish tongue – welcomed them with her still-growing family at her side. Prosperity suited her. She showed them with some pride into a pleasant parlour, brought food and drink and dispatched her eldest to fetch his father.

It was a noisy and satisfying reunion. After six years, Nick was delighted with the success of the Rokesby courier service. The two veterans were flourishing and the family obviously content, the men in good heart. He thought the first part of the scheme beginning to take shape in his mind would work. He allowed two days to be shown and to admire the work being done, and on the third day, rode with Tobias over to Rookham.

There was little left of the Gothic pile at Lower Rookham. The stone had been used to repair the church and make the foundations for the mansion Inigo Jones had raised on the south-facing hill above it. The Palladian facade of this new house glowed in the afternoon sunshine as they rode towards it. Toby's jaw dropped. He had not, in the end, taken up Nick's offer of the estate. He had instead installed a reliable manager and contented himself with curbing the wilder extravagances of the young Welshman. The result was a little gem of Italian architecture nestling back in its setting of English countryside, the folds of the Warwickshire hills sheltering it from the English weather.

They reined in and sat staring at it. Presently Toby said, "It's certainly a statement."

Nick laughed. "Inigo Jones was here. Yes. Well, Toby, what shall we do with it? I can hardly hand it back to the Queen."

"Perhaps the Lady Rosalyne would like to live in it?"

Nick shook his head. "Let's look inside."

The inside matched the outside. Empty of furnishings, the marble floors echoed with the sound of their booted feet and as they trod up the sweeping double staircase, Nick's insides quaked with laughter. Leaning on the balustrade of the landing, he was reminded of his first visit to Angelica's house in the Veneto, a young man on the verge of discovery. There were the niches, the columns and painted panels, the dome with its tiny cupola letting in the light – only four years, but it all seemed a long time ago. No, he would not want to live here, but his son might.

"I'm glad we came," he said to Toby. "I needed to see for myself before I made up my mind."

A peremptory summons to Court awaited Nicholas back at Fletcher's Piece. He sighed and mounted the stairs to change out of his muddied leathers. He had no great expectation that Elizabeth would keep her word to send for Rosalyne. Unless her

177

promises were ratified in paper and ink, she had a convenient habit of forgetting them. He intended to remind her and dressed accordingly. He had ignored the whimperings of Carey's fashion-conscious tailor and chosen instead to have his new doublets cut to follow the natural line of his body. He disliked the droopy padded breeches affected by most of the Court-flies and kept to the breech-hose and thigh boots he was comfortable in. He was not above adornment, however: the black velvet was embroidered with love knots of gold ribbon and slashed with apricot satin. Tasselled gloves and a cloak lined with sable and he was ready. He buckled on his sword, clapped his hat on his head and went down to find Nero also dressed to kill with gold-knotted mane and saddlecloth, his plaited tail brushing his hocks. Hob stood at his head, equally spruced up, the reins of his sturdy little pony in his hand, and clearly intending to come too. As usual.

"You consider yourself indispensible, I see," said Nick. "Perhaps you are right. Who needs a handsome equerry when I have you?"

Hob doffed his cap with a flourish, replaced it and cupped his hands for a leg-up. Nick ignored him and vaulted into the saddle to lead off at a smart trot.

In the passage outside the Audience Chamber, he passed de Maisse, the French Ambassador, coming out. The man looked stunned.

He stared at Nick for a moment before he recognised him, clapped his hands and said, "*Merde*! What a woman! Ah, pardon me. I meant to say, of course, her Majesty is graceful in all she does." He smiled, bowed and tittuped away on his high red heels. Nicholas was shown in and saw what de Maisse had meant. The Queen was déshabillé, still in a very grand dressing gown of silver gauze. Its sleeves were slashed with scarlet taffeta and pendant with many other little sleeves that she was twisting in her hands. Under a matching headdress, her red wig had two huge ringlets either side and she wore pearls and rubies at her throat, merely drawing attention to the fact that her robe was open all down the front, exposing most of her bosom.

Raddled and magnificent, and forced to be civil to the ambassador, she had now worked herself into a fine tantrum. Bess Hamilton, the new assistant to the Mistress of the Robes had been found to be pregnant and straightway banished from Court, the man responsible was in the Tower. The Queen was jealous of the good name and behaviour of her ladies-in-waiting; her courtiers had been guilty on more than one occasion.

Including the unfortunate Essex, thought Nick, thanking his stars he had not fallen in with Toby's suggestion.

"You have your wish, Rokesby. I need someone to take that silly chit's place. I have sent for your wife and I look to you for her behaviour."

"When, your Majesty?"

"As soon as may be. You seem to have kept a rein on yourself thus far – another few weeks won't kill you. Leave us."

As he bowed himself out, Nick could have sworn he heard her mutter, "Men! Brains in their britches!"

He set about opening up the manor house at Richmond, hiring servants and a major domo and a small army of gardeners. He wrote a passionate letter and tore it up, sending instead a simple affirmation. Every nerve-end felt exposed – he would not even express the hope her health was fully restored lest it be misinterpreted. Marlowe's words still worked on him, the twin evils of lust and jealousy had to be kept at bay.

How will she be? he wondered. In the weeks after their loss, she had been remote, saying little. He had sat with her hand cold and unresponsive in his, unable to reach in and share their grief, try as he would. She refused to take comfort from him or offer any. "Time is a great healer," said the doctors and wiseacres – hah! What did they know? "Be patient." Of course he was patient, but he was afraid. It was not her body he yearned for, though God knew he desired it, it was the comradeship, the shared laughter and the talk. Surely not gone forever, with their child? He missed the delicious pleasure of sitting on their bed watching her dither between this gown and that, the female concentration on washing and powdering and crimping, the smell of the oils she used, her own particular smell. He missed watching her body disappear under layers of canvas and bone and velvet and lacing, knowing the flesh and delicate tracery of veins beneath it. He missed most of all coming to her to talk of their day, her wisdom in the exchange of ideas, her steadfast understanding, her ready wit, her gaiety. To him, she was the quintessence of woman, enticing, forbidding, wanton and frighteningly intelligent.

He fretted and paced, watching the weather and the hourglass, almost oblivious to the aftermath of the short-lived rebellion. As the time drew near, he haunted the docks, watching for the first sighting of the *Snipe*. She came at last, six weeks later, on a fine spring morning, her canvas spread, a dazzling white quilt against a blue and cloudless sky, heeling to the wind. Hob and Tobias heaved a sigh of relief. For the past weeks they had been living with a man who behaved as if his fine linen shirt were a coat of nettles, short-tempered and working like a demon. Now, perhaps…

Chapter Twenty-Three

Rosalyne brought with her William and Jack, escorted by d'Arblay and another Melville kinsman, Red Rob, together with a personal maid unknown to Nicholas. Nick could hardly wait for the gangplank to be lowered, he leapt the last few feet and raced up to take his wife in his arms. She stayed still in his embrace until he stood back, and looked past him at the coach standing waiting in its livery of black and gold, the Rokesby arms blazoned on its side.

"Do we go straight to Whitehall, my lord?"

"No, my love, the Court is moved to Richmond, we go home!"

Straight-backed, she moved to the gangplank, put her hand lightly on his proffered arm and walked ashore. She allowed him to hand her into the coach and sat back. "Your sons are eager to greet you, my lord."

Nicholas, looking like a man slapped in the face, turned and knelt with arms outstretched.

"Welcome home, Jack." Jack, no longer a demonstrative child, stood on his dignity and suffered the embrace. William waited his turn.

Chilled, he welcomed the others in turn, and beckoned up the horses waiting behind the coach. Hob brought up the two smart little Welsh cobs that Nicholas had provided for the boys (black, of course) and they sat with backs ruler-straight, flushed with pride.

Tom Percy stayed behind to see Shadow of the Wind and the other horses safely ashore. The party arranged itself, Rosalyne and her maid with their boxes in the coach, the other two men to ride behind. Last of all trotted the valiant Butcher, grown fat on the rats he had caught on the ship. Tobias stayed where he was, on the dock, this was not a scene he could intrude upon. He poked Hob sharply in the ribs; the little man's face was a picture of dismay.

Trelawney was standing on deck. He exchanged a look with Tobias and tilted his head at the tavern. *Yes*, thought Toby. *I'll find out from you later.*

Hob scrambled for his horse to catch up with the cavalcade making its way west to the bridge. "Women," he grumbled. "Nothing but trouble."

They set off along the dockside to the music of the shipbuilders, less now than in former times, towards the city. The coach rumbled over the bridge, its splendid coat-of-arms enough to gain space between the tightly packed stalls and tall houses, the people falling back respectfully. It came to an abrupt halt at the end of the bridge, causing a considerable bottleneck. The crowd closed up behind the riders, eager to see. Nicholas was well known and liked in those parts, a good actor and a wealthy man who was not above drinking with them in the taverns and spreading some of his largesse around.

Nick dismounted, handing the reins to Hob. He squeezed past the coach. The Rokesby coachman was a burly Sussex yeoman, picked for his size and his soft hands on the reins, as obstinate as they come. "Sussex won't be druv," was his favourite maxim. He was arguing with a captain of the Queen's Guard, who was pink with annoyance. Behind the officer was ranged an escort of some twenty men, their arms and breastplates blinding in the sun.

Elizabeth doing it in style, thought Nick, with a grimace.

"All right, John," he said. "Stand quiet." The horses were beginning to stamp and fret and an angry murmur came from the growing press of people. The captain recognised Nicholas and addressed him with relief and a flourish of his sword in salute.

"We are come to escort you to the palace, my lord. Orders from her Majesty."

"We are honoured, captain. Perhaps you will allow us off this bridge? On with you, John."

The coach moved on and Nicholas went back for Nero. He swung into the saddle and turned with a wave and a smile. A ragged cheer went up and the captain looked grim. The Queen would hear of this.

Nicholas closed up to lean into the coach. "It seems we shall not be going straight home after all, sweeting," he said. "We shall see. I pray you, keep patience."

She was looking straight ahead. "It seems to me, my lord, that I am still a pawn to be moved on their board, will I or no, an earnest of your behaviour. I pray *you*, my lord, you keep *your* patience. And your promises."

Nick drew back, deeply disturbed.

The Court had moved early to the palace at Richmond where the Queen liked to spend some of the summer months. The escort and their party trotted past the lane that led down to the river and Richmond House, and drew up some way further on at a pair of tall handsome gates, bearing the Queen's gilded coat–of–arms. The captain halted.

"Her Majesty will receive the Lady Rosalyne and her sons, my lord. You will be summoned anon."

"The boys stay with me."

The captain eyed the implacable line of the mouth and gave way gracefully. The gates were opened and Nick had just time to say to his coachman, "Stay at my lady's bidding. No trouble." John touched his cap, flicked the reins and Rosalyne was borne away. Nicholas watched in silence until the trees hid them from sight and the gates were closed. He turned Nero to lead the way back to the city.

Nicholas ordered Richmond House to be shut up again, its flowers and silver and crystal unseen, the delicate dishes and wine untasted. He returned with the boys and Hob and the dog Butcher to Fletcher's Piece, d'Arblay went with Red Rob Melville to Whitehall to keep his ears open and Tom Percy struck up an unlikely friendship with the Keeper of the Orchid House. Tobias held his peace.

Nicholas spent those days of waiting alternately writing letters and pacing the floor. Butcher, who obviously considered his duty as guardian done, firmly re-attached himself to his man. He lay in his corner, his paw over his nose and one eye open, his ridiculous ear inside out, and watched. He stirred only for food and to get in the way when Nick took a very quiet Jack and William out for the required weapon play and exercise for their cobs. At the end of the third day, his man took him on his knee.

"You are a good dog, Master Butcher, and I tell you this. If word does not come tomorrow, I shall go to the Queen if I have to break in."

Word did come, in the person of a glittering and self-important herald. Nick declined to go with him at once, finished William's lesson and went in to dress carefully and pack up his gifts. William provided a letter, Jack a drawing, Tom Percy a rare orchid, and armed with these and his own presents he rode out to Richmond once more.

As so often, Elizabeth received him alone. She cackled when she saw him.

"You come like a hopeful bridegroom, sirrah! Ah, you will find her in good fettle and well content. She is a great comfort to me, Rokesby, I think I shall never part with her. Never fear, you shall see her – in good time. Tell me, what news of the rich argosy you spoke of?"

"Still at sea, your Majesty."

"As are we all, sweet lord, as are we all." Her breath was laboured and stinking, her knuckles white on the arms of her chair, her rings sparked in the sunshine.

"You dazzle my eyes, handsome one, there in all your finery. Go, find your lady wife, have what good you can of her. While you may. What does that poet say – 'Youth's a stuff will not endure…' As you see. Leave us, you weary us."

He bowed and backed away. She raised a hand.

"One word more. You are no fool, Rokesby, as my poor Robin was a fool. Tread wary, my lord. You will not enjoy my protection for long. Look to your wife."

The echo of Marlowe rang in his ears, he was uneasy.

An usher was waiting to conduct him to Rosalyne's apartments, and he walked behind, Hob at his heels, his thoughts warring in his head. Elizabeth's last words seemed to hint of betrayal. Not Rosalyne, no, he would never believe it. Something had happened since he left Scotland. Surely. His heart was beating fast as he approached her door, and he waited while the servant went quietly away. The cobwebs were back, his hands and feet were ice-cold and heavy. He leaned on the wall, fighting this as he would an enemy, with force of will and practised thought. *You do not matter, think of her.* She was changed since – he could hardly bear to think of it – since then. That kind of fruitless suffering could change a woman, he had been told that. He knew pain, that long fearful agony in the Tower – how could you compare pain? A child lost. *To both of us.* He leaned his forehead on the cold stone. Was Rosalyne lost to him?

He was trembling, as afraid as if he were going into battle. *I am my own enemy here, not Rosalyne, not the Queen, not the traps and tricks of Cecil and his intrigues.* Marlowe's words swam into his mind, "stiffen the sinews, summon up the blood…" He straightened, bringing turbulent body and mind to order. *Rose is strong. She lived. My task is to protect her, bring her safe home. Even if she can no longer want me, she has need of me. Very well, to it.* He pulled down his doublet, squared his shoulders and tapped on the door. He waited and tapped again. Presently the maid came out to him to say her mistress was asleep.

Hauling on the rags of his temper, Nicholas said, "Then she shall be awaked." He pushed open the door to see his wife at the mirror brushing out her hair.

"My lord?"

"Rosalyne… Send your maid away."

"I prefer her to stay."

"And I do not." He held open the door and after a hesitant glance, the woman left. He closed the door and turning, caught his reflection behind Rosalyne in the watery glass, dressed in his finest doublet of well-cut black taffeta embroidered with rose, the orchid in his hand. She was wearing a loose furred robe like the one she had on at their first encounter, her hair silken on her shoulders and his breath caught.

"Come to claim your rights, husband?"

Nicholas stared at her. This was worse than he feared. Was she run mad? He had heard of such things. He gathered his wits.

"I come to see how you do, Rose. Is it not to your liking, this appointment to the Queen? I asked only that you be brought back to England – were you not aware—"

"That I was the guarantor of your behaviour? Of course. The appointment is an honour, it suits me well. And you, my lord, are now free to do as you please. In everything."

She had picked up the brush again and was idly brushing a ringlet round her finger. Now she rose and laid it down, pulling her robe about her.

"Of course, if you insist…"

She could not have chosen a better way to cool his ardour. It was a bucket of ice-water over his head.

"Insist! Rosalyne, what is this? Why do you speak so to me – have you not forgiven my arrogant folly yet? God knows you could not blame me more than I blame myself for falling into Mowbray's trap—"

She would not look at him, but stood straight and trembling by the bed. "You are engineering your own downfall, my lord. I heard things at court, wicked, fearful things. They hate and fear you; you are grown powerful and dangerous. They say the King owes you favours—"

"Do you suppose me ignorant of this knavish nonsense? Or that I am not taking steps for our safety?"

"Do what you may, my lord, they will take you down. I must look to myself and the child I have left to me. You say Jack is to go to your kinsman." This was said with such disdain that Nicholas lost control.

"My God, is this the woman who stood by me in the battle, who lay in the long grass and begged me to love her – there was no hanging back then! What ails you, woman, that you speak to me so?"

His anger cooled as quickly as he had spoken, seeing her so pale and fine-drawn, the marks of strain in her face.

"No, forgive me, Rose, I am too hasty. We both suffer, and you have borne the worse pain in this, that I do know. I ask nothing, demand nothing, you cannot think otherwise, only that we stand together in this."

"You do not know me, Nicholas. When I wed you, your star was in the ascendant. Now, I tell you plain, you are heading for the same fate as my lord Essex. Stand with you? Set up a second court at Richmond? That is what they say. Where a monarch fears he kills, even in your vainglory you should know that. Whatever you have done for James, he fears you. I fear you and I fear for myself. You did me no favour in sending for me. Take your pleasure where you will, and trouble me no more. One thing I ask. I wish William brought here to me."

Nicholas realised he had crushed the orchid in his fist, the sap was dripping over his knuckles, a sharp fetid smell filled the room. He opened his hand and it dropped to the floor. He got out his square of linen and carefully dried his fingers. He had himself in hand by now.

"You may leave my sons to me, mistress. As to the rest, be assured my plans are laid. For us both. It would seem you do not know me either. Make no mistake, Rose, you are my wife, my love and my heart's desire, my friend and dear companion, promised unto death. I do not propose to die to suit anyone's convenience, and if I must insist, be sure I shall. You are mine, Rose, as I am

yours – not the Queen's, nor the next man's, and so you shall see."
He reached out to take her hand and put it to his lips. "Trust me,
Rosalyne. I shall see no harm come to you or our sons. I failed
you in Strathyre, I shall not do so again. When all is safe, I shall
come to you again and you shall let me know your pleasure.
Remember this. You may kill me, but you cannot kill my love –
that you have always."

As the door closed quietly behind him, Rosalyne sank down on
the bed, put her face in her hands and burst into a storm of
weeping.

"That was not well done, my lady," came a voice from the
shadows. "You were meant to draw him in, not send him away
with a flea in his ear. You strayed a little from the script with your
warnings, but no harm done, the arrogant young fool took no
heed. Next time—"

"You think there will be a next time? I do know my Nicholas.
He may threaten but he will never force himself on me. He will
not come again unless I ask."

"Unless you ask. And you will ask, my lady. Lift your finger and
we shall learn what are these plans he speaks of."

About to follow Nicholas from his position outside the door, Hob
had heard the outburst of weeping and hesitated long enough to
hear the other man's voice. At first shocked and angry, he listened.

"I tell you again, my husband has no desire for power or taste
for politics, he does not stand in your way—"

"You are naive, my lady. No man with Rokesby's wealth and
position could resist wielding the power he has. He has the ear of
Cecil, don't forget. Remember too, your sons are still at large? That
was a gallant effort, my lady, and it failed. Think carefully. Let
him dangle a while then twitch the thread and reel him in."

"To put his head on the block?"

"You mistake us. He balked me once, I grant you, and I owe him no thanks for that, but things change. We would help him to what he wants. Carrot and stick, my dear, carrot and stick. With Essex gone our path is clear. We have a true claimant to the throne in Arabella Stuart, and if your gallant husband would but use his honey tongue to persuade the Queen to name her as successor—"

"My husband is not interested in your petty schemes, my Lord Seymour."

"But we are interested in his. If these plans he speaks of so readily run counter to ours—"

"What then, my Lord Seymour?" Rosalyne had been speaking clearly and with this she raised her voice. Hob had the distinct impression she was speaking to him. He had heard enough. He padded quietly down the corridor, took to his heels and ran to find his master.

Nicholas was not to be found. Hob reasoned that after that interview, Nicholas would be sore enough to seek the comfort and company of the players, and set off on a round of the taverns, just missing him every time. He persevered into the small hours and finally gave up on his second visit to the Mermaid. Nicholas had gone off with a group of players, a woman on his arm.

"Looks as if he's going to make a night of it," grumbled Hob. His news would have to wait. "I'm for my bed."

Chapter Twenty-Four

Nicholas had indeed made a night of it. Now, still half-drunk, he sat at the back of the gallery amid the wreck of his dreams. The stage, littered with thrown flowers and orange peel, lay empty and white under the moon, the voices of the actors whispered ghostly round the painted columns and the spaces of the pit. His throat was tight and aching, he longed for the relief of tears that would not come. The sweaty bout with the new wardrobe mistress encountered in the Mermaid had left him guilty and despairing. A waste of shame, indeed. The actor's trick of living in a parallel universe plagued him with echoed words. "What's Hecuba to him or he to Hecuba?" Hamlet had wept for Ophelia: playing Laertes, Nicholas himself had wept for her – why could he not weep for Rosalyne, gone from him as surely as if she lay beside his daughter at Strathyre.

Why? Why? Does she hate me so for bringing her to this? My doing, my enemy, my fault.

"I am punished too," he said into the silence. "If I could suffer your pain as well, I would." The gathering cloud hid the moon and the stage grew dark. He shivered. *Shame on you, Rokesby*, he thought. *Shame. You can't even keep your prick in your codpiece. You sit here snivelling – what sort of man are you – this is no way to win her.* He stood up, legs cramped from long sitting. *If she be hard as*

191

adamant, cold as the nether pits of Hell, there must be a way. And if not, there are other worlds out there, waiting. Kit is the lucky one, he thought. *His true love has never deserted him.*

By the time he had walked back to Fletcher's Piece he was sober and had made up his mind. No more waiting on others' pleasure, he would take arms against this sea of troubles and take action. "Always your forte, my dear," whispered Marlowe's voice in his ear.

You haven't seen the last of me, Kit, he thought. *I may join you yet.*

He woke to find Hob hovering over him with cold towels, hot water and his own particular cure for a hangover. He had fallen into bed without drawing the curtains and the fitful spring sunlight was like needles in the eyeballs. He groaned and struggled up, the whole horrible truth of the night before burst in on him. Hob was shaking his shoulder and badgering him.

"My lord, my lord, you must hear this!"

"Is the Queen dead?"

"No, my lord, worse nor that. Drink this and listen – it's a trap!"

The tale was soon told, better than Hob's cure-all for clearing Nick's head. He sat naked on the side of the bed, thinking.

"Who was this man?"

"I didn't see him, my lord. Sounded like gentry. She said his name loud and clear, sir – Seymour."

"William Seymour, by God!"

"You know him, my lord?"

"I do indeed. I thought that matter dealt with." His malaise forgotten, a feeling of pure joy was stealing over him. He began to re-assess the words spoken last night in the light of this new knowledge. Watching him, Hob fetched the coverlet and put it round his shoulders. Presently Nick got up and began to pace the room, wrapped in the fur, thinking aloud.

"Thank all the powers that be I spoke as I did. She knows I won't fail her. Yes, I spoke of plans. Let us feed them, burst them with false report. It can be done. About it. Hob, my horse."

"Not afore you break fast my lord. You aren't going anywhere on an empty stomach. I've hidden your boots."

Nick laughed and clapped him on the shoulder.

"Very well, a hearty breakfast then and quick about it. I thank you for this Hob, I lie in your debt."

"Constitution of a camel," grumbled Hob, hurrying off. "Hearty breakfast after last night? We'll see if he keeps it down."

Tobias came in just before noon to find a sunny-tempered Nicholas dealing with beefsteak, eggs and a dish of sallet with good appetite. *A favourable meeting with Rosalyne, then*, thought Tobias. *Good.* He dumped his satchel of papers on the table and sat down to fill his pipe.

"They've seen sense at Blackfriars at last," he said. "The company can play there next week and rehearse from tomorrow. Just as well from the look of the weather. You'll be giving us your Oberon after all. That should please her Majesty."

Nick had put a whole hard-boiled egg in his mouth. "Mm," he said.

"Is that all you can say? Yes, I see it is."

Nick took a long swallow of ale and sat back.

"Listen, Tobias. I need to winkle Rosalyne out of the palace and speak with her alone. Any ideas?"

"I thought you were with her last night. I heard you come in at cockcrow."

193

"There was a third party present. No, on second thoughts, never mind. You should stay free and clear of this. I have other plans for us."

That afternoon, Carey drew him aside, where he waited at Court for a glimpse of Rosalyne.

"The knives are out, Nicholas. They say—"

"Who are 'they'? And what do 'they' say?"

"'od's life, man, what ails you? Unable to come at your wife? No, no, no need for that, I meant no offence."

"Then give none."

"I come to give you fair warning. It is being said," he went on, eyeing Nick warily, "it is rumoured abroad that you are after the monopolies on grain and coal from Scotland. They say you have amassed a fortune and raise an army in Warwickshire."

Nick snorted. "I see. And I am about to mount a coup, am I? Shall I seize the throne for myself or keep it warm for James? Gossips and old women the lot of them."

"Hush, not so loud. No smoke without fire, my friend. Monopolies are hard to come by these days, and you have—"

"None. Bad for free trade. Tell your rumour-mongers to widen their horizons, there is money to be made but not by talking. I hear what you say, Robin, and I thank you. There is little enough I can do about it. If I could but come near Rose—"

"My Queen-cousin is grown capricious. She teases you. Or perhaps she has good reason. I have learned not to underestimate her."

"What reason could she have?" Nick thought he knew, but he was probing for information.

"She has a nose for danger, Nick. The hunt is up, she senses it, soon they will be baying openly for your blood. You come of good family, Nick, no doubt of that, and you have connections. But your rise has been swift, you are favoured. Like it or not, you have power and to make matters worse you are a fox in the hen-coop here at Court. Men watch their wives with you around. They say—"

Nick burst out laughing. "A pox on what they say! This goes too far, Robin."

"You mean you have not sampled the wares? With a voice to charm a bird from a tree or a snake from its basket? I find it hard to believe."

"When did you last win at cards, Robin? Is this one of your bets? Ah, a blush, I thought so. If you're short of money, try 'Change – there's a fortune to be made on the turn of the tide."

"Too deep for my pocket. You keep your nerve, Nick, I give you that."

"My upbringing, no doubt."

"And your downfall may be imminent, I warn you."

A Rokesby courier had brought a heavy and much-travelled packet. It was impossible to tell its point of origin; it was badly stained and had obviously been wrapped at some time in imperfectly cured goatskin. Nick opened it carefully, hardly daring to hope. It was what he had been waiting for. Not one, but two manuscripts and two letters.

Valetta. on Malta
Sweeting,
Why Malta, you will say? Blame the weather and our English
pirates. Shipwrecks and hurricanoes – we were left rudderless to

195

be pounced on by your pirate friend Piers of Plymouth. Like any lovesick fool I have kept about me those few letters you have vouchsafed me and with these and a little money I was able to buy my safety. I was set down here in Valetta – I confess a little out of spirits – and was cared for by these soldier knights. So well indeed that here I stay – as good a place as any and my muse serves me well. Here is the play we spoke of. Do not allow Master Shakespeare to change one word and play the Moor yourself. Commend me to your wife and to your sons whom I hold with your sweet body in lasting love. They have the best of you both. CM

The second letter was from the Grand Master of the Knights of Malta.

M. Malheur is come in good time. His health gives us some concern. Our climate of hot and dry is of benefit. He mends. O de W.

Alarmed, Nick turned to the plays to read the poet's mind. One was a deeply cynical look at politics and sexual betrayal, set against a background of the Trojan War, the other – Nick could not describe it, the organ-music of the text went to his head like strong drink. The characters leapt full-bodied from the page, its tragic end was implicit in its beginning. He found he was speaking aloud, these were words he would above all, like to speak to his Rosalyne.

"'Perdition catch my soul, but I do love thee. And when I love thee not, Chaos is come again…'"

The play had no hero in the conventional sense, but a central character of towering presence, who had been given unforgettable words to say. No conventional villain either: Iago, complex and compelling, worked behind the scene with crafty words that crept into the mind and did their work. Nick was reminded of a bullfight he had seen in Spain – the bewildered bull, maddened by darts, uncomprehending, charging at what he saw as his tormentor.

The play went on, the cankers grew, it was as if the Moor suspended belief and sought his own destruction, while Iago was a tinkering child rejoicing in the result of his wickedness.

Nick still had not forgiven Marlowe for planting that maggot in his own mind, but he missed him. He missed the mordant wit, the flights of fancy, the outbursts of light-hearted banter. He was worried about the man's health. He read the play again, punishing himself, trying to see it as pure invention. He knew it was not. The poet had done it again. He had taken a surgeon's knife and sliced without pity to the heart of a human failing. He exposed it on both sides, an insane raging jealousy – what had Kit said – the green-eyed monster, and on the other side a sour malicious envy.

No, thought Nick. *That is too simple. This will tease the mind more than the indecision of the Dane. The pace of it! We want to cry out – 'Behind you!' as we do at the demon in the pantomime, and there is no time. Play the Moor, Kit? I don't think so. I may have the voice, but I haven't the courage.*

"You wretch, you manipulated me as cleverly as Iago," he said aloud. "Don't think I don't know why you did it, Kit. I hope you were satisfied." There was so much in the play to digest – for a great soldier to topple so easily, there must be a deeper flaw. There was an uneasiness in his dealings with the Venetians, uneasiness on both sides. Did it have an effect? When treachery was so skilfully suggested, was there an echo? Nick realised he was trying to rationalise his own feelings. He could find no parallel there.

197

"You were playing cat and mouse with me, Kit. You bastard, you wanted to see if it worked. Well, you succeeded, but you cheated, you played upon a different pipe. What man blessed with a woman like Rosalyne does not marvel at it, feel himself unworthy? But I thank you. I am cured. You have shown me the machinery and I am free of it."

The agreement with Nick's kinsman still stood. It was time for Jack to begin his formal training in the Admiral's household. Well-grown for a ten year old, Jack had a curiously tough quality of mind and Nick had watched him straining at the apron strings. The Admiral would keep him safe and judge what he was most suited for. There was an opening on his flagship if he showed aptitude. The boy was wild with excitement and William watched quietly. He would miss his playmate but did not envy him. Nicholas took him aside.

"There is a place for you at Court, if you wish it, Will, but not yet. You must both be safeguarded and I would keep you by me."

"There are enemies at Court, father?"

"I fear so. It is like boxing with shadows. I must ask you never to go unattended. Do you understand?"

"Is mother safe?"

"All the while she attends on the Queen no harm can come to her."

"I miss her."

"So do I, Will, so do I."

Before he did anything else Nicholas called on Robert Cecil.

"The hydra has more heads than we accounted for," he said. "Seymour has not given up. Is the lady Arabella still confined?"

"She is grown very much a thorn in the flesh for Bess of Hardwick. I do not suppose for one moment the old woman would connive at any plot, but she would be glad to be rid of her. Is this serious?"

"He seeks to draw me in by threats. All I say is, he should be watched. I can take care of my own, the rest is for you. I bid you good day."

His plans to consolidate were simple. He intended to strip himself of assets that could be snatched back by fickle monarchs and liquidate the rest. He found a notary and arranged for Rokesby to pass to Jack, who would inherit the title, with Ponsonby and O'Dowd as life tenants. Rookham was made over to William and Strathyre he gave into the keeping of Young Colin and the clan Melville. He called a business meeting with Tobias and John Challoner.

"I propose," he said, "to sell you Cawdor, Toby, and dissolve the partnership. No, wait a moment, let me finish. It will be a paper transaction only, no money need change hands, we know each other well enough. This is a measure to protect the business from any contagion I might bring to it. Lands and monopolies granted can be taken away as fast – the Queen may regret her generosity as she has done with others. No blame for my actions should be laid on you."

"And what actions might these be?" asked Toby. "You're spoiling for trouble, I know it."

"None, yet. I like to—"

"—be prepared. I know."

When it came to dissolving the partnership, matters were a little more complicated. They decided at last on a compromise. Nicholas would be bought out for a nominal sum, dividends would continue to be paid into the Medici bank in Florence in gold, and investment made on his behalf in the solid business of Madame da Gama in Paris.

"From which I deduce," said Toby, "that you are planning to skip the country."

Nick shrugged. "Perhaps, I don't know. I just want to avoid tarring you with my brush."

"What does your lady say?"

"I haven't asked her."

Challoner, who had been very quiet, said, "It is not customary, Tobias, to consult with women in these matters."

"You don't know Rosalyne," said Nick, with a grin at Toby. "I have not asked her because I am scarce allowed to see her and that only in public. It's a state of affairs that cannot go on."

Chapter Twenty-Five

After a day hot enough to grill a lobster it was a lovely evening. From the terrace outside his room Marlowe could see both arms of the harbour, where new buildings were going up, fortifications against siege, built, with the new aqueduct, at the order of Olof de Wignacourt, the recently appointed Grand Master. Like the others behind in the town, they were beautiful symmetrical structures, built to keep out whatever foe happened to be greedy for Malta, and that other enemy, the summer heat. Under his awning, Marlowe lay limp and sweating. He had a ferocious headache. It was impossible to escape the constant noise and the air was full of bustling dust.

He lay on his pallet in the shade and looked out towards Africa. *What a fool I was last night*, he thought. *So much to do…*

A small fleet had come in, bearing the Spanish mercenary Alonso da Carreras with seven hundred prisoners and booty from along the coast of Africa and the Levant. A randy, riotous young man of nineteen he had a robust turn of phrase that had appealed to Marlowe in his current mood.

"Those Turkish women! I've brought back the Bey's mistress – the most beautiful woman I ever saw – he chased us for leagues.

201

He knows I've had her, if he'd caught me he'd have had me taken up the arse by six blacks and then impaled me."

"Ugh," Marlowe had said with a delicious shudder, and the two men had embarked on a round of ferocious drinking. A foolish debauchery. It had brought back the fever that had delivered him to Malta in the care of an alarmed Captain Piers. The pirate had dumped Nick Talbot's friend in the arms of the Knights Hospitaller, taken most of his money and sailed off.

Kit had written little since his illness, but now came the first stirrings. He saw his finished play as in a bubble, a world in microcosm, where a man struggled in thrall to a woman: empires and battles and honour won and lost for love. He saw a fleet of galleys with a tall man standing on the prow of the foremost, a soldier, an athlete, a lover. He saw a barge with silken perfumed sails and a black-haired, black-eyed woman with translucent skin, the veins showing blue. Trumpets came to him, ghostly across the water, battle music and a cry of despair, bringing words, great sonorous words, beating like a gong. *The barge she sat in burned on the water, The poop was beaten gold, purple the sails...* He saw a man in the fullness of his strength, *bestriding the world like a colossus*, and a woman with a dancing walk, a rose full-blown, laughing like a schoolboy. It was another tale of love and betrayal, a man destroyed by his own passion.

As he gazed, the outline of that hot sunlit globe wavered in the heat-shimmer on the water, and he shivered. Dark shadows were closing in, there were winds and icy rain, thunder crashed and boomed. It was that fever dream again when he feared he was going mad. Words had come to him, wild whirling words to match the storm raging outside and in. Not now, not in broad daylight... The nightmares crowded in, the loss of reason, the

202

seventh age of man. He saw his friend's face, the agony as he held his dead child in his arms. Which was worse, to have brought her to womanhood, loving and comely, and then lose her, or never to see that promise fulfilled? "Never, never, never, never…" The words died away on the wind.

He heaved himself up, held onto the wall a moment and turned in to the cool dimness of his chamber. His table was littered with paper and he shuffled the finished manuscript together, pushed it aside and reached for his pen. The paper they made here was smooth and buffed for their records and the words ran free.

Act One. Scene One. King Lear's Palace.

"Come soon, Niccolo. Come soon."

Chapter Twenty-Six

London. Autumn 1601

There was much speculation at Court about the sudden disappearance of James, Lord Seymour. It was said that a safe marriage had been arranged for the Lady Arabella Stuart. "Bess of Hardwicke can't wait to see the back of her," said d'Arblay. Cecil had moved fast.

Nicholas found himself a ship, a well-found three-masted frigate, with a good deep draught and a turn of speed, built of oak and bottomed with copper. A ship for a long voyage. A skipper came with her, an experienced man who had sailed with Ralegh. Nick had her brought from Portsmouth and anchored at Gravesend.

Tobias had grown accustomed to coming down to find Nick already at work, in his shirtsleeves, writing. The Embassy in Venice, his desk in Richmond, and now here. The only difference was the presence of his son William at his side. Toby usually broke his fast at the unoccupied end of the table, drank off his breakfast ale, collected any messages and left.

On this particular morning, Nicholas appeared to have slowed up. Toby raised an eyebrow and his friend grinned at him.

"Almost ready," he said. "Just a few loose ends, and they must wait until I sail. Just the play now."

"I'm glad to hear it," said Toby. "Have you told Rosalyne?"

"Chance would be a fine thing. No. After the play. Perhaps. All must be made safe."

"A *fait accompli*?"

"She will make her choice. Whatever she chooses, William will come with me."

"You know your wife and your own business best, friend. I had not took you for a gambler until now."

Nicholas gathered some letters together and stood up. "We shall see. The wolves are snapping at my heels, Toby."

"And you like to be prepared. I know." The two friends smiled and embraced and Toby took the letters.

William looked up. "I have a letter written for Jack, Master Tobias. Is there a messenger?"

"It shall go with your father's. Is your brother a good correspondent?"

"Not really, but I think he has very little time."

"Or space."

"He will be midshipman soon."

"Then he will have even less. Do you miss him? Envy him even?"

"I miss him but I don't envy him. I don't think the life would suit." And, self-contained as ever, the boy bent again to his task. He was drawing a map.

Toby rolled his eyes at Nick, who shrugged and said with a smile, "He wants to be an explorer like Master Tradescant. *Ça va.*"

Nicholas listened to the hoof beats fading and looked again at his son. Younger than Jack by a few months, he was now the taller of the two, with shoulders and upper chest precociously developed by his early passion for archery. The injury to his arm had put paid to that, and he now pursued knowledge of the natural world and swordplay with equal fervour. As lively and high-spirited as his half-brother, he had a reflective turn of mind that benefited from association with the playhouse and Tom Percy, whereas Jack, the mathematician of the family, had found his niche in the Navy.

I have done my best, thought Nick. *If anything happens to me, they are provided for*.

The Queen sent to bring Nicholas from the playhouse. He went home and changed into more suitable garb and as he later walked through the chill corridors and crowded anterooms of the palace, he noticed the growing anxiety among the courtiers. It manifested itself in a strange way, one faction drawing away from him as if he carried some contagion, others coming close, looking for favour, some asking him to intercede for them with the Queen. *Robert was right*, he thought.

If he hoped to see Rosalyne, he was disappointed. Elizabeth received him alone. He bowed and knelt, she waved her hand impatiently and beckoned him to stand beside her. He smelt her aging body and saw that the white lead on her face – newly applied, no doubt by his wife – was already cracking. An ambassador was expected, Nick did not flatter himself that all her finery was for him. She was dressed in white velvet over quilted white satin, the whole paned and embroidered with diamonds and rubies.

"You are sparing of your presence, Rokesby. Do you not hunger for a glimpse of your wife? She is about here somewhere. Apply yourself, my sweet lord, I had not heard that sons can be got at a distance."

"Your Majesty wishes, as always, to provoke me. The difficulty is not of my making. How may I serve my Queen?"

The white paint cracked further as she smiled, showing gapped discoloured teeth.

"Should a monarch admit to a wrong? No, Nicholas, I sent for you to offer thanks, not tease you. Another serpent in our midst, its sting removed. What reward would you have? A monopoly, perhaps, the Garter? Speak."

"Neither, my Queen. A holiday for my lady wife, permission to take part in plays to entertain your Majesty is all I could desire. May I enquire of your Majesty's health?"

"None of your business, sir. I do well enough." Her face softened. "But I give you the credit, Nicholas, that you do not ask for the sake of crafty ambition or in the hope of future preferment. Oh yes, I hear what they say of you. I do not believe it. Perhaps if they see you in the company of players, you will become a buffoon, not a man to be reckoned with, such blind fools as they be."

"I must be blind, as well, Majesty, I am always hearing of this mysterious 'they' who have voices but no face."

"If you spent more time with us at Court, young man, and less on your own affairs, you might recognise some of them," she said waspishly.

"Those affairs have brought a fine revenue to your coffers, your Majesty. The tax on the alum and furs alone—"

"And where is your gift?"

"If your Majesty would come to the window…" She beckoned him to give her his arm, and walked upright and steady to look out. A pure-bred Arab palfrey stood on the terrace, pale gold with a flaxen mane, her bridle hung with bells and held by a prideful Hob. Obviously delighted, Elizabeth's fingers dug into Nick's arm.

"If you are as cunning a lover as a giver, your Rosalyne is fortunate, Rokesby. I accept your gift. Just the thing for my

Progress." She turned an arch look on him, disastrous in the cruel light. "'My kingdom for a horse!' Is that what you want?"

Nick managed a laugh. "Not the play I had in mind, your Majesty."

Turned suddenly petulant, she stamped her foot. "I would see a new play! None of your repetitions – bring us something new! And yes, you may play – but we would see you take the first part, a leading role…what do they say – 'a part to tear a cat in'. Do it, Rokesby, and then perchance you shall have your other wish."

Wishing Elizabeth and her moods to perdition, Nicholas bowed his thanks, and lifting his head, caught a look in her eyes that made him want to weep. In that moment, he knew why he served this woman, loved her and sought to protect her. What would become of her realm when she was gone? He bent to kiss her hand.

"My Queen may command me in all things."

"If I were thirty years younger, you might regret that, my lord. Come, sit here by me. I have a poem I wish to hear. Read it to me."

It was a long poem by one of the up-and-coming young writers and during his reading a certain bustle outside the door announced the arrival of the ambassador from Spain. Elizabeth ignored it and when the poem was finished, produced another. Altogether, the ambassador was kept waiting a good hour or more. Before she released Nicholas, she went once more to look at her palfrey standing patiently resting an elegant hind hoof in the courtyard and signed to Hob to take the mare to the royal stables.

A young girl looked out of the hooded eyes she turned on Nicholas. "You have pleased us, Rokesby. Which can be a good thing and a bad thing too. If I am cool to you in time to come, take this in true earnest," and she reached up and planted a smacking buss on his cheek. "Off with you – and remember, a new play!"

Alone in the anteroom, Nicholas was careful to rub off the scarlet blotch before running the gauntlet of envious and questioning stares. He rode in silence back to Fletcher's Piece – he had a great deal to think about.

Chapter Twenty-Seven

The Run-through

Nicholas pondered a long while on which of the plays kept locked away he would give to Will Shakespeare. He dismissed the Trojan play as being too cynically wordy and political to appeal to Elizabeth and the only parts for him were Hector or the stupid burly Ajax – Burbage would almost certainly plump for Achilles. He fancied none of them. The Scottish play, then. In the present uneasy climate of James' Court this might well be seen as a Trojan horse. The King might never hear of it of course, but the Intelligence highway between London and Edinburgh was a well-trodden one these days. Again, perhaps not a wise choice. The play about the Moor – and so many other things beside – rubbed on a sore place in Nick's soul. Still, leaving personal considerations aside, it seemed the only one of the three that met the requirements. Nick had a strong desire to speak those words. Perhaps acting it out would exorcise his demons. He stuffed the manuscript in his satchel and went to find Master Shakespeare.

He found him at the Globe, sitting on the edge of the stage biting his nails. Ben Jonson had scored another resounding success with his latest offering, and the Chamberlain's Men were feeling the draught. He looked up eagerly as Nick approached.

"Tell me you have good news – God knows we need a new play, they are sick of revivals – always there must be some new thing. I am working on something, but the ending eludes me—"

"Not here, and not so loud. Take a walk with me in the fields. I shall need your vote in this, Burbage will not be pleased." The playwright jumped down and followed Nick through the lanes into the fields and woods south of the bear-baiting arena. They sat on a log in a glade dappled with sunshine, the roars from the arena carried to them, with the smell of it, on a gentle breeze, to be banished by the scent of wild garlic. Shakespeare stiffened like a pointer dog and watched greedily as Nick unbuckled his satchel. He reached for the bundle of scrip.

"Give it me!"

"A moment. The Queen commands a new play—"

"So do the people! I told you—"

"And requires me to play a leading role."

Will's face fell. "Oh."

"That is why I need your voice. Richard will want this part, by right it should be his – a part to tear a cat in – and it will be, but for the Queen it must be mine. I do admit I hunger to play it."

"What is it – what is the story? Give it to me."

"It is more than the story, as always. A tale of jealousy and love. Murder and treachery. Set in Venice and Cyprus, the tragedy of Othello the Moor."

"I had hoped for a comedy."

Nicholas had decided on a liberal interpretation of Elizabeth's permission.

"Listen, Will. While this is in rehearsal – it's powerful stuff, I promise you – I suggest we do as Richard wants, put on the *Dream*. I would play Oberon, as he says. The people will come to see a knight of the realm make a fool of himself – which, incidentally, I do not propose to do. It will not be 'just another revival'. Titles are box office."

"All right, all right. And you want the Moor?"

"So I am bidden." This was a trifle disengenuous: the idea had taken hold of Nick, he would fight tooth and nail for the role.

"Let me see." Nicholas handed over the manuscript and watched as Kit Marlowe's ghost began to read. Shakespeare's hands began to shake as he mouthed the words, he could barely hold the pages together. He leafed on, found another passage and another, and looked up at last, his eyes glistening, with emotion or cupidity, it was hard to tell.

"By all the gods at once – it's a miracle! Who can have done this – who?"

"We should let it be known you have a new play in rehearsal and keep the matter of it secret. Do you agree?"

"Yes, yes, and the fact you are to play it. Come, quickly, set it before the others—"

"You go on ahead, it is yours. I should not be seen in this. The Queen has commanded and this is your response. Understood?"

Shakespeare nodded, feverishly shuffling the pages together. About to leave, he stood still, and drew himself up, planting his feet.

"You must play this well, Nicholas. It is deserving of the best."

"I shall."

Nick expected, and got, a good deal of resistance to the idea of his playing this plum part. Of right, it should go to Richard Burbage, it was taken for granted that the lead role in any play was his, but he could not gainsay a Royal command.

"For one performance at Whitehall, then," he grumbled. "And that only if you manage to stay on your feet as Oberon and not bump into the scenery." For the previous production of the *Dream*, Tobias had followed the coming fashion and provided a number of ingenious devices. Oberon made his first appearance from a descending moonlit cloud, a magical wood appeared to sprout from the stage and glide from behind the Grecian columns built at each side.

"What need of all these toys," muttered Master Shakespeare. He put his foot down when it came to the rustics' play. "The comedy depends on their own clumsy contrivance," he shouted. "The moon is in Snug's lantern, not some bauble suspended from God knows where – I say again, devil take Master Inigo Jones and his masques!"

"I know that, Will," said Toby mildly. "There is nothing but what the clowns bring to it – I take it you do not object to Master Butcher playing his part?"

The trees were passed as having a convincingly magical effect, but Nick objected to the cloud: in spite of Toby's best efforts it had a decidedly jerky movement. He preferred to glide down on a silvered rope from the musicians' gallery. Unlike the jealousy of Othello, the 'jealous Oberon' did not disturb him, but the plight of the lovers found another sore place. Haunt the environs of the palace as he might, he seldom caught more than a glimpse of his Rosalyne. Once across a crowded Audience Chamber he saw her in conversation with an obviously smitten Italian Ambassador, but before he could come at her she was summoned to do some trivial service for her mistress. Elizabeth was playing a mischievous game with him, Nick knew, and tried not to resent it.

He missed his wife desperately, his empty bed was a constant trial of his will, and almost as much, he missed the long talks with

Marlowe and the music of his voice. He thought he had the reading of the part right, he knew enough of his friend's mind to come near it, nevertheless he would like to have to spoken of it with him.

He fitted rehearsals of *Othello* and performances of the *Dream* into an already punishing regime of work and preparation, so that he fell into bed each night and slept like the dead, too tired even to dream. If Eliza, the woman who kept the wardrobe now that Mistress Molly had retired, had hopes that their encounter would be repeated, she was disappointed. Nicholas was courteous and free with his money but kept his distance. Piqued, she told her friends that the Lord Rokesby was a cold fish, and word went out he was too conscious of his rank ever to be a true player. His performances as Oberon went a long way to contradict this, his fellow players accepted him and ceased to wonder at Burbage giving him such a key role. There was still spiteful gossip, there were those, Iago-like, that whispered of the Queen's favourite and the power of money, but once the scripts were passed out for the new play, the mutterings were subdued by the wonder of it.

Nick's playing of Oberon was both majestic and sly, with a touch of malice that helped distinguish him from the courtly Duke of Athens. Doubling the parts meant a quick change at the end, easily accomplished during the fairies' dance. The debut of Master Butcher was a scene-stealer and received with much mirth as he tugged at his frayed piece of rope, trying to reach his master offstage. Moonshine, struggling with his bush, his stool, his lantern and the other end of the rope, was not the only one to complain when Butcher developed a penchant for thrusting a cold wet nose into the relatively unprotected groins of the other rustics. "This dog, my dog" came out through gritted teeth. The play within a play reached new heights of sheer farce and their audiences loved it. The timing of the revival was good; the public was ready for a simple piece of divine entertainment.

Nick was working on his voice, matured now to a deeper register. He wanted it lower and full of sonority for the Moor, and went to Master Greenwood, a master of rhetoric, for the richness and phrasing he was after. Already taller than most, he exercised to put back the weight he had lost in the last few stressful months. His Othello would be larger than life.

With all the poaching of players and pirating of other people's work that was going on, the Chamberlain's Men decided to rehearse the new play in camera. Nicholas supposed that with so much new talent arriving on the scene such jostling was inevitable.

Inevitable also that word should leak out. Burbage himself was partly responsible: he let it be known that out of a generosity of spirit, he was giving one of the youngsters – a lord and a knight, no less – a chance. Any damage this might have done to future box office and to Nick's performance, when people might come to jeer and throw rotten fruit, was offset when the name of the 'youngster' got out. Nick's Jacques and Oberon had gained him a certain respect and credence and he was liked by the public.

Speculation about the play occupied the gossips in the taverns. It featured a Turkish despot complete with harems, it was about Attila the Hun, it was a daring play of the Pope and the Borgias, it was a tale of Heracles or Odysseus with gods and monsters. This last was favourite, the talkers fancied Nick in either role. What was certain was that anything about recent events, or failed or failing monarchs, especially the Queen's father, was too dangerous even for the Globe, where they occasionally trod a very thin line. Look at their *Richard the Second* – madness.

Nicholas found it odd that with so much talk about the plays, little was made of the playwright. If Will had expected fame and fortune to come his way, he must be bitterly disappointed. He made no fuss, indeed apart from laying claim to the plays, he seemed to shy away from the public gaze. *As well he might*, thought Nick. *For all he knows, Southampton or Oxford or our revered Francis might pop up any minute to confound him.* The fortune part seemed to be working. Will was known to be a warm man, a man of property these days.

Denied the leading role, Richard Burbage persisted in directing the new play as he saw it. He loved the rhodomontade of the great speeches, they might have been written for him. *Probably were*, thought Nick. *Kit may want me to play it, but he must have known it would likely go to Richard*. Inevitably the arguments with Burbage began and went on far into the night, until at last the actor-manager was forced to admit that Nick's reading of the part was at least as valid as his own. Nicholas could bring to the play an understanding of the "subtle arts of the Venetian", and the authority of a warrior, whereas Richard Burbage had never been out of the country. He marvelled where Master Shakespeare could have learned them. "All in the interpretation," said Will airily.

Nick found an unexpected ally in Robert Armin, who was playing against his customary comic role, as Iago. The man who could play Touchstone and Feste could certainly play Iago. Nick was remembering the men coming off the Arab dhows to trade in Venice, Arab not Nubian, not the "nigars and etc" so disliked by Elizabeth that she had had many of them deported. He wanted the lighter colour of a North African, or a Moor of Southern Spain, and a different culture, Moslem turned Christian, a man familiar with the customs and practices of the Turk and the southeastern coast of the Inland Sea. Nick had seen adulterous wives stoned to death in the streets of Morocco, whipping at the cart's tail was nothing to that. Armin supported him.

"Nick has the profile of a hawk. I have seen such men of the desert. The 'thicklips' from Roderigo is a common insult and the 'sooty bosom' may perhaps be Will's nod to the make-up."

"I thought of using bark or walnut juice. Burnt cork is likely to run and leave snail tracks – there will be blood, sweat and tears in this performance, I know it."

Burbage shrugged and let it go. *Let the young cub have his head,* he thought. *Find his limitations. My time will come. Ha! Let me see you do it, Nick, that's all.*

Nick worked with fervour on the polysyllables of the great speeches. Reminded of the precision needed for Shylock's "harmless necessary cat", and the contrast of complex and simple in Macbeth's "let the multitudinous seas incarnadine, making the green one red" (*like the waters of the Tummel,* he thought) he strove for clarity of diction and strong open vowels. Such lines as "Farewell the plumed troop and the big wars" took on a sound like organ music, the repeated "Farewell" made new demands on his tongue. He cursed Kit Marlowe as the language brought him to his knees. Once the technical difficulties were mastered, he came to the biggest hurdle – the anguish and passion and destruction. Could he bear to strip his own soul naked and expose his doubts and fears for the stinking breath of an audience to blow upon?

You're an actor, he said to himself. *There must be a way, or how could any of us survive? A part to tear a cat in, yes, but not to tear ourselves apart.* It would be no use approaching Burbage in this, or the master of rhetoric who dealt only in manipulation. Instead, he sought out Edward Alleyn, Burbage's only rival, he of the silver voice, and asked his advice.

"How to distance yourself?" said Alleyn. "Never dream of it. The man is not you, but you are the man. Keep a small corner of him for yourself, a looker-on that judges your performance. That is what it is, Nick, a performance. It must be always under your governance. Find what lies in you and use it. You will find that it comes best in practice, always you will find that critic in the back of your mind – for the rest, let heart and soul go into that other and give it life. Is this the new play I hear of?"

Nick grinned at him. "I thank you, Master Alleyn, but I am not at liberty to say. I seek only to improve so that I do not make too much a fool of myself before my peers."

"Part of the job, dear boy. Practice, practice, practice."

Alleyn was right. In rehearsal, Nick began to get a grip on this thrashing monster of a part. He lengthened his stride to match the rhythms of his speech, slow, redolent of authority. *The man had a sense of humour*, thought Nick. *"Put up your bright swords or the dew will rust them."* It showed again in his gentle teasing of Desdemona, he could afford a little banter with his men. Perhaps the movement should change as the poison got to work, become faster, less coordinated.

The scene where Iago first introduces his theme of jealousy worried Nick. Iago seemed to cave in too easily to his general's demands, it was clumsy. In the second run-through, as Robert Armin spoke the lines leading up to, "It were not for your quiet nor your good…to let you know my thoughts," Othello began to frown. He grew irritated and angry as Iago hinted at loss of good name in man or woman: "Who steals my purse steals trash…"

On Othello's line "By heaven I'll know thy thoughts!" Nick took Armin by the throat, snatched out his dagger and set the point over Armin's heart.

An actor to his backbone, Armin carried on. "You cannot, if my heart were in your hand; Nor shall not, while 'tis in my custody."

"Hah!" and Nick thrust a little harder. Armin's eyes rolled and his hands went up in surrender. Nick pushed him away and Armin gulped for breath and found his lines.

"O beware, my lord, of jealousy. It is the green-eyed monster…"

"Good, good," roared Burbage. "Makes sense. 'Heart in your hand'. Keep it in. Again."

"Not quite so enthusiastic this time, Nick, if you please," said Armin, rubbing his throat. "We poison only in jest, remember…"

As the speech went on, Nick turned abruptly away, eyes downcast, shaking his head, his hands brushing the air as if plagued by flies. He could not believe it, he would not, he fought back – but… The line "She did deceive her father marrying you" went in like a knife, his hands dropped, the dagger fell. Armin picked it up on, "I see this has a little dashed your spirits," and offered it back. Nick stared at it with dull eyes and took it like a sleepwalker. "Not a jot, not a jot," a man in a dream. Armin hammered on, Othello's resistance weakened, his peace of mind destroyed by those first doubts. He would have proof, it was promised him.

Nick broke off at this point. Here was his greatest difficulty.

"Why does he place Iago's honesty above his wife's? This harping on his 'honesty' is like Mark Antony's 'honourable men', it produces the opposite effect."

"On the audience," said Armin. "It's for them to see."

"Othello's not a fool. Why can't he see it?"

"Where we love, the wisest of us are fools." This came so near Nick's own misgivings that he was silenced. Burbage was looking at Othello's next long speech.

"We'll have a mirror, a fountain, perhaps, where he can see himself. This might be his Achilles' heel, might he wonder – we've all done this – 'What does she see in me?' There is this constant playing on his most vulnerable spot, the only chink in his armour. The man's a soldier, not a lady's man like Cassio. He cannot caper nimbly in a lady's chamber, nor does he want to. He is the honest one, he expects honesty in others."

"And in his wife," said Nick. "Especially in her. One tiny doubt –"

"Yes!" shouted Burbage. "She deceived her father, not just once, she must have done it many times, seen Othello behind his back, sneaked out – I can make a lot of that—"

"There is his pride," said Armin. "His manhood is under attack—"

"It makes him angry," said Nick, his voice unsteady. "He cannot endure that. But he is in love – new to him perhaps – he has scaled the heights of a different passion. The first sight of her after this would tear him apart."

The two men stared at him. He grew slowly red.

"What I mean is, she comes to him when he is off-balance. He is in pain. He sees her at that moment in a new light. Every word and deed is suspect, she is digging herself in deeper."

"That is where Will has been so clever," cried Burbage. "We know she is innocent – or do we? I was not convinced of it until the last, with Emelia. Then the tragedy is at its height, and then again when the scales fall from the Moor's eyes. Oh, brilliant! Masterly. The man's a genius."

Nick sat down heavily on the edge of the stage. "I need a break. Yes, Dick, a fountain. Let me see how swart and ugly I am compared with young Cassio, let me wonder at her response to me as her lover – she seems to have enjoyed it. There are ways to counterfeit virginity."

"I know that and you know that, but would Othello?"

"Undoubtedly."

"Would you think in this way, Nick?" said Armin curiously.

"No. But I am not Moslem turned Christian, I have not spent my life as he has, my boyhood in slavery, the rest waging war. I have not used whores for relief as he must have done. He asks, 'Why did I marry?' For love, that's why, first love in his middle years and it will crucify him."

"You need a break. And I need a drink," said Burbage. "B'r lady, this takes as much thinking about as the Dane. Watch yourself, Nick. You are in danger of getting too drawn in. This is not just about Othello. It is about how easily a mean-spirited man can destroy a reputation, Cassio's, Desdemona's, how lives can be lost and destroyed by foolishness and ambition and one man's envious spite. Over-shadowed, I grant you, by the toppling of a great man. His fall is monstrous and the cause is petty—"

"It is trivial and not trivial," said Nick. "One small pebble in the path of a siege tower and we have a wreck."

"I'll have a large small beer," said Armin, and turned a cartwheel. "Let's find Will and stand him a drink."

Chapter Twenty-Eight

Court life seemed to suit Rosalyne. She had regained some of her looks and had been seen dancing with the young and dashing envoy from Paris. Indeed, she had been laughing, reported Carey.

"Don't let the playhouse and whatever else it is you're up to, keep you away, my friends," he said. "While the cat's away, you know…"

Nick snarled and presented himself as soon as that afternoon's performance was over. His Oberon had been more malicious than mischievous, and Burbage had warned him not to let the Moor contaminate the King of the Fairies. He felt it was beginning to seep into his whole life. If he could but see his wife, speak to her, hold her…

He went alone and on foot, William was safe with Hob and Tobias. He had not dressed for a Court appearance, he was in rehearsal clothes and climbed the stair to her rooms unchecked by the guards, who knew him by sight. No matter how long Elizabeth kept her Mistress of the Wardrobe dancing attendance, he would wait it out. The game had gone on long enough.

He sent away the maid who answered his knock, a younger, prettier one than before, he was glad to see, and stretched out on the bed. He was tired but did not fear falling asleep, he was too keyed up for that. His main worry was keeping a rein on himself, he did not wish to alarm her. He banished Othello from his mind, thinking instead of Strathyre and Richmond, how she had come to him before the battle in boy's clothes, how she had cared for his wounds and shouted with laughter at Marlowe's jokes. They had lain in the long grass at Richmond and made love – no, better not think of that. But he could not help it; they had been so long apart. Did she still blame him for the loss of their child? Had she ever? There must be no reproaches. He formed words in his mind, sentences – the door opened and she was there.

No need, after all, for words. She was in his arms, lips, teeth, hands, seeking and finding. A force unreckoned with took them both to the very edge, the little death. Nicholas was the first to recover himself. He leaned up on one elbow and she put her palm across his mouth, drawing it down until her fingers slid between his lips.

"No words yet. Show me."

At some time in that night of rediscovery, she whispered, "I thought you would put me aside, Nicholas. I am told there can be no more children. Elizabeth—"

"I thought you held me in disgust for what I allowed to happen. You have given me a son, beloved, and we have Jack. It is enough."

"You were not to blame."

"You were cold to me. I was afraid."

"I was afraid. You were in danger. I heard talk, and Elizabeth – she was testing us, I think."

"Playing with us, rather. It shall not go on."

She yawned and stretched against him. "This has been like that first night you came to me from the playhouse, shy, fumbling for words. Not for long. It was like bringing a young tiger into my bed."

223

"I have learned a little art since then, lady."

"A tamed tiger, then?"

"To be led by you, a true lover in all things."

"True?"

"And if I have not been?"

"I should hold you blameless. It has been a long time."

Nick shook his head, laughing. "Too good to be true, mistress. I confess to the odd slip. If I had known you to be so complaisant, I might have been more liberal."

Her fingers dug into his flesh. "Did I say 'complaisant'? You are mine."

"Forever yours."

Let Marlowe's words distil their venom, he thought. *I am armour-proof. I know my Rose, I know her past and so long as I am her present, I am content.*

He missed the morning rehearsal and very nearly the afternoon performance as well. The Queen sent two men-at-arms to summon him from Rosalyne's bed at midday. "She has eyes everywhere," he said, hastily pulling on his clothes.

"The cat stretches out her paw – beware her claws, Nicholas."

He presented himself unshaven, still in his black fustian, now short of button or two, and threadbare hose, bent the knee and bowed his head to hide a grin. Elizabeth might scold as she would, he did not care.

"So, my Lord Rokesby, you have found your wife out."

"In what, my Queen?"

"You are a saucy fellow, Rokesby. In her chamber, in her shift – would you put me to the blush, sir?"

"I humbly thank your Majesty for your gracious protection of my wife in these troubled times."

"And now you have no need of it?"

"I do not say so."

"No, but so you mean. I declare I am sick of her moping face. It was at my behest she was set to entertain de Valois. I hoped to cheer her, but to no avail. Back she comes, 'Patience on a monument' – is that the line?"

In the grip of euphoria, Nick almost laughed, and caught himself up. "Your majesty has it pat. But a poor description of my lady."

"She is restored then. I am glad of it." She sighed. "What is it you men do to us? I forget. Get up, man, take her to Richmond, we remove there soon."

"I thank your Majesty."

"Devil take your thanks. She will not breed, they tell me. Were I to counsel you – but no, you have found your cygnet, have you not?"

"Your delicacy does you credit, madam. As always."

"A telling afterthought, you young monkey. Out of my sight, before I box your ears."

"Command me in all things, my Queen."

Yes, Elizabeth thought watching with a sour face as he bowed himself out. *All except the thing that would please me most.* Not even keeping his Rosalyne mewed up at Court had succeeded in turning him into a courtier or a statesman. He reminded her of the young Leicester or Ralegh, untameable. She sighed and sent for Robert Cecil. There must be a way.

Nick's make-up for Oberon took a full half-hour and he was running late. He sent a messenger hot-foot to Hob to fetch his mistress to Fletcher's Piece, and slid down his silver rope with only a moment to spare. Oberon sparkled, his magic worked, the Duke was smugly uxorious with his Amazon queen. The quick change was made, the lovers were put to bed at last, sprinkled with their fairy dust and even faster, he tore off his costume and hastened back to Deptford. Rosalyne was fast asleep in his bed. He slid in beside her, meaning to remind her who he was, and fell deeply asleep himself.

Supper was put back an hour until they woke and came down, every bit as smug as the Duke of Athens. Tobias welcomed them with great solemnity, then surprised Nicholas by picking up Rosalyne and whirling her round with a whoop, Butcher barking madly at his feet.

"Welcome home! Let Bacchus reign tonight!"

It was not all honeyed words and the fruits of Paradise, how could it be? They had been a long time apart. Nick's life and work had expanded to fill that hideous gap, Rosalyne was reunited with William. The resulting demands made for clashes and recriminations, both worn down by the long absence, the easy companionship seemed gone. Nick persevered with his search for the heart of Othello and put off the time when he would have to reveal his plans to his wife.

One evening late, for want of something to say, he broke an uneasy silence to ask her opinion.

"What would a woman do, accused of adultery?"

She dropped her sewing and rounded on him like a wildcat.

"Do you so accuse me? What cause—"

He flung up a hand, half-laughing. "I am answered. No, sweet, it is this play. I find some inconsistency—"

"You expect a woman to be consistent?"

"You are. In general, in my small experience, if a woman be not devious, she is consistent."

"In a play, she may act as suits the playwright's purpose."

"Yes, but it does not satisfy. This playwright speaks truth."

"Show me." He handed her the manuscript and sat gazing into the fire as she read. After a while, she looked up.

"I see what troubles you. We have a woman who begins by defying her father, daring all for love, and at the first threat, she is submissive. You want her to fight harder?"

"I don't know. That is why I asked."

"Not just to make conversation then?'

"We were always wont to talk over a difficulty, Rose."

She smiled suddenly and came to sit on his knee. "So we were. Like this, not sat apart like strangers. M. Malheur wrote this, didn't he?"

Nick started, almost tipping her off his lap.

"Why do you say so!"

"He had some of it written at Strathyre. He asked if I thought you were of a nature to be wrought upon by jealousy."

In spite of his dismay, Nick asked, "What did you say to him?"

"I said, how could I tell, without giving you cause? I should be much surprised, I think."

Nicholas stood up, suddenly, catching her to him as she fell.

"That is it! You have it – she is much surprised. This is not the man she thought she knew. He has hit her, he is a man, and strong. What else might he do? Have we not seen, Rose, how a beaten wife will deny all? Emilia can tell her the ways of men and she will not, cannot, believe. So, at last, we can believe her innocent and the tragedy grows more poignant. I wonder, can our boy player understand? He has intuition, he must be made to see it."

"Nicholas, can you leave your play a moment and tell me – where is Christophe? I thought you were rehearsing Master Shakespeare's new work?"

Nick turned away, his hand to his head. "Oh lord, this is a pretty pucker. Listen, Rose—"

"Is this some secret you have kept from me?"

"From all the world."

"You would say, for my own safety."

Nick closed his eyes briefly. "No. For Kit Marlowe's."

"Kit – But he is dead!"

"And must remain so. It is a long story, sweet, begun just after we first met. Did you never wonder where I went?"

"I asked but no-one knew. There was talk of a rich patron. I could not show too much interest, I was soon in need of a husband." He reddened and she laughed. "I do not mean to reproach you. William is your gift to me. Tell me this tale."

"No, I have said too much already. M. Christophe Malheur is a mad Frenchman fleeing his creditors, he wrote bad verse and is now in Africa. Or somewhere. Kit Marlowe is murdered. Forget him, Rose. For all our sakes, forget them both."

"Does Tobias know?"

"No, no-one. I beg you, not a look or a sidelong glance. 'I would an if I could.' The littlest hint goes round this city like wildfire. If Will Shakespeare can hold his tongue, so can you. I swear I will tell you all, but not here, not now. Promise me."

"I promise. But I shall have it out of you in the end."

"So you shall, if you will hold patience. It will be hard. This play will set the town by the ears."

"I believe you. I see it working on you like a fever." She drew him to sit by the fire and poured wine for him. "Strange," she said thoughtfully. "This play seems to have given us back to each other – as we were wont to be."

228

"Hearts and minds. You are my garden of delight – it is a relief to me to trust you with this secret that it is not mine to keep."

She crossed to draw back the curtain. "We have talked the moon into the sky. To bed, to bed."

About to put down his cup, Nicholas stood still. "Did Malheur read you anything else?"

"Of course, some tale of three witches. But I have forgotten it, I promise you."

"Those words, once heard, are hard to forget."

"I trust you will find it so on opening night. Come to bed, I do not usually have to ask you twice."

Master Butcher rose from his nest by the hearth, put out one leg and stretched all four one after the other, yawned mightily, shook himself head to tail and trotted over to stand by the door, panting gently. They both started to laugh and he joined in, barking and frisking.

"He will wake the house. I see I must play the householder, damp the fire, lock the doors and take this wretched dog out."

"A good dog. He chooses not to foul the rushes."

"Just leaves his bones in them. I'll come presently. I need to think."

Outside in the damp chill, the rising moon began to pale the stars.

"On such a night…" said Nicholas. He sat on the stone by the pump and watched Butcher nosing around, looking for rats long chased away. A sleepy bird cheeped, rousing others. *One note*, thought Nick. *That's all it takes for them all to sing. One word, and all is lost.*

Things were starting to come together. All the orders and messages winging their way to and fro in the hands of the Rokesby couriers had slowly shaped into a discernible plan. On one level Nicholas was in touch with bankers, academics and diplomats, on another he dealt with freethinkers, radicals and vagabonds. It would be the ending of the old life and the beginning of a new. His stints at the courts of Paris and Venice stood him in good stead, as did working for Robert Cecil. He wondered what Cecil was up to, he was ominously quiet.

Chapter Twenty-Nine

In fact, Cecil had found himself unable to satisfy the Queen's demands that Rokesby be reeled in and made use of. Dealing with that young man was like wrestling with a Moray eel, impossible to get a grip on and potentially dangerous. Elizabeth herself made it more difficult by showing him favour. He could not be tempted with money, he refused to take office or a seat on the Council, the Queen had loosed her grip on his wife – the only useful lever they had. Cecil was puzzled by Nick's refusal of the monopolies offered him. The new legislation would have made them a timely weapon against him. *Freetrader!* he thought. *Privateer, more like.* For himself he would not care if he never set eyes on Nicholas, Lord Rokesby again.

"I underestimated him from the start," he grumbled to himself. "Faulds did warn me. Making use of that courier service was another mistake." He suspected that Nick had a network every bit as good as his own, and several ships into the bargain. This thorn in his flesh managed to keep the Queen's favour in spite of his elusive behaviour and Cecil went behind her back strongly to oppose offering him the vacant seat of a Knight of the Garter. He had a candidate of his own with useful Scottish leanings.

Like one before him, he felt like asking, Will no-one rid me of this troublesome...play-actor? No rhetorical question after all, the idea took root. Rokesby had grown too powerful, perhaps he had been over-hasty in alienating him. Too late now, he knew his man too well to think of coaxing him back. Rokesby had distanced himself from Scotland, he had avoided entanglement with Essex. He seemed impervious to the treacherous rumours Cecil's spies had set circulating. It was time to do something positive. An unfortunate accident? Another fatal brawl? No, the wretched youth never started a fight, he was good at finishing them. That fool Mowbray had taken years to provoke him – that had been a fiasco.

Robert Cecil, busy spymaster, had so many tangled threads in his hand that he made another serious mistake. He sent for Robert Poley, and separately, Ned Faulds. Plenty of dark alleys round the Globe.

Poley was a man who liked to play both sides against the middle, and he had developed a healthy respect for Nicholas Talbot. Wooden-faced, he took the money and his instructions and picking his time, he sidled up to Nick on the crowded dockside.

"Watch your back," he muttered. "Word is out. I doubt I'm the only one to be set on."

Nick looked down at him. "Your paymaster and mine, I suppose. No longer, if you choose… I have a task for you myself. Fancy a trip to Bruges? Leaving tonight."

Poley nodded eagerly. Bruges sounded a safer place than the City of London or the South Bank. Plenty of dark alleys round the Globe. He fancied himself a good judge of men and did not think Nick Talbot would have him tipped overboard on the crossing.

Ned Faulds was cut from different cloth. An experienced agent and Intelligencer of some standing, he rather liked Nicholas

Talbot. He had watched with some admiration as the youngster threaded the labyrinth and did not underestimate his talent for getting out of trouble. Faulds held his cousin Meg in affection and knew she had offered Nicholas solace in times of need. He took his fee and instructions with a studied indifference, therefore, folded his hands and did nothing. Time, perhaps, to retire and buy that little place in the south of France.

Busy as he was, something in Faulds' demeanour had alerted Cecil. He twitched another thread in an attempt to find out what exactly Rokesby was doing. Meanwhile he would give Faulds and Poley a week. If they failed, there was a new breed of hungry young men at the foot of the ladder who did not know Rokesby and would not scruple. He thought wistfully of the Antolini twins, those infamous brothers now somewhere in Sicily. *A pair of assassins to rely on*, he thought and stopped there. This was surely not his style. He preferred the subtle approach: he was allowing Rokesby to drive him to extreme measures.

"Give him enough rope," he said aloud. "Yes, let him overreach himself. He is grown so high-stomached, he must fall." He set traps and tripwires and trusted that if all else failed, Rokesby would bring about his own downfall.

And of course, there were always those dark alleys…

Nick had read *The Prince* in company with Marlowe and knew well enough how Cecil's Macchiavellian mind worked. Put on his guard, he was polite, never servile, he could not be seen seeking favours; he was generous, but not so much that it could be thought a bribe. His manner, if austere, could hardly be seen as arrogant. He avoided private conversation in corners and flirted only with his wife. So much for the Court. Elsewhere he was careful not to walk under scaffolding or alone in those dark alleys. He was seldom alone anywhere, and without his knowledge the faithful Hob tasted all their food.

All this took its toll. Nicholas began to feel beleaguered, as if he were playing several roles at once. He turned to the one role that loomed so large in his imagination. For Nick, this play had come to epitomise once again the power of words. In the hands of a master like Marlowe, the words of a plain-speaking 'honest' man worked by implication, serpent words that wormed into the mind and stayed there. The rolling thunder of Othello's speech, reminiscent of Marlowe's 'mighty line', caught at the heart, equally seductive. *We should take care*, thought Nick. *When we first learned to speak, did we intend it to be used as a weapon, a bludgeon or a stiletto, an opiate or a cup of poison?* He shook his head. *At this rate, I shall turn dumb, afraid to open my mouth.*

"Choose your words wisely, William," he said to the boy at his side. William looked up from his work and Nick was struck again by the fierce intelligence in the eyes so like his own. The boy had grown again this summer, he was going to be tall. He had Rosalyne's oval face and sculpted mouth, the cheekbones and jawline were his father's. The tip of his tongue showed at the side of his mouth as he wrote: he frowned now, and drew it in.

"I am trying to, Father. M. Malheur told me. 'It is a tool to be used with skill and forethought,' he said."

Nick sighed. "M. Malheur is a master craftsman, Will. In his hands the tool can be dangerous."

"He said the same, 'Be careful how you use it.'"

Why do I bother, thought Nick. *Kit is always before me.*

"I interrupted you," he said. "I'm sorry." William flashed him a blinding smile, shook his head and returned to his writing. The

234

tip of his tongue crept out again. Silenced by a rush of feeling that ran too deep for words, Nick left him to it and went to find his wife.

Chapter Thirty

The war of the Theatres

Between his preoccupation with his part in the little world of the Globe, and the wider world of his other plans, Nick had hardly noticed the friction building up between the Companies. Henslowe was building a new theatre in Cripplegate to add to his empire that could take custom away from the South Bank; Ben Jonson was having considerable success with the Children of the Royal Chapel. The Rose appeared to have a host of new plays to offer, and when they were stuck, fell back on a series of 'sacred' plays to fill in. Two of Nick's fellow actors of the Chamberlain's Men were successful playwrights, without Will Shakespeare's commitment to the Globe, and wrote for other companies, Henslowe's among them. Always desperately short of money, they sold their work where they could. Thomas Dekker, a robust player not much older than Nick, was doubling Montano and Ludovico and brought to the latest argument a new comedy.

Most of the Globe shareholders were gathered in the Mermaid to discuss the rotation of performances once Will's new play was ready. They were waiting for Nicholas, who was less punctual than at former times. Dick Burbage had not come, he had a slight chill and was cosseting his voice. Master Hemynge came in his place to state the case for the finances, with a sheaf of papers under his arm and Nick arrived in a flurry of friendly catcalls. They sat in a corner well removed from the noisy crowd surrounding Ben Jonson and sent for ale.

"Thinks he owns the place," grumbled Will Shakespeare, scowling at the noisy group round Jonson. Thomas Dekker still had not come. They settled to discuss the rotation of the plays without him, in spite of the fact that one of them was his. It was easier perhaps to talk of them in his absence: his latest, *Satiromastix*, was perhaps too much a provocation of Jonson to be considered. He and Philip Marston, his friend and fellow playwright, and arch-enemy of Jonson, were of course wild for it to be performed. Hemynge preferred *The Shoemaker's Holiday*, a rumbustious comedy and a proven success.

"It is not new," said Will.

"Last year is new enough, we have not played it for a while. If we play neither, he may leave us for Henslowe. *Othello* is new."

In the end, they decided to alternate *Hamlet*, still playing to packed houses, with *Othello*, *The Shoemaker's Holiday* and *Twelfth Night*, to remind the people of Master Armin's Feste, lest he be booed and hissed off the stage as Iago.

"Two old, one new and one newish," said Master Hemynge. "They can't cavil at that."

"They will," said Shakespeare gloomily. "They will. With Jonson and the others churning out material at the rate they do — we are like spiders or the wretched silkworm, ever spinning words."

"A useful analogy," said Nick. "You must put it in your next play." Shakespeare glared at him. What he would have said was lost in the turbulent arrival of Philip Marston. He sat himself down, ordered a round of drinks and began to argue. About to leave, Nick was made to sit down again and was seized upon by Hemynge with a list of figures. He missed the beginning of the quarrel and the jibe Jonson made, becoming aware of it when a bench went over and Marston could be seen at Jonson's throat. Blows were exchanged, Jonson with his bricklayer's hands getting much the better of it. In the ensuing fight Marston was knocked to the ground. He scrambled to his feet, pulling out his dagger and at this point Nick judged it best to intervene. He snatched up his cloak and dropped it over the furious Marston's head, imprisoning his arms. Unable to distinguish friend from foe, the man struggled and fought, Nick seized his wrist and the dagger fell on the table. Jonson picked it up with a flourish.

"I am the victor here, I think," he said with a sneer.

"You would do well to take your strutting elsewhere for the moment," said Nick. "Let tempers cool."

"Let him think twice before he lampoons my plays! Pissing against the world, am I?"

"Must you always have the last word?" asked Will. "We shall see – just wait until—"

Nick cut him short. "Come on Philip. The Elephant for us. We'll drink to your new comedy."

"Call that a comedy?" shouted Jonson after them. "A travesty, that's what it is!"

Marston struggled in Nick's restraining grasp. "He has my dagger. I'll–I'll—"

"I'll see you get it back. Your wit will hurt him more."

Marston began to calm down. "Yes. Yes, I know just the thing. Just you wait, you congealed lump of bombast!" he shouted over his shoulder.

"Quiet, quiet, for pity's sake," pleaded Will, wringing his hands. "There is enough trouble."

"Tom should have been here," complained Marston. "We could have taken them down, him and his cronies."

"Here he comes, in good time," said Nick. "You missed all the fun, Tom."

"Fighting again?" sighed Dekker. "When will you learn? You should have—"

"Fie on the lot of you! I'm for livelier company – and I'll thank you to keep your hands to yourself next time, *Sir* Nicholas!" So saying, he flounced off down the street, giving the finger to the watchman who rounded the corner. Dekker shrugged and went after him.

"If that is our meeting ended," said Nick, "I'm for home. I've been too long already."

Will Shakespeare, left standing alone, watched him swing off down towards the river. Sometimes he hated Nicholas Talbot.

Chapter Thirty-One

Westminster. Opening Night

On the opening night of *Othello*, Dionysus, god of players, came down and touched them with magic, scattering his largesse on actors and audience alike. They could do no wrong. What was missing of scenery and lights, their sophisticated audience willingly supplied. It was night in the blaze of candles as Iago drew his dupe forward to begin his mischief-making.

Nicholas they did not recognise: outside himself, he *was* Othello the Moor. He came softly out of the shadows barefoot, his face and body part of the darkness, his black hair close-curled like a bull, a dark kaftan folded about him – roused from his bridal bed perhaps – a gold ring in his ear, a heavy bracelet on his bare arm. A quiet consultation with his two ancients, his anger contained, and he made his exit, point made. Robe whipped off and boots pulled on, his second entrance was controlled, powerful, even amused. He spoke in a voice that was violet and indigo, with a brazen edge born on the battlefield. Hypnotised, they listened as he spoke of a life so totally foreign and beguiling that, like Desdemona, they would have followed him to perdition and back. Iago's smears and Roderigo's insults faded into insignificance until Brabantio alerted them with his pinprick: "She has betrayed her father, and may you." Burbage had kept his promise and made much of his opportunity. The barb planted so skilfully would be remembered. For now, their sympathy was all for the Moor in spite of his alien looks.

The sun shone in Cyprus, they could smell the sea. Their instinctive liking for the gallant Cassio, a courtly mannered man like themselves and, like themselves, not above trifling with women, became tarnished with a little contempt for a man who could not hold his drink. They held their breath as Iago's poison began to do its work and gasped as the Moor's true nature revealed itself in his agony like a blare of trumpets. Someone cried out as he struck his wife. However raised up and powerful, even if she played him false, for a Moor to strike a white woman! Fickle as ever, their allegiance changed. They were proved right, Desdemona was innocent, how could they have doubted? They sat quiet as her husband padded towards her bed. The words came deep and slow. "It is the cause, my soul. Let me not name it to you, you chaste stars…" A pause, and the voice rose in all its beauty and pain, "else she'll betray more men". It was a cry from the heart and there were men in the watchers who heard it and shuddered. The women watching trembled as the dark face approached the pale mouth for that last kiss. "So sweet was ne'er so fatal…" She woke – surely he could not do it?

But this was not the end of the tragic waste. Othello must see just how he was betrayed, not by his wife, but by his honest friend, played upon, the chink in his armour found and penetrated. Nicholas and Armin between them had shown them how Iago, almost by accident, as he had with Cassio, stumbled on the flaw and gleefully exploited it. Roderigo had been easy, a rejected and resentful lover, a tool ready to hand. Cassio had exposed himself, had been a bow at a venture that found the target. How easy then, to find the man of another race, another culture, under the skin and inflame him with the slur on his manhood and the abuse of his love. Iago, who had no concept of such love, had found it surprisingly easy. Almost contemptuously, idly, with no idea of the self-doubt of a true lover, he had meddled with an emotion and a nature he did not understand. No wonder then, he chose to remain silent at the last. Nicholas, his terrible outburst of grief over, straddling the body of his faithful wife, spoke his last words. No justification, no apology, a simple acknowledgement. "I loved not wisely, but too well…and threw away a pearl richer than all my tribe." The hidden dagger went in, the watchers groaned.

"All over bar the shouting," murmured Burbage from the wings. "Follow that, if you can, Dick." Perhaps he would let the lad have the part after all.

The Queen sent for Nicholas after the performance. Exhausted, he had no time to do more than change his clothes and she threw up her hands at sight of him and cackled.

"Upon my soul, Rokesby, you stand revealed in your true colours – no gilded court-fly here. A barbarian and an adventurer. What, shorn of your love-locks? Swart as the devil himself. You have affrighted your poor wife – she fled the scene. I see it has been cruel in us to keep you from the playhouse. Play on, my Lord Rokesby – something a little more cheerful next time, if you please."

"Life is not all comedy, your Majesty."

"You have the right of it, more's the pity. Those of us who deal daily with its woes seek solace in laughter, you play-actors should know it, none better. Let Master Armin but slip on an orange peel and I am content." She paused, became serious. "It is a fine play,

242

Rokesby, and a fine performance. I pray you in future make me shed tears of laughter not grief. There has been enough of that."

"Your Majesty may command me. Is Rosalyne—"

"Commanded to bed. We have missed her company of late. She will send."

Of all nights this was the one Nick would miss Rosalyne. His first great leading part – he wanted to go over every nuance with her, the actor's cry – "How was it?" He could only bow himself out gracefully and go and find his fellows.

Chapter Thirty-Two

An invitation came from Rosalyne, still to Nick's disgust kept in close attendance on the Queen. They were to meet on the grassy terrace overlooking the Thames, the scene of their betrothal. Still rather darker-complexioned than usual, he came into the garden and hesitated. Rosalyne was pacing at the far end and turned at his step. A moment later, she was in his arms in a flurry of stiff muslin and jewelled silk, the scent of her filled his senses.

"My Nicholas, not a Moor at all!"

"A play-actor, sweet, as you first saw me."

"I loved you then as I do now."

"Were you affrighted, love? I admit it freely, I have been."

"Of what?"

"Of losing you, or that part of myself I value most. That play works on the mind, sows doubt and suspicion where there is no cause."

"Do you doubt me, Nicholas?"

"I think, not now."

"Lord Seymour—"

"Is dealt with. I know of it."

"Come, my lord, we waste time, we are too much apart."

An usher called from the end of the terrace. "My lady, her Majesty wishes your attendance."

Rosalyne spat a very unladylike word. "So much for promises. She plays with us, Nicco, for her own amusement. I must obey."

"A word, before you go. I am leaving—"

"You are leaving me?"

"No, sweeting. I go to make us a new life, if you will, away from the whims of princes. I will be back for you, never fear. While the Queen lives there is scheming. And I no longer trust in James. He longs to be popular, he will scatter favours like autumn leaves. It means trouble. How enamoured are you, my love, of Court life, of wealth and position? I don't say it does not become you, but it sticks in my throat."

"We were content once at Strathyre, were we not? No, no, I know there can be no going back. I have no friends here."

"I am answered. Be patient, Rose, our time will come again, I promise. Quick, a kiss to seal it."

She looked back once as she followed the equerry, with a smile to stop his breath. He watched her go, amazed at himself. How could one woman, one kiss have this effect on him. Nick Talbot, knight, adventurer, hard-headed businessman, to be reduced to this. *Exalted, rather*, he thought. *Kit Marlowe knows. The heights and the depths, he knows them both. We shall have much to say to each other.*

The last doubts stilled, he was free to pursue his plans. He paid his tolls and taxes and, ostensibly on the Queen's business to drum up trade, he boarded the *Seamew* with William, Hob and the dog Butcher at his heels, bade farewell to Tobias and sailed for the continent.

Chapter Thirty-Three

The fever came again, worse this time, with pain in his lungs. He coughed desperately, trying to breathe and blood came in a rush to stain the sheet. Someone was bending over him, there came a sharp aromatic scent and he slid into darkness. A storm raged outside and within the stout walls Marlowe fought for his life. He was not finished yet. After the old king's raging there had come a time of peace. He had written little, fragments only, plays he knew he would never complete. Now he had a new idea, a rounding off. He would not die yet.

The long-awaited ship sailed into the harbour, flying its black and gold flag. Marlowe made his slow and difficult way down to meet it. The familiar figure ran down the gangplank and leapt ashore, halting at sight of him. A pause, and Nicholas came on, arms flung wide and eyes full of tears, to envelop him in a bear-hug.

"I should never have let you leave me," he said, his voice muffled against his friend's hair.

"Nonsense! Your climate would have done for me long since. I do very well here. Come, your news – I am starved of it…"

Nicholas had come to him to tell him of the triumph of *Othello* and talk of his plans for an enlightenment. Settled in his lodging,

246

domestic and political news disposed of over a flagon of wine, Marlowe laughed at him. "You are a mad fool, Niccolo. The time is not yet. You will get yourself killed. And what of my Anthony and his Egyptian queen?"

"Burbage will play it. I shall be doing it, if at all, in French. I say, words, not wars. What have you been telling me if not that. That is what I have come for. I need words from you, Kit, to feed my presses, feed the mind, the people are hungry for hope."

"Teach them to reason, not hope. Educate them. Entertain them and they will learn. Your troupe of mountebanks will do more to open their minds than any philosophical treatise. If you must waste your money on printing presses I can't stop you. Why not just give it to the poor?"

"I want 'the poor' to help themselves. I was poor once and you helped me to help myself. Come Kit, these are just idle thoughts and you know it."

"Not at all. My plays hold a mirror up to nature – let humanity once recognise itself and there may be a chance." He looked at his friend and disciple across the table. The fledgling actor had grown into a man with wider horizons and a vision. He was not going to give it up. Marlowe sighed. "You will persevere then with your forlorn hope. I must admire you for it, my friend. And when you fail, as fail you will, there are other worlds to conquer."

"I must, at least, try."

"So be it. You shall have your words."

The poet had seen the distress on the young man's face at sight of him. These days he remembered more and more those times in Verona, when his Niccolo, a mere stripling, had cajoled, persuaded and inspired him. He had fallen in love with the agile good-looking lad with the beautiful voice, had done his best to seduce him and jealously watched him grow and develop beyond his influence. Now he loved him for what he was and took some credit for it. Emaciated and sick, easily tired, he knew that a frightened Nicholas had gone to the Knight Hospitaller in charge of the Infirmary and what Sir Roderigo would have told him.

"It is the white plague, *signor*. All that can be done is being done – our hot dry summers agree with him. A hard winter may bring the end."

A small grey cloud of daddy-long-legs drifted past, legs dangling, to join the other heaps of dead insects lying in the angle of the wall. Nick shuddered.

"Has he any particular friend?"

"One of the lay brothers – Aloysius. He scribes for him."

Nicholas gave his short nod. He had brought a heavy bag of money and he set it on the table with a chime of gold.

"For your care of him. I am guilty, Father, that all I can do is offer money. He is my beloved friend – I would stay if I could."

"I absolve you the guilt. I understand you have family and a mission. These things are important to him, too. Finish the tasks you have in hand, come again when you can."

Brother Aloysius proved to be a fresh-faced, gently-bred youth, who greeted Nicholas with a shy smile. "M'sieur Malheur honours me with his words."

"He is writing still? That is the best medicine."

"It is indeed, though at times in the grip of it, I fear for him."

"A fine frenzy – I remember it well."

"Such words, such thoughts! He sees our poor human condition and holds it up for the world to see. You will take the words, my lord, spread them?"

Reassured, Nick nodded, gave him a purse of gold "for a few luxuries" and hastened back to his friend.

At their parting, Nick did his best to conceal his grief, a last loving embrace, and Marlowe sent his lovely boy away knowing he would likely never see him again.

Chapter Thirty-Four

London. 1602.

The dismal wars dragged on across Europe. It was hard to tell by now what they were about: land-grabbing here, a religious wrangle there, a prideful power struggle or two. Taxes went on rising, the only things that seemed to flourish apart from prostitution and the pox. The precious stone set in a silver sea groaned under the burdens of tax and falling trade and looked to her defences and elsewhere for profit. Michaelmas came and went, the Queen finished her Progress, staying with the Sidneys, almost bankrupting them with this second visit in two years. She tired suddenly and Christmas was spent partly at Richmond and partly at Whitehall for Twelfth Night. Elizabeth was dissatisfied with the play, a comedy by Ben Jonson, and retired early. Rosalyne was pleased to be back in sight of the Thames and kept watch for the *Seamew*'s sails. She had letters from Nicholas, long passionate letters, quite in his old style, decorated with drawings and enclosing words and pictures from Will. She was in touch with Tobias, who seemed to know where her husband was, and entrusted him with her replies, all the things she had not been given time to say, and a budget of news from the Court. She heard things said of Nicholas, things men dared not say to his face, and she began to understand. He bowed the knee to both Elizabeth and James, they said, and was biding his time. He had a standing army in Scotland and the West Country, he was seeking friends and allies in Europe. Sides were taken, positions taken up. Rosalyne suspected Robert Cecil of fomenting the rumours. She wrote of them to her errant husband.

One of the ladies-in-waiting, a friend of the disgraced Bess Hamilton, told her how Bess had angled for Rokesby's attention.

"I know Bess," she said, with a sidelong look. "What she wanted, she always got. More than she bargained for, this time. Who will the babe favour I wonder?"

Rosalyne slapped her face and the screams echoed down the corridors.

The English envoy just returned from Venice was so circumspect in his comments as to imply the worst. Nicholas had been seen much in the company of the Princess d'Alighieri, known to be his former lover, and again in Paris at the Comedie, escorting the leading actress. He had been seen in Bruges, hobnobbing with an older woman – a Jewess, would you believe? Rosalyne could hardly slap every rumour-monger. Like Elizabeth, she learned to keep her counsel and say nothing.

Rosalyne's thoughts were often with Jack, he had all his father's adventurous spirit and had joined the Admiral's flagship in Portsmouth. She had long loosed the reins, and now she fretted but let him go. She had entrusted William to Nicholas, he had gone with Hob and she had no-one left to talk to. Tobias always seemed a little distant and she missed Mistress Melville. She found she missed Nick's odd friend just as much, the poet who had graced Strathyre with his words and his voice, a brave man who had stood over Nicholas on the battlefield and yet could talk to

251

her as a friend and an equal. Where had he gone? Everyone she loved seemed to have disappeared. She walked on the terrace and waited for a sail.

It came at night. At the turn of the tide the *Seamew* slipped up the river and hove to in midstream. A slice of the old moon leaned its back against one of the tall twisted chimneys of Westminster as two dark figures rowed to the foot of the Privy Stair. The taller of them stepped out and ran silently up and through the door, to emerge presently with someone enveloped in a cloak struggling in his arms. The door was closed quietly behind them and the boat pushed off, rowing back to the ship. In no time she was gliding back the way she had come.

Next day, All Fools' Day, all hell broke loose. Richmond and Whitehall were in uproar as the black frigate reached the open sea flying a flag that might as well have been the Jolly Roger.

Nicholas Talbot faced his wife across the table of the tiny panelled saloon, his hands on the chest between them, the lamp swinging on its gimbals above their heads, to and fro, light and dark. Rosalyne's face was stark white, her pitch-ball eyes blazing.

"You madman! What have you done?"

"I have stolen you away. I am taking you with me into exile. I mean to show—"

"What! How shall we live—"

"Like gypsies perhaps. Like ordinary folk. Free."

"Free to do what?"

"To shape our lives as we want them, Rose. I can show you worlds you have not seen, Paris, Venice, the Inland Sea. Further perhaps, Africa, the Spice Islands – Eldorado!" He flung his arms wide. "Trust me, the world can be ours, sweetheart. If you can love me as you did."

"William—"

"Halfway up the ratlines, if I know him, the monkey." He sobered. "If you mislike it, you shall be set ashore at next landfall and taken back safe and provided for."

"And you?"

He shrugged. "I shall follow my star."

She came into his arms. "You fool, Nicco, you lunatic, lovely fool. So, I am to choose between you with nothing but the clothes on my back and a rich empty prison, am I? You are my husband and lover and friend. I have missed you, Nicholas, I choose you. Again. It has been a long time."

He swung her up to smile into her face. "I am not such a fool as all that. Look." He set her down, and keeping one arm about her, threw open the chest. Ribboned scrolls lay on top of a heap of gold and jewels. "Behold, my squirrel's store, or part of it. Plain Nick Talbot, merchant adventurer, has money in the banks and a ship to take us where you will – to Paradise, under the stars."

Rosalyne was crying and laughing at once. "You devil, you led me on."

"I needed to know. And I couldn't resist showing off. It's the actor in me."

Hob pushed open the door and wobbled in with a bottle and beakers. Nick rescued the bottle and poured.

"A toast!" cried Rosalyne. "To love and adventure!"

Nick raised his beaker, his eyes sparkling. The woman he loved was back, the serious talk could come later.

"'Excellent wretch! Perdition catch my soul, but I do love thee.' To us." *And to Kit Marlowe, who started all this*, he thought.

253

Chapter Thirty-Five

Malta. Autumn 1602

Letters came to Malta with news of the presses in Paris and Bruges and Milan, set up in houses that hid in their basements other presses that disseminated new ideas and new discoveries. Kit Marlowe heard of a troupe of travelling players that had started at the *Comedie* in Paris and was working its way across the continent to Italy. In his fever dreams he heard the thump of those presses and the melody of his friend's voice. He saw a tall broad-shouldered Harlequin with russet hair escaping under his black cap, a laughing raven-haired Columbine at his side. Nicholas was busy.

When the poet was too weak to hold a pen, he dictated to the Welsh lay-brother who cared for him and wrote a beautiful hand. He was not there tonight, he was singing in the new vestry. The voices of the many boys on the island rose in counterpoint to the deep chanting of the Knights, and the sound carried on the still air, quiet after the storm.

The isle is full of noises, scribbled Kit Marlowe. *Sounds and sweet airs that give delight and hurt not.* "Oh my poor monster, to be alone and unloved." He laughed suddenly, remembering. "Of all parts to wish for, Niccolo, Aguecheek, with hair like flax on a distaff! 'I was adored once too…' The falsetto does not suit you, my dear. You loved me, the world will love me. I am content. But come, my messenger, my sweet Ariel, come."

In March, the Year of our Lord 1603, Sir Robert Carey rode from London to Edinburgh in four days, on a relay of post-horses ready and waiting, to carry the news of the Queen's death to her successor. A remarkable feat.

Christopher Marlowe, poet, playwright and gentleman spy, died within a week of Elizabeth, an unbeliever to the last.

Nobody remarked on Kit Marlowe's second passing.

April 1603. 'Will you have an Epilogue, or a Burgomaster's Dance?'

Nicholas stood on the cliff above Valetta, looking out to where the *Seamew* lay at anchor, her sails furled like folded hands, rocking gently as a gull on the swell. He could see Rosalyne, a tiny figure leaning on the taffrail, William would be in the crow's nest as usual, Hob and Butcher no doubt in the galley. Midshipman Jack Talbot was on another ship far away. He would see him again.

A heavy packet had gone to London with a Rokesby courier and a letter.

Not all at once, Will, you will know the time. Do them justice, see them played well and you will have your reward. Truly the staff is broken, this pen will write no more. I pass it to you. NT

Nicholas was thinking, *It is at an end. James is crowned. He may join England and Scotland and call it Great Britain, but nothing is changed. He will seek to buy popularity with favours – all the old ways. Men bought and sold. No, I shall not go back.* He turned aside and made his way to the stony mound where the poet lay buried. He stood with bent head, lines running through his mind.

"Take him for all in all, We shall not look upon his like again…"

Nick's part was played. Eager young men like himself were manning the presses, the players had scattered, carrying the words. He had done his best to ensure immortality for his friend, and now, disenchanted with the old world, he was ready for the new. The new-found lands beckoned, the *Seamew* was victualled and waiting, all that remained was this last farewell.

The sun was setting, wind and tide right. Nicholas spoke the words as they should be spoken.

"Goodnight, sweet prince, And flights of angels sing thee to thy rest."

He drew his pistol from his belt and pointed it to the sky. "Bid the soldiers shoot." He fired and a cloud of white-winged birds burst clattering from the cliffs to circle up, up on the spirals of air.

Nicholas turned his face to the west and went down to join his ship.

A New World and a new beginning.

Bibliography

The Life and Death of Robert Devereux, Earl of Essex. By Prof G.B.Harrison

The Cecil Papers at Hatfield House

Elizabeth 1 by Emeritus Professor J.B, Black, Aberdeen University

Ben Jonson of Westminster by Marchette Chute

The English Succession

HENRY VII m
r. 1485–1509

James IV [1] m. Margaret Tudor m. [2] Archibald
King of   6th Earl of
Scotland   Angus

James V m. Mary of   Lady Margaret   MARY TUDOR
King of   Guise   Douglas   r. 1553–8
Scotland   m. Matthew
                             Earl of Lennox

Mary Queen of   m.   Henry Stuart   Lord Charles
Scots   Lord Darnley   Stuart
1542–87   1546–67   Earl of Lennox
                                            d. 1576
                                            m. Elizabeth
                                              Cavendish

JAMES I   m. Anne of
r. 1603–25   Denmark
(VI of Scotland)   d. 1619

Henry   Elizabeth m. Fredrick V   CHARLES I   Arbella Stuart   m
d. 1612   Elector   r. 1625–49   1575–1615
                     Palatine

HOUSE OF HANOVER

Elizabeth of York

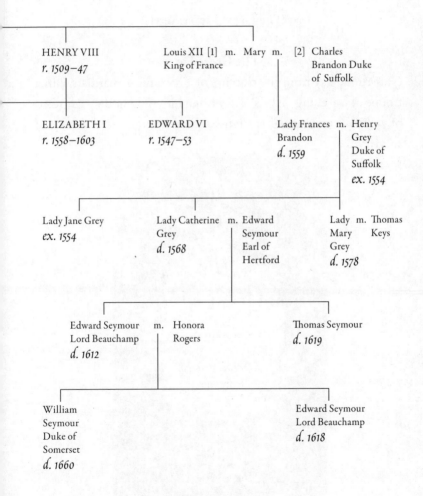

HENRY VIII
r. 1509–47

Louis XII [1] m. Mary m. [2] Charles
King of France   Brandon Duke
                             of Suffolk

ELIZABETH I
r. 1558–1603

EDWARD VI
r. 1547–53

Lady Frances m. Henry
Brandon   Grey
d. 1559   Duke of
               Suffolk
               ex. 1554

Lady Jane Grey
ex. 1554

Lady Catherine m. Edward
Grey   Seymour
d. 1568   Earl of
                  Hertford

Lady m. Thomas
Mary   Keys
Grey
d. 1578

Edward Seymour m. Honora
Lord Beauchamp   Rogers
d. 1612

Thomas Seymour
d. 1619

William
Seymour
Duke of
Somerset
d. 1660

Edward Seymour
Lord Beauchamp
d. 1618

MORE FROM M. STANFORD-SMITH

Enjoyed *Flights of Angels?* Read more about Nicholas Talbot's adventures in the first two books in the Great Lie Trilogy:

The Great Lie Trilogy

The Great Lie

Nick runs away from the clutches of a tyrannical guardian with a troupe of travelling players. They bring him to London – a hotbed of political and sexual intrigue, where he must find a way to survive…

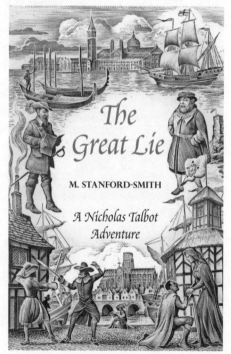

Sea of Troubles

Nicholas is heartbroken – his home burned down and the love of his life married to another. In this second adventure he looks for more than transient thrills but his ability to find trouble is unerring…

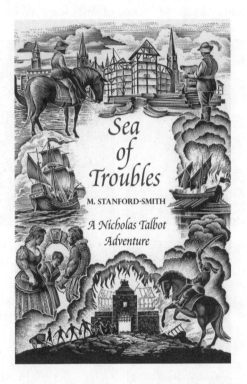

All Honno titles can be ordered online at
www.honno.co.uk
twitter.com/honno
facebook.com/honnopress

MORE FROM HONNO

Short Stories, Classics, Autobiography, Fiction

Founded in 1986 to publish the best of women's writing,
Honno publishes a wide range of titles from Welsh women.

All Honno titles can be ordered online at
www.honno.co.uk
twitter.com/honno
facebook.com/honnopress

PRAISE FOR HONNO'S BOOKS:

"Hooray for Honno!"
Sarah Waters

*"Honno so magnificently lives up to the headline
— "great books, great writing, great women!"*
Glenys Kinnock

*"Ashford borrows the 'mischievous spirit' of Austen herself in this
thoroughly entertaining mingling of fact and fiction."*
Anna Scott, Guardian

"a marvellous compilation of reminiscences"
Time Out

"A cracking good read"
dovegreyreader.co.uk

"Illuminating, poignant, entertaining and unputdownable"
The Big Issue

"sucks you in straight away."
Chick Lit Club

"… a wonderful, miniature gem of a novel"
Historical Novel Society

All Honno titles can be ordered online at
www.honno.co.uk
twitter.com/honno
facebook.com/honnopress

ABOUT HONNO

Honno Welsh Women's Press was set up in 1986 by a group of women who felt strongly that women in Wales needed wider opportunities to see their writing in print and to become involved in the publishing process. Our aim is to develop the writing talents of women in Wales, give them new and exciting opportunities to see their work published and often to give them their first 'break' as a writer.

Honno is registered as a community co-operative. Any profit that Honno makes is invested in the publishing programme. Women from Wales and around the world have expressed their support for Honno. Each supporter has a vote at the Annual General Meeting.

To receive further information about forthcoming publications, or become a supporter, please write to Honno at the address below, or visit our website:

www.honno.co.uk

Honno
Unit 14, Creative Units
Aberystwyth Arts Centre
Penglais Campus
Aberystwyth
Ceredigion
SY23 3GL

All Honno titles can be ordered online at
www.honno.co.uk
or by sending a cheque to Honno